RELEASE OF MAGIC

RELEASE OF MAGIC

THE LEIRA CHRONICLES™ BOOK TWO

MARTHA CARR

MICHAEL ANDERLE

DISRUPTIVE IMAGINATION™

Copyright © 2020 (as revised) Martha Carr and Michael T. Anderle
Cover Art by Jake @ J Caleb Design
http://jcalebdesign.com / jcalebdesign@gmail.com
Cover copyright © LMBPN Publishing

LMBPN Publishing
PMB 196, 2540 South Maryland Pkwy
Las Vegas, NV 89109

Version 2.00 June 2020
eBook ISBN: 978-1-64971-012-3
Print ISBN: 978-1-64971-013-0

RELEASE OF MAGIC TEAM

Thanks to our JIT and Beta Readers

Erika Daly
Kimberly Boyer
Keith Verret
Kelly ODonnell
Joshua Ahles
James Caplan
Melissa OHanlon
Peter Manis
Paul Westman
Micky Cocker
John Raisor
Thomas Ogden
Alex Wilson

Editor

Ellen Campbell

From Martha

To everyone who still believes in magic and all the possibilities that holds.

To all the readers who make this entire ride so much fun.

To Louie, Jackie, and so many wonderful friends who remind me all the time of what really matters and how wonderful life can be in any given moment.

And finally, a special thank you to John Nelson of the Austin, Texas Police Department who patiently answers all of my questions. I hope I made you proud. Thank you for your service.

From Michael

To Family, Friends and
Those Who Love
To Read.
May We All Enjoy Grace
To Live The Life We Are
Called.

CHAPTER ONE

The explosion from the necklace took its toll. Leira *still* heard a mild buzz in her ears days later. The drive back to Austin was mostly in silence except for occasional laughter from the troll and the loud sound of chewing. In Missouri, Correk reached back and grabbed the nearly empty box of Cheez Its, scowling at the troll. Yumfuck looked up surprised. "What?" he squeaked. His fur was matted from a mixture of chocolate, jerky and salt.

Correk shook the box, grimacing at the troll. "You've eaten almost everything." Leira furrowed her brow and glanced at Correk. "You know we can buy more."

"It's the principle of the thing."

"The principle of road trip etiquette?" Leira rubbed her temple, willing the mild headache to go away.

Correk reached into the box and pulled out a handful of the tiny squares, throwing them into his mouth. He quickly made a face and looked around for something to drink. "These are just a form of drier Cheetos," he said, gulping down Dr. Pepper.

"We've hit a new level of snacking if we're elevating Cheetos to fine dining. I'm not sure if we've gone up or down though," said Leira.

Correk handed the box back to Yumfuck who crawled inside of it and chewed his way out the other side. He fell asleep on the back seat of the custom Mustang, his paws outstretched and his mouth wide open in a food coma. The car quickly fell back into silence.

But somewhere during the long stretch in Oklahoma, Leira finally said what she had been thinking since Somers had managed to incinerate himself.

"I'm thinking I failed this mission." She tapped a finger on the steering wheel. "The killer is dead and the necklace is missing. I got there just in time to be a witness and that's about it."

She looked out at the setting sun across the prairies that ran alongside the highway. The remaining light was throwing purple shadows on the winter ground.

The beauty of the scenery was doing nothing for her mood.

"We don't measure failure the same way on Oriceran," Correk said tersely. "It's not about the right or wrong, just the consequences. And by that measure we accomplished half of the assignment."

"No more killer, I get it. You realize that thanks to erasing the last minutes of that party no one knows exactly what happened to Bill Somers or the dean. It's going to be a permanent cold case. The dean's family will never know."

"Not much can be done about that," Correk told her. "Beyond what the Order of the Silver Griffins were willing to do. It was nice of them to hold that little service on Montrose Beach and pour the ashes into Lake Michigan. Someone took the time to remember both of them."

"Even if we couldn't tell where Somers ashes ended, and Dean Muston's began." Leira shook her head. "There has to be some kind of spell that would let us leave the dean's family at least with a false memory of what happened to him like a heart attack and a nice funeral, even if it's a lie. Somers only had that odd little friend, Randolph. He looked like an easy mark for a simple spell."

"We've learned the hard way that when we meddle with magic, even with good intentions, other problems pop up," said Correk. "As for the necklace, it will surface. It's far too powerful to stay hidden forever."

"Small comfort. Like knowing someone has an atom bomb somewhere out there and when it goes boom, we'll know where they were keeping it all along." Leira watched an old Crown Vic weaving in and out of traffic along the highway, narrowly missing bumpers. "Would love to pull that asshole over," she muttered.

"If you continue to take what happened in Chicago personally, it'll be harder to focus. Let it go and put your attention on whatever we're supposed to be doing next."

"There's no *we* at this point, Correk. We have no leads of any kind. You go back to your world and I go back to mine."

Yumfuck let out a loud snore in his sleep and curled up into a ball, his fur sticking to the seat.

"With a troll."

"Okay," she admitted, "that's a sizable wrinkle, but I got myself into that one. Besides, your life in Oriceran will call you back at some point."

"Hopefully not quite so abruptly. But yes, if my king and queen asked me to return, I would oblige. So far, that is not the case."

Leira gave Correk a sidelong glance, pushing her dark bangs off her face. "They have some other plan already, I guess?"

"I am assuming the same, but I don't know. Look, that conversation can wait. Are we not going to talk about your mother?"

"Again with the *we*." Leira pursed her lips, irritated. A groan went up from the troll, his legs running in his sleep.

"I can be of assistance. There's still a lot you have to learn. Not only about who you really are, but how to use all of that to your best advantage."

Leira bit her bottom lip, pulling out from behind an eighteen-wheeler to follow a long line of different colored pickup trucks cruising down the left lane.

The silver Dodge truck directly in front of her had a single large star in the back window. It felt good to know they were getting closer to home.

"I lead this investigation," she said finally. "I call all the shots, and you keep the magic to a minimum so we don't both end up on some tranquilizer drip swearing we're not crazy, right alongside my mother."

"Agreed," he answered. "We'll find a way to get her out of there."

"That's not what has me tied in a knot." Leira gripped the steering wheel. "It's what fifteen years in a psych ward has to have done to her."

"There's no way you could have known your mother was telling the truth. We've noticed your species prefers to believe in what it can see and has been known to react badly to alternate theories. An entirely different world of species that can perform magic could be seen as an enormous threat. If your sci-fi movies are to be believed, your government's first reaction would have included cages and vivisection."

"Maybe that's just the over-caffeinated idea of some writer on a deadline," said Leira. "I keep holding on to the idea that if she's half Light Elf..."

"Everything says she must be."

"*If* she is, her other-worldly DNA helped her out. Maybe she figured out a way to create some kind of life for herself in there. Fifteen years..." Her voice trailed off.

"We'll figure out the rest of this another day," Correk reassured her. "Come on," he said, holding up his fist and smiling.

"Let me do one of those strange handshakes. Don't leave me hanging."

"We call it a fist bump." She returned his smile, despite everything weighing on her mind. "You picked up a lot of lingo from one visit to the bowling alley."

"That's more like it." He looked around the car. "Do we have any of the Nacho Doritos left?"

"That's why you want to stay, isn't it?" She sighed, "Our junk food has sedated many a foe apparently. You're the only one who would know what's left in the snack bag back there. Maybe Yumfuck didn't get into everything. I gave up on it back in Southern Illinois." She tapped the brakes. "Thought I'd lose a finger going for a stuffed pretzel bite."

"Those things are addictive. I suggest when we get back to Austin one of the first things we do is look for some real food."

"You mean pizza, don't you?"

"The waitress assured me it covered every major food group on this planet."

"Pizza for breakfast again, it is. But this time we're going to try my favorite."

"Which is?"

"You'll see, the suspense is worth it."

Eireka Berens sat at a round wooden table topped with Formica in the dayroom of the Claridge Psychiatric Hospital flipping over cards looking for the ace. Her long brown hair hid her face and she made a point of not making eye contact with anyone.

The small ward had no more than fifteen psychiatric patients at any given time. Ten of them were long-term, like Eireka, and she had learned how to form alliances with each of those patients, if not friendships. The other five were a constantly rotating cast of characters who had tried something stupid to harm themselves, or had pissed off their family just enough with their bad choices that they wanted them gone for a little while.

A tall male orderly dressed in a white uniform right down to his soft-soled white shoes strode into the room and clapped his hands sharply.

"Time for six o'clock medication. Okay everyone, you know the drill. Line up to the right of the window and the nurse will place the medication on your tongue, handing you the glass of water. Swallow the pills, stick out your tongue, lift it so that we can see that the medication is gone and this will all go smoothly."

He clapped his hands sharply again. Once, twice. "Come on people, dinner tonight's burritos, everybody's favorite. We don't need anyone holding up the line or causing trouble. Ms. Berens, go get in line."

Eireka got up slowly and shuffled toward the line. She had mastered the look of the drug-induced haze years ago. Her paper slippers made a *skitch, skitch* noise against the worn-out linoleum floor.

The redheaded girl in front of her was young and looked nervous. She was a new admittance, came in just last night, and she kept looking furtively from left to right, wringing her hands. She was crying hard enough that a sheen of snot glossed her lips. Eireka wanted to reach out and comfort the girl. She figured she had to be about the same age as her own daughter, Leira. But the risk that someone would notice and discover she was faking her torpor was too great.

"Maggie! You're next!" The orderly was doing his sharp clap again, trying to get the new girl to move forward in line. All it did was make her cry harder, an irritating whimper coming out of her trembling lips.

"Burrito night!" An oversized woman with wiry gray hair sticking out all over her head was stomping her feet in the back of the line. She was also a fairly recent addition to the ward, but

Eireka had a good idea that she was at the start of a very long stretch.

The old woman had had enough and started shoving the people directly in front of her in line, still yelling *burrito night* at the top of her lungs. Three orderlies immediately rushed her, restraining her and dragging her out of the room.

"Burritos in your room tonight, if you're awake enough to know they're there," one of the orderlies laughed.

Eireka took the opportunity to surreptitiously raise her hand and gently push the crying girl in front of her, moving her forward as if she had no will of her own. *Even if it's the last good thing I can do.* It was the one really good thing her mother had given to her, and she had done her best to pass it on to Leira. *Never back down from doing the right thing,* she thought. *Never.*

Eireka caught a glimpse of the thin scars that marred the soft, white underside of the girl's arms.

The rumor was that her parents were wealthy and well-connected. *Definitely a tourist,* thought Eireka. As soon as her involuntary hold was over, they would find her a more comfortable place where they could hide her away.

When Eireka got to the top of the line the nurse barked, "Name."

"Eireka Berens."

Eireka opened her mouth and held out her hand for the glass of water. As the nurse handed her the water she let two of her fingers brush against the woman's skin and whispered one of the few spells she had learned from her mother.

"Invisibilia," she muttered. She took a sip of the water and then opened her mouth wide, the three capsules still on her tongue clearly showing. The nurse gave a sharp nod and barked "Next!"

Eireka had learned over time that the spell only lasted for a few seconds and was really only good for creating an illusion on smaller things. She had tried to use it once or twice to make it look as if her bed was occupied, when she was still intent on breaking out. But it never lasted long enough or was big enough to influence people who weren't in the room when she cast the spell.

It took a few stays in isolation in a padded cell before she decided to stop trying to escape and instead focus on making things better for herself. She still held on to the belief that one day her beautiful, funny and clever daughter would figure things out, and come and get her.

She knew Leira Berens was on the police force, but it had been a few years since she had seen her in person. Leira had come over four years ago to tell her that her own mother, Mara Berens, had disappeared.

The weight of those words had crashed over Eireka, taking her breath away.

"You're alone!" she had gasped, shocked and alarmed.

Eireka reached out, grasping her daughter's arm in desperation. She tried to tell her where to look for her grandmother but the second Eireka started to talk about Oriceran again, Leira pulled back. Even stood as if she was ready to go. Determined to go.

Still, Eireka had persisted and tried to tell Leira how to create a doorway, ask the elves for help. The orderlies overheard and dragged her away. They gave her an injection that left her groggy for a week and made it impossible for her to pull off a spell of any kind.

Leira had visited her mother again, months later but Eireka could see the toll it was taking on her daughter and clasped her hand tightly, whispering, "Don't come back. Get on with your life and forget I'm here."

Leira had protested, but Eireka had been thinking about what to do for months.

"Invisibilia," she had whispered, clinging to her daughter's hand, conjuring the image of an empty space where her mother sat. She held onto the image as hard as she could, knowing the intensity of her feelings would help push the idea further into Leira's heart.

It wasn't as if she expected Leira to forget about her, but she knew the spell would help shroud Leira's feelings for her and help her only child get on with her life. So far, the spell was working.

Still, Eireka Berens had never given up hope that someday her daughter would be ready and figure out her true heritage in time to free her mother without exposing them both to danger. Then together, they would find out what had become of Mara Berens.

Every day she woke up wondering if today was that day.

"You're crazy. Thin crust all the way." Correk folded the slice like he'd seen people doing at the large table next to him, pushing half of it into his mouth.

They were sitting on metal stools at a long, thin stainless-steel counter outside of a low-slung red brick building in Austin. It was a warm winter morning, the kind Austin was famous for. Large neon letters over their head spelled out Home Slice Pizza. Correk still had a knit hat pulled down over his ears and his long hair was pulled back into a ponytail.

The waitress gave him a thumbs up as she leaned through the window service and refilled his Dr. Pepper.

"Good call leaving the troll in the car," he said. "But when he smells the grease he's going to be pissed. We need to bring a peace offering."

"I'm the one who said thin crust is better. Roll it out thin, till it bakes into a giant cracker for a crust. You didn't seem to mind deep dish back in Chicago," Leira pointed out.

"That's before you took me to Home Slice," he replied, looking around the small restaurant on the south side of Austin. The thin white paper plate in front of him was soaked through with grease.

"Stopping for more pizza before we got back to my place was your idea. Granted, a really good one. I have to admit this is not half bad. This is as close to New York style pizza as you can get here in Austin."

"Yo phone is bluzzing," mumbled Correk.

Leira winced, watching the grease run down Correk's chin. "Chew with your mouth closed, dude!"

He pointed a greasy finger in the direction of a pile of vibrating small white napkins.

"Swallow, Correk, swallow. Hello? Hagan, slow down, what is it?" Leira leaned toward the small window and waved at the waitress. "We're going to need the rest to go."

"What is it?" asked Correk, wiping his hands. "This grease is tenacious."

"That was my partner. There's a case. All hands on deck."

"How does he even know you're back in town?"

"I called when I went to the bathroom to check in. It's a cop thing," she said with a shrug. "I'll drop you back at my place. The troll's piece is coming out of your share of the leftovers."

"Not a chance, on either one, Leira. Okay, he can have my pizza. But if I'm going to stay here on Earth for a while, then I'm going to stay by your side as much as I can." He held up his hands to stop her from saying anything else. "I understand it's a police investigation, but I'm not sitting around your tiny house with a troll for hours on end. And no, sitting out at the bar is not much better."

"Fine, I don't have time to argue. But we're still dropping off the troll and you stay back by the car. Under no circumstances do you interfere. I mean it," she warned, throwing down a few dollars for a tip.

"Do you normally get this agitated at the start of a case?" Correk scooped up the box, as they headed for the car.

"Normally, I make a point of not rushing. That's the way you miss clues. But these are special circumstances. A child is missing, presumed kidnapped, and one person is already dead. We have a window of just a few hours before this could turn into another homicide. Besides, this is not the moment I want more people to realize magic is a thing, it's gone local and Siegfried and Roy were *really* out of this world."

"Only Siegfried." Leira scowled at Correk and slid into the front seat. "But yes, I get your point," he said, buckling up. Leira turned on the lights and siren and gunned the car out of the parking lot.

CHAPTER TWO

There was yellow and black tape around Pick One Up's parking lot, stretching out to the street. Patrol officers were standing in front of a small crowd on both sides of the minimart, holding back the lookie-loos who had walked over from the nearby cookie-cutter subdivision a block away. The day was turning out to be one of those hot winter days that were pretty typical for Austin.

Leira scanned the crowd as they pulled up and parked behind the short line of black and white Austin police cars. It was her usual practice when first arriving at a crime scene. Never know what kind of clue is sitting right out there in front. *The oddest things become important later.*

She quickly formed a visual map of the area in her head. Behind the blocks of starter home ranchers and two-story houses was a dense patch of woods that was full of homeless people who rarely came out during the day. Leira had cruised past this area many times in the middle of the night, checking on leads and seen the small crowds milling about in the parking lot. Hagan swore they even had a generator to power up stolen cell phones and keep a small refrigerator going.

The taqueria truck in the far corner of the lot would have been buzzing with activity till sunrise. "Guarantee there was a line of hungry people with just enough for a breakfast taco," she said quietly. "They would be the best witnesses."

Correk already knew better than to say anything and got out to stretch his legs but stayed by the Mustang.

Leira looked at the uniforms standing near the door of the mart, quickly spotting Detective Hagan. He was taking notes, nodding his head, rolling his hand, trying to get the two officers in front of him to talk faster.

He was clearly pissed off. He saw Leira as she ducked under the tape and started waving frantically in her direction. There was a sheen of sweat on his face. Leira recognized all the signs of a case going sour, fast.

"Was there more?" Hagan turned his focus back to the two officers, his eyebrows raised and his pen poised in the air.

"Hey, Detective Berens," said the younger officer.

"Ritchie."

"If we're done with the pleasantries," Hagan snapped.

"We're done, Detective," the officer said.

"Anyone go into the woods to talk to the transients?" Leira turned her attention to the line of woods just a few blocks away. The tops of the older oak trees were visible from where they stood.

"Not yet, no," Ritchie said.

"Well, then, grab a few more people and see what you can find out," Hagan said impatiently, waving again, this time at nearby officers.

"Hold on," said Leira. "Don't head out just yet. Look, they're not suspects. They're possible witnesses. Don't treat them like suspects. Don't mess with their belongings. Don't threaten anyone with anything. Don't find reasons to arrest anyone. We need them to cooperate and we need them to want to do it now.

Is that understood?" She waited till she got an affirmative from every cop.

"You have an hour to find something," she said. "If you can do it in less time, that's better. Don't edit what you hear, just write it down. Let us decide what's useful."

"Now, go. Go!" Hagan ordered. He pulled a handkerchief from his back pocket and mopped his face and the top of his balding head. "Hate these fucking cases. Only monsters steal kids."

"Where's the dead guy?" Leira already knew he must be inside of the store. There was a swarm of technicians in blue booties circling around the front counter, bending down, meticulously retrieving things and dropping their findings into clear evidence bags. Still, she wanted to hear what Hagan had to say about it. Cases involving children always got him wound up, and he had to talk the whole thing out for Leira to get the bits and pieces she really needed. It was a process.

"The owner. He's behind the counter. Damnable thing. He died on his knees, still propped up. His head is resting on the shelf back there. Near as I can tell, the dumb fucker bent down to get a sawed-off, but never got back up. The gun is still there, under his head. Well, what was left of his head."

"And the child?"

"His six-year-old niece. A Lucy Kate." Hagan flipped open his small notebook and read from his notes. He was reluctant to type anything into the department-issued tablet. Everything about him was old school. "According to his daughter… That's her sitting in the patrol car over there doing her best to pull it together."

Leira looked over and saw the young woman sitting in the back seat with the door open, resting her head on the seat in front of her. *Reality still hasn't sunk in*, she thought.

"According to his daughter, he was babysitting while the mom worked a night shift stocking a Walmart." Hagan tapped his notebook. He was already chewing on an idea. Leira gave him a moment to put it into words.

"The money from the register is gone," he said, scowling, "but you should see it in there. Neat and clean. No fuss. Except for the blood splatter from the victim, nothing else is out of order. It's like the killer waited for the store to be empty. No sign of anyone rushing out or hiding behind something."

"Or they let him pass," said Leira. There was a well-known code among the homeless in the rougher parts of Austin. See nothing, do nothing, say nothing. "And if that's what happened and whoever this is didn't shoot any of them..."

"Then this is more personal, and he would have known about the code. Fuck me." Hagan pushed the palm of his hand against his belly. "Damn heartburn."

"This gives us a place to start," said Leira. "Let's go look inside."

She glanced back at Correk who was leaning against the Mustang, carefully observing everyone around him. It was a sign of Hagan's frustration that he didn't say anything about tall, blonde and handsome waiting for her.

Correk locked eyes with Leira and gave her a nod, his eyes briefly lighting up, glowing from within. *He's itching to use magic.*

She turned away, letting the thought go, and pulled on a pair of blue gloves and booties before stepping into the store.

"Found anything yet?" she asked the older technician, Harriet who was carefully picking something up off the ground with tweezers. She was known to be no-nonsense and really didn't give a shit how someone else was feeling. Leira liked working with her.

"Oh, hey Leira. Nothing definitive. So much useless DNA in this place, including way too much old semen. What are people thinking? The little girl was sleeping back there..." She pointed toward the door behind the counter that was open slightly. "No signs of a struggle or any resistance. She may not have been awake."

Leira glanced at the food racks closest to the door. Several of them were empty. The same was true of a few of the boxes of candy just underneath the front of the counter. "There were people in here," she said, pointing.

"You know this because..." he asked.

"Because the shelves that aren't near the door are all full like they were recently stocked, but everything close to the door is just about picked clean. Easier to grab and go. But there're no bloody footprints. No one went near the body, including whoever shot him."

Leira stepped carefully around the counter. "Okay if I go back here?"

"Yep," said Harriet. "We're done. I told the coroner to wait till you got a look for yourself. I know how you like to see the crime scene. What's it saying to you?"

"That they wanted the girl. This guy is collateral damage." Leira bent down to get a better look at the dead man. His finger was resting on the trigger. He'd been inches from coming out ahead. "Miss is as good as a mile," Leira whispered.

"The mother came rushing in, hysterical, and had to be dragged off and medicated," Hagan said. "No father to speak of. Mother swore up and down the father wouldn't have cared enough to do this."

"You know, the thing that bothers me the most, is that whoever did this knew not to shoot any of the homeless people standing around. Even if they were all outside, which is unlikely, he would have still been visible, but nobody cared." A warm curl of anger grew inside her, spreading out to her limbs. "This wasn't personal. It was professional," she spat.

She glanced down at her hands and saw her fingertips start to glow cherry-red through the thin blue latex gloves. She balled her hands into fists and looked away, unsure whether her eyes were glowing. She needed to get to Correk.

"Excuse me," she said, stepping carefully back around the counter, keeping her head down.

She hurried out the front door of the Pick One Up, shoving her gloved hands into the pockets of her leather jacket. Correk stood up straighter as she got closer, a look of concern on his face.

"The magic is coming over you, isn't it?"

"You knew this would happen? Why didn't you tell me?" she asked, exasperated. She pulled out her hands, ripping off the gloves to look at her fingertips. There was still a faint glow.

"How bad is this going to get?"

"There's still so much to tell you. Volumes. Remember, my original job was not to help a half-elven cousin learn to control her powers. It was to find a killer and a necklace. Take a deep breath," he said, taking one himself. "Think about the first thing you learned. Feelings control magic. It's all tied to your DNA, your very cell structure. The more you can focus, the more you can bend and shape the magic and use it purposefully."

Leira took a step back, shaking her head. "No! No! I'm not using magic to solve a case," she insisted, pushing her dark hair out of her face. "What are you thinking?"

"That you have a case to solve."

"What happened to worrying about the Order of the Silver Griffins? Aren't there still some pretty severe repercussions for playing Bewitched? And how would I explain any of it? I suppose we would do another amnesia spell!" Leira was talking faster and faster, pacing in front of Correk.

"You're considering it, aren't you?" Correk was keeping his voice low and measured, trying to calm her down.

"What in the hell are you doing, Leira?" Detective Hagan had stomped his way across the parking lot but Leira, for once, wasn't paying enough attention to her surroundings.

She shook her head no at Correk.

"Where I'm from, we put the preservation of life ahead of all things. Especially the lives of our children."

"That was a low blow, Correk," Leira said through clenched teeth. The anger started to rise inside her again, taking over her thoughts. This time she could feel her eyes glow, and the world around her became crisper, clearer. It became easier for her to see how all the events connected and what to do next. She started to calm down but instead of resetting back to her normal state she felt something new inside of her. A new power, a presence.

She held her hands out in front of her and watched as symbols appeared on the backs, glowing as they got more prominent. She could feel the power surging through her body.

"What the fuck?" Hagan stumbled and then spun around to see if anyone else had noticed, turning back to shield Leira from the nearby crowd. Fortunately, most of them were too busy looking toward the crime scene.

The coroner was finally removing the body, and a long black plastic bag on a gurney was rolling out of the store.

"How did you do that?" Hagan clamped his hands down on the top of his head, still clutching his notebook, mussing what little hair he had left. "Are you really Leira?" He seemed to finally take note of Correk. "Who are you? What are you? Fuck! Is this like Body Snatchers?"

"Hagan, Hagan." Leira reached out and grabbed his arm. He tried to pull away, a look of alarm on his face. She hated seeing that in his eyes. "Enough with the B movie logic, Felix. It's still me."

"You want to explain what just happened?" asked her partner.

Leira took in a deep breath, letting it out slowly, shaking out her hands.

"That doesn't really do anything," said Correk. "Your hands didn't just go to sleep."

Hagan leaned in close to Correk and hissed, "Are you some kind of alien?"

"Really not my favorite description," said Correk, wiping a little spit off of his face. "I prefer visitor or traveler, or in Leira's case, cousin."

"Enough!" said Leira. She shook her head again. "Hagan and I have worked dozens of cases like this one, successfully I might add. I may be getting better at this, but I really have no idea what I'm doing. If we waste time on this and I'm wrong that could spell disaster."

"Waste time on what? What could you do?" Hagan looked back and forth at Correk and Leira. "I *am* still your partner, am I not?" His face was reddening with anger.

"Seems you made a similar speech to me," Correk observed. "Something about trust and not keeping secrets?"

"You can be a real asshole at times," she retorted.

"She only says that when you're right," Hagan said. "Spill it. Are we all becoming visitors?" His sarcasm was mixed with a healthy dose of worry. "Am I changing?" he asked, patting down the front of his shirt, checking his pockets. An old green peanut M&M came rolling out.

"It's not like losing your keys, Hagan. And you're not going to start morphing into something."

"Unless you want to," Correk added.

"Not the time to tease the ignorant Earthling." Leira gave him a menacing look. She looked at her partner and said, "There's a lot I want to tell you, but not now. It's too much, and we have to focus on this little girl. Some douchebag of the first order has taken a little girl. That comes first."

"Well, what was he saying about using magic? We're running out of time. If it was a professional, they're on the move. They won't stay in the area long."

"Why can't it be you, Correk?" asked Leira. "You have hundreds of years of experience."

"Ack, damn heartburn!" Hagan pounded on the middle of his chest. "I've got to stop eating so much junk food!"

Correk looked up at Hagan's bloated face. "Cheetos caused that?"

"Not the time," said Leira. "But yes, you should slow your roll on the faux food. It's got some slow-burning consequences. Now tell me, why not you?"

"The short version is that I'm running out of power. If the girl isn't still nearby, I might not be able to pull it off."

"And the longer answer?"

Correk let out a sigh. "I had hoped to wait to tell you this. But I suspect you are far more powerful than I am. Even with Earth's limited power I believe you'll be able to find her. You are more amazing than you realize, Leira Berens. If I'm right, the half of you that's from my world is from a very, very rare strain. An ancient and powerful one I might add and it would mean we are not really cousins. I was just hoping you could learn that gradually."

"Oh geez." Hagan was bent over, his hands on his knees, taking deep breaths.

"Felix, you either get it together or I call your wife."

"That's cold, Berens. She'd only tell me to remember my deep breathing exercises from meditation time. That's right, people! I've been learning how to meditate. Never realized I'd be using it to be cool at a showdown of alien versus predator."

"Thanks a lot," said Leira. "Yes, that was fucking clever. You still have it, Hagan. Now, tuck in your balls and let's do this."

"Fine, I will hold my shit together. I'd love to see what you'd tell her, anyway."

Leira turned back and stared at Correk's face for a moment, but she already knew what she was going to have to do. Time was running out.

"What about a fireball? Those seemed to work for you."

"It's a ball of light and that's more of a tracking device for what's happening in the present moment. Not useful for seeing the past. You can do this."

Correk took a step toward her and held out his hands. "I may not be able to generate enough energy to do this myself, but we can connect our energy and I can at least guide you through it. Go on, put your hands in mine."

Leira hesitated. "What if others see us? We whammy them later?"

"That's up to you. For now, we find the girl."

"I'll stand behind you two," said Hagan, mopping his face. "For once my size is going to be an asset."

Leira put her hands into Correk's and immediately felt the energy surging back and forth between them. Instinctively she pulled back, but he held her hands tightly.

"Focus," he said.

"On what?"

"Every event, every emotion, every act leaves behind a temporary trail of energy. Focus on the stronger ones that are closest to you right now. Do you feel them?"

Leira felt the warmth start behind her eyes and saw the same happening to Correk. She felt the calm come over her and the world around her became sharper and clearer.

"Use your feelings to reach out and see the trails of energy others have left behind."

Suddenly, glittering trails in different colors began to emerge everywhere, some more faded than others. A few pulsed with energy. Leira took a deep breath and felt Correk nudge her, guiding her toward those streams of light.

The first one was erratic and as Leira connected to it she could feel her mind jumping around from thought to thought. It got harder to make sense of anything.

"A schizophrenic," she said, looking up at Correk. "Someone who's homeless. He headed back toward the woods."

"Very good. I agree. Try again," he said. His face was tense and she could tell he was using the last of his energy to help her. "It's not about me," he said sharply. "Focus! You can do this." He was practically shouting.

"Can you quiet it down a little?" Hagan took another look around, but everyone was still busy up near the store.

Leira focused on Correk's face and stopped fighting the surging of energy. Suddenly, she had a 360° view of the world around her, but it wasn't in the present moment. It was different chunks of time from the past twenty-four hours. She felt an urge to go searching through the streams of light again but felt Correk's instruction to let her feelings guide her through the maze.

"Trust the process," he said.

"Oh great, we've gone late-night infomercial," said Hagan.

Leira let herself relax and felt the energy increase. The symbols under her skin glowed, creeping up her neck and on to her face.

"Mother of God!" Hagan's mouth dropped open and he stared at Leira's face. "Just when you think you've seen everything. I thought little Yumfuck was mind blowing."

"The more meaningful the event, whether it's a tragedy or celebration the stronger the trail it leaves behind. These trails have the ability to influence how you feel if you're not careful." Correk's voice was low and soothing. "Look for the steady stream of energy that still glitters and sense the darkness around it. Both from the time of night when the crime occurred and the murder."

Leira let her energy brush against the different trails, absorbing the feeling of being homeless or a petty thief or a drug addict, quickly discarding each of them and moving on. She found one that was a tangled knot, hidden by all the other streams. Leira cautiously approached it, touching it with her energy as if it were a flaming hot stove. The moment her stream of golden and bronze energy brushed against the midnight blue tangle, sparks sprayed out, surprising her. She instinctively drew back as if she was actually burned.

"Found it!" Leira felt a moment of exhilaration even as a darkness crept over her like a poison. She could see the brilliant blue glittering stream of Correk's energy reach out and shove the darkness away and felt what it was costing him. His energy was ebbing. She wanted to stop and ask him if there was some kind of permanent cost to him, but she felt his energy grip her by the arms and she refocused.

A child's life was in the balance, and they were too far in to back out now anyway.

"You are a powerful being. Rise above this." It was Correk's voice inside of her head. "You influence the darkness. The darkness does not control you. We do this by trusting in our own feelings."

Leira felt a peace she had never known before. It felt like a sharp, cool breeze swirling around her. She reached for the tangled knot of energy again. This time, she felt confident and in control. The same feeling she got every time she was about to leap forward and take down a felon running away from her. Her energy reached out and touched the darkness.

When she did, thoughts crept into her mind that she knew didn't belong to her.

"The dead man," she gasped. "It was revenge. The owner's sister slept with the wrong man. Wait, there's more." The tangled knot gave off sparks again, but this time Leira was prepared and held the energy. "The dead man stopped paying his protection money. He didn't know anything about the affair. They were making an example by killing him. Taking the child was a last-minute decision. The child was sleeping," she said.

"You can see that?"

Leira ignored Hagan and kept focused on Correk's face. No images appeared in front of her but still, she knew what the killer was thinking and where he was headed. "They're going to move her out of town."

"Can you tell where she is?" Hagan was squinting at Leira as if that would help him see what was inside her head.

"She's being held inside of a small, rundown house on the northeast side of Georgetown, about thirty-five miles from here. There isn't much time."

Leira slowly pulled her hands away from Correk's. She was trembling and felt like she might throw up.

"Swallow hard," Correk said. "The feeling passes. It's the drain of energy, like you just ran a marathon."

"I know where she is," said Leira. "I can't give you the address, but I can drive you straight there."

Hagan ran his big, meaty palms across the top of his head. A nervous habit when he was trying to figure something out. "Do we take a caravan?" he asked.

"No, there's no way to explain how we got the tip."

"Let's roll," said Hagan. "I'll follow you."

They pulled away from the crime scene, not explaining to anyone. Leira waited until they were a mile away before turning on the lights and siren. Hagan followed her lead. She pushed the gas pedal all the way to the floor, screaming north up I35.

When they got to the exit for the stretch that curved around Georgetown's older section, Leira cut the lights and siren. Hagan quickly did the same thing. She turned on to a narrow gravel road that wound through an old stand of pecan trees tangled with undergrowth. A quarter mile down the road, Leira slowed the car to a crawl. Even though she had never seen this road before, it all seemed familiar.

"How is that possible?" she whispered.

"It's the more distasteful part of brushing up against other people's energy. A part of their, I suppose you'd say personality mixed with their memories, lingers with you. I'm afraid I'm not going to be much help with magic. I'm running too low." He flexed his hands open and shut. "However, I do have an effective right cross."

"For once I wish we had the troll with us." Leira stopped the Mustang and jumped out.

"Did I mention that trolls have been used in battles before? You don't bring a troll to something like this unless you're prepared to bring a mop to clean up the mess."

Leira gave him a startled look. "That would have been useful information to know a little sooner." She thought about Thomas swinging around from the end of a tree branch.

"That may have been an oversight on my part."

"You think? Never mind." She shook her head to try and clear her thoughts. The mixture of other people's thoughts was still swimming through her own, making her a little nauseous. "Focus," she told herself.

Hagan parked right behind the Mustang and got out, taking a long look in every direction. "There may be sentries posted in places we don't expect. From your description, as spooky weird as that was, they sounded like professionals. The kind of professionals I don't think we see often. At least not what I'm used to."

"The sense I got was your standard issue psychopath with a little money and firepower. A lethal combination," Leira said. She drew her gun from the shoulder holster and started walking up the gravel road, scanning from left to right. "You stay back by the car, Correk. Not the time for iffy magic. Sometimes a nice solid piece of flying lead is what's called for."

"I'd argue but I don't have my bow and arrow with me. But if I did..."

"I know, I know. You'd be formidable." Leira held up her hand to stop them from saying anything else and held her finger to her lips for a moment, signaling to Hagan to follow right behind her.

Even though the house wasn't visible yet, she knew it was

there. She even had a sense of how many guards there were. As they got closer to the house, the feeling of dread she had felt before began to nag at her. *The killer is still in the house.*

Leira turned back to Hagan and whispered, "There's only one guard with him."

Hagan had his gun drawn and looked calmer than before. He was getting used to the idea of yet another magical creature in his midst, even if this time it was Leira. A sheen of sweat was visible on the top of his head.

"How would you know that? Don't answer. My brain already feels like it's melting. Help, I've fallen into a Marvel comic and I can't get out." He held up his hands like he was under arrest.

"Humor is good," Leira said. "Come on, let's do this."

She got to a stand of tall cacti and was about to turn the corner when a wall of energy hit her in the chest, knocking the wind out of her. She doubled over for a moment, catching her breath.

"What now?" Hagan stopped, looking concerned. He tried to peer around the tallest cactus but all he could see was a broken down single-story wooden house with a rotting front porch. He looked back at Leira. "You getting more magic brain waves?"

"Feels more like a cosmic warning."

She stood up, ready to push through it, using the memory of the connection with Correk to find a way to swim upstream against the steady pulses of the dark energy. It hit her hard again, right in the center of her chest, and threatened to push her back. But this time she was ready. Instead of fighting it, she allowed the energy to pass through her.

"Stay right behind me."

"Normally, I'd be insulted but under the present conditions, sure, why not?" Hagan replied. "Who knew I'd be the novice at my age."

Leira could feel her energy draining but she pressed on.

"Wish I'd eaten more carbs this morning. Thank God I'm a runner."

"I have no idea what anything you're saying has to do with what's happening right now, but I'm always on board. At least for the carbs. If it helps, I took care of that for both of us," Hagan said, giving a quick pat to his belly.

Leira sensed the change in the energy field and felt a rip opening. The heavy, dark energy was parting in front of her, creating a path.

"Correk, no," she said in a hushed voice. *Correk is clearing the way. What will this cost him?*

"What is it?" Hagan looked around quickly, but he couldn't see any movement from the house. "We need to cover this ground quickly," he said. The dry lawn was crunching under their feet. Every noise sounded amplified to them, and he was acutely aware of the number of windows staring back at them from the house.

Leira used two fingers to point toward the left side of the house. Hagan gave her a nod and bent low, moving as fast as he could toward the east side of the house.

Leira scaled the right side of the porch and easily swung over the rotten railing. She heard the familiar whine of a bullet whizzing past her head. She hit the floor of the porch, cracking two of the old boards, and rolled against the house, just beneath the windows. She crawled past the window and stood up with her back against the house. She leaned forward and craned her neck, trying to catch a glimpse through the window. It was going to be impossible to take a shot without knowing where the little girl was located.

The current of energy she had followed to the house came rushing through her like a gust of strong wind, sweeping into the house. From inside the house, she heard a choked gurgle, followed by gasping.

Leira hesitated, but only for a moment. The killer knew they were there, which meant the girl was in even more immediate danger. There was no time to waste. She took a look through the front window, ready to fire, using her newly found ability to get a faster, clearer assessment of the room in front of her. On the floor in the front room were two large men clawing at themselves, gasping for air, turning shades of blue and purple.

The back door of the house splintered as Hagan kicked his way in with one good solid kick. He entered the front room, gun drawn. He quickly spotted the two men and glanced up at Leira. He put his knee in the middle of the larger man's back and pulled his cuffs out. Leira entered through the front door, rushing in and covering him while he secured the second man.

Neither man resisted and within seconds, both of them had passed out from lack of oxygen. Hagan patted each of them down quickly, removing three small guns, an assortment of knives, and a pair of brass knuckles.

"Regular murderous boy scouts. They came prepared," he observed.

Leira could sense they were running dangerously short of air. Magic still had them by the throat. "Correk, stop! They're down," she yelled.

"I thought you told him to stay by the car!" Hagan looked toward the door but didn't see anyone. He shook his head. "Magic monkey business. Can't say I'm not grateful for it. Stopped these mooks from shooting at us. This is why I eat so much," he said.

The larger man began to stir. Hagen pulled him to his feet.

"That's the killer," Leira told him. "Keep your eye on this one," she added, pointing toward the other man who was still unconscious.

Leira held her gun in front of her as she went to search the other two rooms in the house. She could sense that there was no more danger, but she wasn't willing to take a risk on brand-new magic. In the bedroom, someone had pushed an old, wide wooden dresser in front of the closet door. Leira shoved it aside, scraping the floor. She opened the closet door slowly, gun drawn, ready for anything.

The missing girl was pressed up against a back corner. She looked dirty and frightened, but unharmed. Leira quickly holstered her gun.

"It's okay, it's okay. Lucy Kate, right? Okay. Hello Lucy Kate," she said in a soft voice, her hands held up in front of her. She crouched down and reached for the girl. Lucy Kate drew back, terrified. An idea came to Leira and she summoned the energy, the magic, and gently reached out toward the girl.

"This may be a really stupid idea."

Her eyes shimmered briefly and Leira could sense a ripple of energy flowing from her toward the girl. Leira inched forward saying, "You're safe now," over and over again, until she had the girl safely held in her arms.

It took some help from Correk to get the two large men, still dazed from the lack of air and Correk's magic, in separate unmarked cars. Leira deposited the girl in the front seat of the Mustang. The girl drew her knees up under her chin and wrapped her arms around her legs.

"How do we explain all of this?" asked Hagan. There were large sweat stains under his arms. "I'm not even sure what happened. That'll make it tough to fill out all that paperwork. Besides, we have to explain why we went off by ourselves and didn't tell anyone what we were doing. What excuse do we have for being out here and *tripping* over this in another jurisdiction?" he asked sarcastically, making air quotes with his hands. "You have a magic spell for that?"

"Yes, we call that lying," said Correk. "Works pretty much the same way here as it does on Oriceran."

Leira noticed Correk was leaning against the car and his skin was even paler than usual. "You're going to need some food, and this time something that resembles actual food. No arguments."

"Our story..." said Hagan. "Somebody start this mythic tale for me."

"How about..." Correk started.

"How about we got a tip and were so close to the area we drove on up to take a look. An anonymous informant told us they were about to pull out. No time to call it in. A six-year-old girl was at risk. These two goons can talk their fool heads off about something invisible strangling them and we'll do our best shrug. Everyone got it?" Leira asked. She raised her eyebrows, her mouth in a straight, determined line.

"Simple. I like it," said Hagan. "Gonna be a shitload of paperwork."

"Always is," she replied.

"Even a few discussions about jurisdictions and cooperation."

"Yep," Leira agreed as she got in the car. Hagan was still muttering, walking back toward his older Oldsmobile. He got in and started up the engine.

Leira started up the Mustang and did a sharp U-turn, spitting gravel, eliciting a moan from the back seat. The little girl looked up at Leira, worried.

"It's okay," Leira said softly. "He can't get to us from back there."

The little girl was sitting in Correk's lap, holding on to the side of the seat.

Leira looked over at Correk. "This is almost too much for me," she said. "We can tell a lie to the Captain and given the outcome, they'll buy it without a lot of fuss. But what about these Silver Griffins? Won't they be along next to tell us to cut it out?"

"Possibly. Likely."

"Great," Leira said, turning on the lights as they pulled out onto the paved road.

"Sometimes you have to take a risk and break the rules," Correk said, looking out toward the road.

"You don't strike me as a rule breaker. And, in case you can't feel this one, I'm not either, usually. Feels too much like lying. That's another thing I'm not a big fan of." She looked in the rearview mirror and saw Hagan closely following her as they cruised out onto the highway, pushing eighty-five miles an hour. It wouldn't be long before they were back in Austin. "So, what do we tell them? The Griffins?"

"They already know what we've done. They'll tell us what to think, and soon."

Leira looked down at Lucy Kate. She felt an unexpected twinge she wasn't used to after a case. "This whole feeling thing is a rough roller coaster ride," she said softly.

"It suits you. Cousin."

"Yeah, I caught that earlier. Kind of cousin. Both elves." She glanced at him. "We'll be circling back to that, don't you worry."

"You did the right thing, no matter who finds out."

"Yeah, well, so did you," she said.

CHAPTER THREE

The sign that hung on the door to the large, open room said PDF in large black letters. It stood for Paranormal Defense Force and was comprised of a small group of hand-selected magical creatures whose ancestry went back to Oriceran.

One of the requirements though, was that each hire had to have been born on Earth. Magical beings made ordinary human beings very nervous, in general. It was why they kept the small department off the books. The PDF was the ultimate black-op.

There were jokes around the department about what PDF actually stood for. On bad days it was joked the PDF stood for *put down fast*. A reference to the days when human beings liked to dissect anything they didn't understand. On better days, PDF stood for *presto digitalis frenzy*, an incantation every magical child learned that made someone cluck like a chicken.

At least once a year, someone got fed up and made a human general, or worse, a Congressman from some small state who had just learned about their existence and insisted on a tour, flap their arms and crane their neck, gulping in air as they crowed at the fluorescent lights overhead.

The *never was, never will be* spell was getting a workout from PDF.

Even so, there was an unspoken agreement that once someone had let loose with a childish prank, they'd give it a minute or two before reversing the spell and erasing the memory. That way everyone got one good selfie in before the fun was over.

It helped that all the members of the PDF looked as ordinary as any other mid-level manager who worked for the government, even if they did have the ability to turn somebody into a toad.

The two women sat in front of the oversized virtual screen hanging in front of them, puzzled at the data scrolling by just above their heads. It looks like unintelligible green symbols in straight lines but they understood every word. Their eyes followed along as their concern grew.

They were sitting in a nondescript, low-slung grey brick building that was tucked in the back of an office park decked out to look like different companies that sold manufacturing equipment in Alexandria, Virginia just across the river from Washington, D.C. It was a government front for an enterprise that was known only as the G4 Project, including the PDF. The witches and wizards, and a handful of elves that worked there liked to refer to it as Area 51, but only when their human coworkers weren't around.

That line usually got a snicker or a raised eyebrow out of any new hire. Part of the requirement, after all, was you had to have some non-human blood.

"You sure this isn't the work of the Silver Griffins?" asked the younger woman, dressed neatly in navy blue slacks and blazer. She wrinkled her nose and squinted at the data still coming in. "I can't remember in the five years I've been here ever seeing so much unregistered magic phenomena. Lois, you've been here longer. Does this ring a bell?"

Lois scowled at the other woman. "I'm not old in witch years you know, Patsy," she said, pushing the thin brown frame of her glasses back up her nose.

Patsy smirked and let out a snort. "Okay, whatever. You didn't answer my question. Any of this look familiar? I mean, geez, that has to be a right good explosion, right? We should report this to the G4 section manager."

"Now, hold on to your britches, there, Patsy. They're just a bunch of government humans. The worst kind! Very literal! Long-winded! They'll call for a study! You've seen what they do when they hear that one of our kind is out using their natural talents. They run amok! What if this is some naturally occurring gases, or something?"

"Ha! That's a good one. Remember what happened back in '04 when those elves managed to make the fireworks hang in the air over the Super Bowl? That nice Light Elf, what was his name?"

"Justin Timberlake."

"Yeah, that's the one. Sang at the halftime just as the fireworks went off and hung there, glittering in the sky."

"So pretty! Sure, I remember. Saw it live on TV and said to Earl, Earl, that sure is pretty but it's gonna cause trouble. Don't you know my phone rang just a minute later? Didn't get to see the end of the game."

"Thank goodness for Justin's quick thinking and that so-called wardrobe malfunction!" Lois let out a peal of laughter, bending over in her chair.

"One little nipple and everyone forgot about the fireworks. Humans," Patsy chortled. "See all of those swirls and triangles and the sparkling explosions next to the one that looks like a ferris wheel gone crazy?" asked Patsy, pointing at the symbols streaming in front of them, reflecting off of Lois' glasses. "That's an explosion in the middle of downtown Chicago."

"Huh. I thought that was just a large use of magic like an artifact or a group of wizards performing a spell together."

"Well, in a matter of speaking, but when it's combined with the swirls it means a big magic kaboom. Now, seeing as how all the morning programs haven't spit out their coffee and run as fast as they could to Chi-town I'd say someone also did a pretty neat job of covering it up. That, I'll bet you my tenth row Aerosmith tickets, was done by the Silver Griffins. The big boom doesn't read like them, but the cover up sure does."

"What do you think it all means?"

"Someone powerful is using magic out there," said Patsy. "From the looks of it, not your average Oriceran. Hmmm, interesting."

"We have to report it. That's our entire job description," said Lois.

"No doubt. It's how we phrase it that will matter."

"You mean, like we maybe don't mention the use of an amnesia spell..."

"Good example, yes. And, maybe we dig around for a few facts first. Look in the Chicago Tribune for anything weird that happened that day."

"That works for me. Just sounds like we were doing our best to do an even better job."

"Totally agree."

"Uh oh."

"What now?" Patsy pushed her long blonde bangs out of her face.

"Look!" Lois held up her smart phone. "Front page of the Tribune from the same day as the explosion. Just under the fold. Two people mysteriously disappear from a college soiree. A professor and a dean. No history of mental illness it says. Total mystery. No traces found."

Patsy looked up at the screen and pulled out her wand, a government-issued willow branch left over from the glory days of the 1970s. Totally old school and not as effective as the new ones made on 3-D printers, but it got the job done. Besides, it was the only type approved for use within the small bunker of a building. They were required to leave them in their lockers at night.

Patsy waved the wand around in short swirls and occasional sharp pokes in the direction of the screen that was part paranormal magic and part modern technology.

"Oh, that's bad. That's bad indeed. Two deaths for sure, and it's the same location as the big kaboom. Well, the humans will not take this well at all."

"Unless the two victims are not of their kind. They tend to take that a little better."

"A lot better. Quit Googling so much. Give me a chance to think." The green letters flittered across the screen, letting off sounds like children's toys, with high-pitched whines, clicking and whirring.

"Maybe we could run it past the gnomes in magical forensic accounting first."

"Not a bad idea. Very discreet group, those gnomes. They seem to know how to handle the touchy government types. And they dress so well, with their little suits and bowlers."

"You mean touchy humans," said Lois.

"Well, that goes without saying, but when you mix it with mid-level government managers, well, kaboom!" Patsy wiggled her fingers in the air, rolling her eyes.

Lois shrieked with laughter followed by a hiccup, not uncommon for her. "You think it's that girl? You know, that detective in the wild, wild West?"

"If you mean Texas, maybe, but I doubt it." Patsy pulled her wand out from where she had tucked it neatly into the back of her bouffant. Lois' government issue willow branch hung from a delicate gold chain at her waist, right next to her ID badge, always at the ready. "You still have that connection in the Silver Griffins?"

"My cousin? Of course I do. Not many ever choose to retire. You know that. But she's never one for gossiping, particularly since there's a rumor going around that the PDF ratted on a few magical beings last year."

"Yeah, I heard that one last time I was in Hanover County. Lovely spot for a kemana. Best tomatoes on the planet."

"Those are from Oriceran seeds and there's a little magic in that Hanover soil, you know."

"Who doesn't know that?" Lois was always irritated at having the obvious pointed out to her. "Best BLT there is."

"What were you doing in Hanover? Was it work?" Patsy asked, pushing the topic further.

Lois looked at her over the top of her glasses and said quietly, "You know these walls have ears."

Patsy pulled her wand back out and with a flick of the wrist, swirled the air around them.

"You have a minute, girlfriend. What were you up to?"

"Recharging of course, although those damn tomatoes were a good enough reason. I know they like to keep our energy levels at a minimum, but they don't have our best interests at heart. I figure out ways to drive toward Richmond every few months."

"I hear you. Who *did* rat out those wizards last year?"

"I heard it was their own stupidity. Got a little high on some Oriceran weed and were found making a light show out of fireballs around the Capital. Had to tie them all up till they came down off the high, otherwise they would have kept sneaking in spells. Juvenile stuff. Of course, they had no memory of it. That O weed will make you forget your name. Still, no one believes me when I tell them it wasn't us who told on them."

"Ah crap! What was that?" Patsy slid out of her chair, almost plopping on the floor before rebounding to her feet. The symbols were taking on different shapes, spitting new data across the screen.

"More unauthorized use, but this time in Austin, Texas."

"Well, that *has* to be her. What was her name?"

"Hang on, I have it right here," Lois said, shuffling papers.

"Your fascination with putting things on paper baffles me."

"The humans love it. Here it is. Leira Berens, an unaffiliated magical being. Recently detected and in the company of an actual Oriceran. A Light Elf. Very interesting times, Patsy."

"You can say that again." Patsy swirled her wand, stirring the air again. "Hey, did you hear about the joke Harvey played on those visiting generals last week? Made all their voices sound like they were sucking helium!" Patsy laughed, almost choking on her gum. "I thought I would pee my pants!"

"Better be careful or they'll gas this place with us in it and we'll end up in some cheap science lab."

"Didn't you hear? A group of us put up sensors last month to detect anything hinky. Never trust a human who's still breathing, I say."

"You mean like your husband?"

"Especially him!" Patsy snorted. The air around them stilled once more, and the recording devices that whirred constantly in the background taking down every conversation picked up where they left off.

"Back to work," said Lois. "Break's over."

"I'll get that report about Detective Berens right over to HQ. Someone will have to tag her. Make it easier to track her whereabouts." Patsy rolled her eyes when she said it. She was making sure she used what she liked to call her 'official voice'.

Any witch or wizard worth their wand knew how to get a GPS tag to track whatever they wanted it to track.

"I'm getting hungry, you? Want something from the machine?" Lois lifted the wand hanging by her side. "Yummina," she said.

There was a loud rattle from down the hall as the old vending machine shook and then leaned forward on two legs, followed by a thwack as a package of Oreos slid out and came zipping through the doorway, landing neatly in Lois' hands. "They should give in and leave them in a box for us."

"Where's the sport in that? Get me the vanilla cookies. I love those."

Lois rolled her eyes. "Almost not worth the effort. Vanilla. Okay, Leira Berens, we've got your number." Lois swirled the air with her wand before setting a pen to magically fill out the paperwork. "What they don't know, we won't have to hear about."

"Agreed."

Leira took a quick look around, checking to see who else was around the precinct. Almost everyone was out checking leads, eating lunch or just generally elsewhere. Leira was riding her desk, filling out paperwork on her laptop. It was taking forever.

Nothing like solving a case a little too easily to make the higher-ups cough up more paperwork, more interviews. It wasn't that everyone wasn't happy with them, and there was talk of a commendation for her and Hagan. It's just that by nature, law enforcement is skeptical of anything that ties up too neatly. On the other hand, as long as Leira didn't write something that waved a red flag at everyone, she was pretty sure they would all happily move on to the next case. The bad guys were arrested, the child was returned safely, and the news reports were making them out to be heroes.

No one likes to shoot down the hero, if they can avoid it.

"Gaw, I hate paperwork," Leira muttered, resting her head on her arms for a moment. She popped back up and looked around again. "Am I gonna do it? I think I am."

Leira stretched her hands out on the desk, pressing down as she took a deep breath and let it out. She felt the warmth behind her eyes grow and everything around her take on a sharp focus. The edges of her hands began to glow and the faint outline of ancient symbols appeared just under her skin.

"Just this once. It will only take a minute and then it'll be done. Come on, focus and breathe deeply. You can do it."

"Fuck, Berens! It was easier to absorb the fact that you might be half alien than it is to find out you've taken up meditation and are getting in touch with your inner self!" Hagan dropped a case-book on his desk loudly, startling Leira.

She stood up quickly, knocking her knees against the desk.

"What the hell!" The clarity left her instantly, and she could feel her heart pounding in her chest. "Hagan wear a fucking bell, goddammit!"

The reversal from conjuring up the magic from deep inside of her, to suddenly shutting it off abruptly left her lightheaded and she had to stand still for a moment, waiting for the room to stop spinning.

"You okay there, Berens? Not like you to be caught off guard."

"Yeah, well, a lot has changed." She rested her hands squarely on the desk and sat down slowly as a wave of nausea came over her and just as quickly left. *This magic thing is going to take some getting used to.*

Hagan flipped open his notebook, dropping heavily into his chair with a sigh and a grunt. He flipped through a couple of pages and looked back at Leira. "What the hell were you up to?" He looked surprised. "Tell me you're not so stupid that you were trying to do magic in the middle of a police precinct."

"Not so fucking loud, if you don't mind."

"Oh, so *me* talking too loud is what you're worried about." He lowered his voice. "I get you using magic to find the girl. There was a time factor there, and the men who took her didn't give a rat's ass about her well-being. But what exactly are you working on right now that would make you take a risk like that? Last time

I checked we have a probable suicide, and a pretty open and shut, husband killed the wife case."

Leira drummed her fingers on her desk, trying to put off admitting what she was up to, but there was no getting around it. She decided to go for it and sat up straighter, looking him in the eye and said, "Paperwork." She gave him one of her better dead fish looks, pressing her lips together, daring him to say anything.

Hagan stared back at her and for a moment it seemed as if his anger was going to erupt. Leira braced herself for the argument and took a quick look around to make sure there was still nobody around to hear the conversation that would entail magic, paperwork and other planets.

Hagan wrinkled his nose. Then his mouth opened, and he was laughing so hard his belly shook.

Leira wasn't sure if she was insulted by this reaction and crossed her arms over her chest. "You want to tell me what's so funny?"

Hagan tried to tell her, gulping air, but was taking a few false starts before he could get out a complete sentence. Leira waited, her frustration growing, and she wondered if there was a spell to shut her partner up. *Bad thought, Leira. No practicing magic on friends allowed. We're just going to make that a general rule. Otherwise everyone back at the bar will eventually end up as a cockroach or rat. Well, maybe a dog and or rabbit. I really do like those people.*

Hagan wiped his eyes with the back of his hand and took a good look at Leira. "You're thinking about what you can turn me into, aren't you? Don't bother lying to me. I've been a detective way too long not to know when somebody is thinking about what they'd like to do to me. The only difference is you might pull it off." He looked her up and down, checking for anything peculiar, arching an eyebrow. "Changing someone's basic structure has to be against the law, somewhere."

Leira smirked. "Don't worry. I'm too much of a rule follower

41

to change your ass into…" She stopped, trying to consider exactly what she would've turned him into.

"And not that you exactly know how yet."

"And not that I exactly know how yet," she admitted. "But I wouldn't."

"But you're still going to take the shortcut with the paperwork. I know you. Once you've made up your mind, and set the course, there's very little that will make you turn back. Even common sense and apparently the chance of getting caught performing higgledy-piggledy." Hagan wiggled his fingers in the air and rolled his eyes.

"Please tell me that's not what I look like when I perform magic."

Hagan ignored her and pushed away from his desk to get a better view of the captain's office, which was still empty. "If you're going to do it, you better do it now. This is your window and I'm not sure how long it's going to last. I'll be your lookout."

"It says something really good about our relationship that you didn't make doing *your* paperwork part of the deal. Or you just knew I was going to do yours, too."

"Sister, after the past few days there is nothing in this world that I'm entirely sure of anymore. If I saw you levitate and spin around I don't think I'd be surprised."

"I'm not sure flying is part of the deal."

"What about invisibility? Or x-ray vision? Oh, oh, oh, what about bending steel or shooting out spider webs from your wrists?" Hagan held up his arms and aimed his wrists at different parts of the room. "Zing! Ping! Wazing!"

Leira couldn't help herself and smiled at him.

Hagan stopped what he was doing. "Well, that's new. You actually gave a genuine smile. I haven't seen you do that much, if it didn't involve dragging some felon off the hard pavement."

"Leira 2.0," she said. She shook her head and gave her more

usual crooked smile. "I know, I know. I'm evolving. I suppose it was bound to happen."

"I'm not sure you're what Darwin ever had in mind in terms of evolution, but I'll take it. Now, are we going to get this show on the road, or not? Let's get this paperwork done." Hagan rolled his chair around till he was sitting next to Leira. "This won't throw off your spell or anything, will it? I don't want to get any runoff. It'd be hard to explain to the wife, much less the Captain."

"Something tells me that won't be a problem," she replied. "But I can't exactly guarantee it. Correk's waiting for me back at the guesthouse and without him we're just doing magic for jollies without a roadmap."

Hagan rolled his chair to the edge of the desk. "I'm still in. Let 'er rip."

Leira stretched out her arms and shook her hands. "I'm sure those few inches will make all the difference." She ignored Hagan and looked back at the screen again. She felt the warmth slide up from deep inside of her more easily this time. It was getting easier to call on the magic and conjure up what was becoming a familiar feeling.

The energy rushed through her, feeling like it was filling her veins with something warm and tingly. Everything in the room became more distinct and she could focus on the task at hand. Thoughts about what happened yesterday or worries about what might come next dropped away. Hagan stared at her, his jaw dropping open as her eyes began to glow. The symbols appeared under her skin but this time they even vibrated.

"Holy mother of God." Hagan's head turned side to side, looking at the monitor then Leira and back, wondering if this was after all, a good idea. "What if we're unleashing something? You know, like those ancient mummy curses. I have got to stop watching those movies." His hand instinctively drifted toward his gun, just in case.

Leira was no longer paying attention to anything in the room except the computer screen. Every question in the report came to her without reading it. The answer came to her just as easily and at the same moment she thought it, it materialized on the screen.

Hagan watched what was happening and saw page after page of the report getting filled out in just seconds. He was torn between two feelings. One of relief that he wouldn't be spending his evening eating bad food, trying to stay awake and finding new ways to explain how they found the girl without having to use the words magic or hocus-pocus. The other was a feeling in the back of his mind that there was no way this could end well.

"Maybe this will be more like X-Files than Independence Day. Right? No, the aliens all die in both of those," he said. "I'm not going to let that happen to you." He knew she wasn't registering what he was saying, but he meant every word.

"Done."

Hagan's eyes widened. "Even mine?"

"Yours, too."

"How'd you get past my password? Was it magic?"

"It doesn't take magic to figure out that your password is maple bacon and you never change it." Leira stood up and stretched." We should get out of here so we don't have to look busy when someone walks through. I won't hit the send button for a few more hours to at least buy us some credibility. We can't do this all the time because they'd wonder how we suddenly learned to type so fast."

Hagan stood up and pulled his jacket off the back of his chair, folding it over his arm. "Agreed. You know, Leira," he said as they made their way out. "This is more than my old brain can take in. At this point I'm just rolling with what happens and trusting that you won't blow us up. Or if you do blow us up, I don't see it coming."

"Always the optimist, Felix. I'll do my best."

"Patsy, come take a look. There's another blip on the screen. Our girl is getting a little loose with the abracadabra." Lois pushed her glasses up her nose and frowned at screen.

"Oh geez," said Lois. "Any word back yet from that first report we sent in?"

"Not that I know of. I even tried a couple spells to see if I could listen in, but those government types aren't as dumb as they used to be. It was all kind of muffled and hard to hear."

"So, what were you able to make out?"

"That's the oddest part. They didn't seem all that upset. From what I could tell they see Leira Berens as a potential asset. Go figure."

"Go figure," Lois echoed, amazed. "Just when you think you've heard everything."

"Next thing you know they'll be offering her a job."

"Remember the old days when they used to burn us at the stake? Then they went through that whole stage of trying to cut us up and study us?" Lois shuddered.

"Thank the heavens for Hogwarts and chocolate frogs."

"Yeah, but Rowling took a big chance spilling all of those inside secrets. Someone might have started to wonder how she knew so much."

"Humans are slow. Bet the gates are open for years before someone starts to ask those kinds of questions."

"In the meantime," said Lois, lifting up her willow wand, "How about a little TV?" She waved her wand and the data pouring across the screen was replaced with The Price is Right.

"Much better. Oooh, they're still on the showcase."

"You think we should alert the big guys that the detective is using magic on a more regular basis?"

"How do you think she's able to pull so much energy?"

"Now, that's a very good question. Eight thousand! Say, eight thousand," she yelled at the image of Drew Carey floating across the room. "Drat, I was over."

"Why didn't you use your wand?"

"Not as much fun. You're right, let's keep this to ourselves for a little longer. You still have that artifact your grandfather used to hear better? Let's see if we can find out more before we rat out one of our own, just in case."

"Just in case."

CHAPTER FOUR

L eira pulled into the parking lot at Costco and turned off the engine. She was trying to choose her words carefully.

"What?" Correk looked at her. "I can see a lecture of some kind approaches. You didn't have to come with me. Look, Scott gave me a map and a bus schedule."

"You can't get in Costco without a membership card, and they all know it. It's why they brought it up in the first place. They have a habit of testing new people to see how many favors they can get out of them before you say no. I'm the only one at Estelle's who's a member. It was their Christmas present to me last year."

"Interesting. An exclusive meeting hall for shopping. Oriceran has something similar but it has far darker intentions."

"This is more like shopping at Target but in bulk sizes. You show up to get a cake and push out a cart full of jeans, a few books, yoga pants, a case of beer and a twelve-pack of steaks. I usually end up with a shopping hangover."

"We can use your plastic card. It will be alright."

"You're dying to see if they have an as seen on TV aisle, aren't you? We can't do that again. Look me in the eye. No!" She gave him a stern look and waved her finger sharply back and forth.

"You could stand to relax a little more. It could only help you with learning magic. Okay, yes, I want to see more gadgets. They're like cheap magic tricks for humans."

Leira rolled her eyes. "Tell me again, who exactly told you this would be a good idea? I want names. Fuck, it's like giving a box of matches to a pyro and then being surprised at what happens next."

"Normally, I don't find it useful to do what I think you Earthlings call tattle."

"Well, you're going to have to do something about those ears or wear the hat again." Leira pulled the knit hat out from under the seat, brushing off crumbs the troll left. She held it out to Correk, raising her eyebrows, giving it a shake.

"You have another idea?"

Correk didn't answer. His eye glowed and symbols appeared around his hairline. His ears slowly rounded.

"Whoa, did you just change the structure of your ear? You didn't even say anything!"

"No, it's just an illusion. Not everything has to be spoken. Some things can just be felt, imagined. We call it a glamour spell. The gnomes lent me a book. If you touch them…hey! Don't put out your hand." He batted her hand away. "You're not feeling up my ears. I assure you, the points are still there. Now, if that's your last objection, let's get in there!"

"Way too excited about Costco."

The troll climbed out of Leira's pocket, neatly rolling over the top of the front seat and into the back disappearing to the floorboards below.

"You realize, that wasn't a good sign. He looked like he had a plan before he went over the back of the seat."

Leira waited, but when it became clear Correk wasn't going to answer she said, "Spill it. It was Mitzi, wasn't it? She has a crush on you, you know. What she doesn't realize is that if you keep buying in bulk like that, those six pack abs are going to become more like a tootsie pop."

"What?"

"It's a candy. Like a lollipop with a surprise inside. Hard on the outside." Leira stopped herself at the last moment from pointing at the outline of Correk's abs clearly showing through the long sleeve shirt. Instead, she knocked on her head. "But chewy on the inside. It doesn't take long. One of our better weapons of warfare."

"They said you'd say that."

"Aha! I knew it!" Leira practically jumped off the front seat, banging her hand against the steering wheel, letting out a sharp honk from the horn. A mother dragging a reluctant toddler behind her jumped and turned around to glare at Leira.

"Sorry," Leira said, holding her hands up like she was under arrest. She lowered her hands and said, "I knew who the *they* are. It's the usual list of suspects from the bar. Mike? Craig? They give you a list of their own?"

A smile spread across Correk's face.

"Now what?"

"I may be from another planet altogether, but family operates pretty much the same way everywhere I've ever been. Well, maybe not for the gnomes. They don't talk as much and they all look alike. I'm not even sure how they manage to tell each other apart. And they share everything…"

"You have a point buried in there somewhere?" Leira turned in her seat and got up on her knees so she could get a better look over the seat. She could sense something was happening with the troll. That, and the loud chewing noises were causing her concern. "Be careful with my car, little dude," she muttered.

"It's like you're in their clan. They've adopted you and you've accepted." Correk pulled a list out of his pocket. "And yes, I have a list. They said it was the only way to shop in this large bazaar.

I'm splitting a bag of tube socks with Craig, and Mike assures me you can get Cheetos shaped like little balls in giant containers. And I'm looking for the Double Stuffed Oreos."

"You look way too happy when you say these things. Oh damn, what have we done? You are a Light Elf in the royal court. You don't wear tube socks or eat orange, crusty air."

"I believe the saying is, when on Earth, do as the humans do."

Leira leaned further over the seat till she could see the troll. He was chewing on an old green wad of gum.

"Nom, nom, nom." The troll was at first delighted, munching away, but then a look of confusion spread over his face. He pulled one end of the gum out of his mouth, watching it stretch. He pulled his fingers apart and stared at the gum stuck on them.

Leira looked at the wet, sticky hairball and felt herself gag. The troll shook his hand, letting out a high-pitched exasperated squeak. It wasn't long before the gum was stuck all over him.

"Uh oh, yum fucked."

"He sounds defeated," said Correk, glancing back.

"He's got gum in his green hair. This won't end well."

"Give him a chance. They're very resourceful."

The troll tried rubbing his hands on the floor. Crumbs and bits of dirt were ground into the gum, cutting down on the sticky texture. A happier, "Mah, fuck hmph." He threw himself onto the floor of the car and rolled around like a log from one end to the other. The troll stopped and looked down at his body, now covered in a rainbow mashup of crumbs. He patted his belly and trilled softly.

"I've seen gunshot wounds that weren't that gross. Is it safe to try and take food away from a troll?" she asked. She slowly lowered her hand toward the troll's mouth.

"I wouldn't. I've never known it to end well. What's he eating?"

Leira quickly took her hand back. "Fuzzy gum. I don't suppose it'll hurt him."

"Have you fed him lately?"

Leira's face warmed. "Oh crap! I guess I own this one. What do you feed a troll? Can they eat Kibble?" She slid back into her seat.

"Not sure what a kibble is but they're little tiny garbage dumps. Scavengers. They eat whatever they can find. On Oriceran it's nuts and berries they find in the forest and the scraps others have thrown away. Works out well for everyone. Here," he said, gesturing at the vast blacktop full of cars, "there's not much forest. You're going to have to find food for him."

"Then we're in the right place to solve this one, both short term and... whatever the hell long term turns out to be. Fuck, I didn't think of that till just now. Do trolls live a long time? No, wait! Don't tell me!"

"What's a Topo Chico?"

"A fancy Mexican fizzy water. That's Estelle's order, isn't it?"

"See? This is what I mean." Correk slapped the piece of paper. "You really know these people, inside and out."

"They've all taken to you, too. Come on, we'd better get going. Looks like quite a list you've got. Who needed a giant bag of frozen fruit?" Leira opened the glove box and rooted around till she found a small rag with a few grease stains. "Better than nothing."

She leaned over the seat and scooped up the troll, giving him a slight shake before wrapping him in the rag. Only a few crumbs fell off. "This time, he's all yours. Think of it as shared custody. This trip was your idea, so you watch him."

"Fair enough, but he won't listen to me like he listens to you."

"I can live with that." Leira opened the car door.

"So, we're not going to talk about your mother yet. I was trying to wait but it hasn't come up." Correk got out of the car.

"What is there to say? I keep rolling it around in my head. Trying to figure out how to get her out without anyone dragging her right back in again. I don't have power of attorney over her.

Even if I did, she was committed by the state." Leira shook her head and started walking toward the oversized warehouse. "The only thing I've come up with is to magic her out of there."

"That's not really a thing." Correk caught up with Leira, even trying to find a pocket where he could keep the troll hidden and happy.

"Hang on," Leira said. She ran back to the Mustang and opened the trunk, pulling out a green hoodie. "This'll work. Put it on and he can sit in the pocket. Do you really think we can't use magic to get her out of there?" There was a catch in Leira's voice.

"There's a limit to everything, I assure you. However, I suspect your powers are more than capable. Eventually. You don't have enough control yet for us to be sure that we wouldn't end up making things worse. Then, there's the Silver Griffins."

"Someone would notice I messed with the order of things and send a bolt of magic."

"That's one way of putting it."

"Do you have a better idea?" There was a hopeful note in Leira's voice that wasn't normally there. She wasn't used to feeling so vulnerable and asking for help.

Correk stopped near the entrance. He put his hand on Leira's shoulder. "I have been a part of much more difficult journeys. We'll find a way."

Leira stood still and closed her eyes, searching for the feeling that was always with her these days. The buzz of magic. *We'll find a way.*

"Okay," she said, shaking off darker thoughts. "Time to get our oversized shopping on. Get a cart and meet me back near the front in thirty minutes. That's plenty of time. Probably too much time. I'm not guaranteeing we're getting everything you pick up."

"I have money from your family." Correk pulled a wad of cash out of his pocket. Leira saw the curve of his stomach and felt herself flush.

Have to stop doing that every time I see the man's skin.

"That helps," she said, flustered. "Put it back in your pocket and grab a cart."

"You know, we could still be cousins."

"Alright, alright. That helps. Fuck. Grab a cart, already. One of those rolling metal cages. You put what you want to buy in that."

"I saw them at CVS. They're amazing."

"Go figure. No one ever stole a shopping cart and took it back to Oriceran. You travel through a portal from another world and ooh and aah over a shopping cart and Cheetos. Hey! No gadgets," she yelled after him, as she reluctantly watched Correk head off toward the home goods section.

"The tube socks are in the other direction! I know you can hear me!"

A woman turned to see who Leira was yelling at and smiled. "Men. They say they don't like to shop but put them in a Costco and they go nuts."

Correk quickly abandoned his first cart. A front wheel kept spinning in circles making it drift to the right. He considered applying just a little magic but thought better of it. He turned around, retracing his steps in the direction of the front of the store to get another one.

"Try a pig in a blanket?" A rangy, thin woman with spiky blonde hair wearing a blue Costco apron stood behind a tall, narrow table with a hotplate full of little wieners stuffed in crescent rolls. She was holding a pair of tongs in the air, yellow bracelets jangling around her wrist.

"Beg your pardon?" The smell made him stop. That and the troll squirming to get out of his pocket. Correk clamped his hand down over his stomach, holding the troll as still as possible.

Correk raised his fist to cover his mouth and coughed, "Nesturnium."

"I thought that only worked when I did it." Leira was right behind him, whispering over his shoulder.

Correk jumped and almost lost his grip on the pocket.

"It does but hope springs eternal. Dammit! Announce yourself!"

"You mean, like with a card? Not the way I roll. Helps to be able to sneak up on people. Hang on, come here."

Leira bent over so her face was closer to the pocket.

"How close do I have to be when I say it?"

"Not that close."

Leira straightened back up, waving at the old man walking by, leaning on a cane. "Hello," he said, tipping his hat with way too broad a smile.

"Well, that was awkward," she said, her face warming. "Okay, from here is good?"

"Perfect. Right where you are," said Correk through clenched teeth.

"No need to get twisted about it. Simple mistake. Things like that happen all the time on this side of the portal."

"Any time you're ready," he said, annoyed.

"Okay, okay." Leira was enjoying the moment. *So much better than touchie-feelie.* "All right, that's enough." She took in a deep breath and let it out slowly. "Nesturnium."

"It isn't necessary to do the whole deep breath thing first."

"I know but I like the dramatic pause. Makes it seem like a bigger deal."

"Not really."

"Sure it does. Wiener?" Leira grabbed a toothpick from the clear plastic cup the woman was holding and speared a hotdog, holding it up to Correk's mouth. "Careful biting down. Might be hot."

Correk wanted to protest or at least look more dignified. "Smells too good," he said, and bit down hard.

"Careful! Don't want to take the toothpick with you," said the woman.

"Listen to the sample lady. Besides, they'll let you have two. You can even have mine if it means that much to you." Leira saw the look on his face and rolled her eyes. "Oh come on, it means that much? Sure, fine." She speared another one, dipped it in the ketchup and held it up. "Slower this time. Even in Costco there's a certain etiquette, you know."

"Even better with the red sauce. Why are you back over here?" said Correk through a mouth full of dough and hotdog.

"I can always wait till you swallow," said Leira, looking away. "It's a crime scene in there. You're near the produce section. My next stop."

"You're checking up on me."

"No, that's hopeless. You're like a dog in a warehouse full of shiny squirrels. You're going to chase after everything. My plan is to stop you at the point of exit."

"It's nice of them to feed us while we shop in their market."

"Oh, you have no idea. Meet you up by the front. Tick tock. I'm headed to the groceries. I'll catch you later."

"Does that mean we're near the Oreos?"

"In the neighborhood."

"They're over by the back wall, three aisles over," said the sample lady, smiling at Correk. She was pointing in the direction he needed to go.

Leira watched the way the woman was ogling Correk. "Your fan club grows larger everywhere we go. I don't quite see it," she said, squinting her eyes. "Get going. Don't want to be in here all day."

"I was headed to the front to get a better cart. The old one had a broken wheel."

"The worst," said Leira. "Twenty minutes left on the clock," she said, patting her wrist.

"Is that some kind of sign language?"

"Leftover signal from another era. Never mind, get going."

Correk worked his way toward the front of the store again and found the carts. He pulled another one out, testing it in every direction.

"Careful. Thoughtful. I like that in a man." The woman smiled at him with crimson lips, batting false eyelashes attached to smoky eyes.

Correk offered a strained smile and pushed the cart away quickly, sliding a hand into his pocket to check on the troll. "Women on this planet…" he muttered. "There are so many of them in constant search for a mate."

He turned at the mattresses and got disoriented, weaving his way down the lawnmower aisle before popping out next to a display of no-name cookies in large plastic containers. He stopped and looked at them. "Probably not."

He looked across the wide expanse in the center at the tall aisles on the other side. From that vantage point it was easier to see that at the end of every third aisle was another sample lady.

"Well, it's kind of a plan." He maneuvered his cart to the far wall of the store, checking his list. The first sample station was serving tiny quiches in three varieties. He gave the lady a half smile, arching an eyebrow as he got closer. "I know I'll hate myself later. Using Elven charm for extra servings of free food."

"Why, hello there. Bless your heart," said the tiny, round woman standing on a stool so she could more easily work the microwave next to her. "These come thirty-six to a bag in the frozen section just behind me. Two minutes for half a bag in the microwave and you have yourself a party!" Her voice was high pitched, almost a squeak.

Correk took a small napkin, trying to decide what to try first.

"Oh, take one of each, darlin. It's early. I have plenty. Nice big man like you. You need a little snack."

Correk easily palmed one of the quiches into the pocket in his hoodie where he felt two small hands grab on and pull the morsel away from him.

"Are we near tube socks?"

"Honey, just work your way down all the food aisles and you'll see them in a big display in the middle, halfway down. Can't miss it. You single? I have the cutest niece!"

Correk smiled and turned quickly, pushing the cart in the direction of the Oreos. He wheeled down the third aisle, easily spotting the large packages of Double Stuffed, amazed as he took in the different sizes and flavors of just that one cookie. He went further and looked at the Chips Ahoy, Pepperidge Farm and Keebler.

"That is not at all what an elf looks like. Like they mashed a troll and a gnome together and put a little pointed hat on it. What are these?"

He opened an oversized bag of Deluxe Grahams, sliding out two, putting one in the pocket with the troll, biting down on the other. "Not bad, even if they have their Oricerans wrong."

"No sampling the stuff that's for sale." A large man with a bushy moustache wearing the familiar Costco blue apron stopped at the end of the aisle with his hands on his hips. "Make sure you buy those and stick to the free samples till you get out of the store. Some people," he muttered, as he walked away.

"Got it. Only eat what the sample ladies give you in the store."

Correk made his way up and down the aisles, listening to the pitches, stopping for a small paper cup of chicken chow mein, 'ready in ten minutes, all in one bag', and another paper cup with cherry cheesecake, 'just take it out of the freezer and you're done', and a hot and spicy wing, 'perfect for game day', that left him holding his mouth open, fanning his tongue till he came across the samples of Gatorade, 'to replace all of those electrolytes after a hard workout', grabbing three of them and drinking them down as fast as he could.

In between, he managed to find the things on his list,

marveling at all the varieties. "Look at all the different kinds of pizza! Surely, Leira will understand." He got one of each and tossed them into the cart, making his way to the next sample lady.

By the time he got to the front of the store he had found everything on the list, but there was a growing gurgle in his stomach. The troll trilled softly and a tiny hand poked out of the pocket, the palm outstretched, looking for more food. "Oof! I don't know how you do it."

The little hand waved faster. Correk pulled out another graham cracker and shoved it into the pocket. The little hand retreated. "Mmmmm. Yumfuck."

"Hello, good day," said Correk, trying to smile at the ladies passing him who seemed more amused than offended.

"It's about time!" Leira was leaning against a large pile of men's khaki pants. "You don't look very good. What did you do? Oh, you tried everything." She shook her head. "Such a rookie. You're riding home with your head out the window. Come on. Did you manage to get any kibble for the troll? Forgot didn't you. No worries. Saw that one coming a mile away. We're going to try a little Purina. He ate fuzzy gum. This will be a big step up," she said, as she pushed her cart up to the nearest register.

CHAPTER FIVE

The remodeled Chicago Avenue Pumping Station in the heart of Chicago's Magnificent Mile, the shopping mecca by Lake Michigan, was also the regular meeting place for the local Order of the Silver Griffins. It had been for well over a hundred years since the station was still functioning in its original capacity as a public utility. Back then, no one gave the building a second glance. There were so many other things to distract, like the World's Fair and a new invention that debuted there called the Ferris Wheel.

The Ferris family were proud members of the Order going back thousands of years and clever engineers. A wizard cousin helped build the pumping station and started the ball rolling to make it a safe haven for witches and wizards passing through Chicago in need of a place to rest.

Fortunately, as it changed hands, eventually becoming a theater, it still came under the purview of a friendly witch or wizard family. The thousands of tourists who schlepped past the building every day on their way to the Water Tower and the dancing fountain that spit water up and down several flights in the middle of the escalator, never knew they were so close to so much hidden magic.

The humans were impressed with a clever fountain that shot water the same way, at different intervals all day long. Spit, spit, spit. Imagine if they could have seen into the depths of the Chicago Avenue Pumping Station, especially at the annual Christmas party.

More than one instance of snow thunder was too many witches and wizards dipping into the whiskey punch. There was a general rule that no wands were allowed but no one ever listened. The elders always stood in the back and kept watch, just in case things got too far out of hand. After all, the Order's credo was to keep magic hidden. Not dress up like Santa just to fly over houses for a laugh.

In the back of the station, one flight down, sat the vault that was built before the station and was even the reason for planting the large stone edifice on top of it. To keep the contents safely hidden away.

Today was no different.

An older witch looked up from what she was doing to the noise over her head. She was wearing a navy blue suit and flat shoes and a badge hung around her neck from a lavalier that said, docent. A fancy word for guide.

"It's Peter Pan again. The matinee is just getting started. Humans are obsessed with flying fairies. They're okay, I suppose, but really, a dime a dozen on Oriceran."

"It's a nice fairytale," the other witch replied. She was dressed in long charcoal gray yoga pants and an even longer powder blue puffy coat that went to her ankles. That's what pegged her as a local. Perfect to blend in with the shopping crowd outside in the cold winter air. "Now, go be the lookout. Don't let anyone wander down here."

The wand made of fir tucked into her deep coat pocket was what pegged her as a witch from these parts.

The wizard kneeling next to the younger witch was casting a spell on the vault to get it to open. "Expandoria," he said, waggling his fingers. The solid three-foot thick door creaked open an inch but not quite far enough. It was far too heavy for anyone to force open without magical ability. The charm on it would make machinery useless as well.

"What's with the jazz hands?"

"Sorry, I've been playing with my kids lately. Showing them little spells. Have to train them early."

"Well, a little focus would go a long way right now. If anyone found out we grabbed the necklace there will be trouble."

"I know. I get it."

"Are you sure no one saw you do it?" The witch was carefully holding a braided necklace with a diamond-shaped lavender colored pendant. The edges of it were covered in soot but otherwise there wasn't a scratch on it.

"Positive," said the wizard. "I got to it before the smoke cleared. Everyone was still trying to get their bearings after the blast. I told you that was going to happen."

"I know, I know. The whole ending was no real surprise. Tragic but not a surprise. Good thing you thought to cast that spell over the broom closet in the back or we would have been toast along with those two humans." The witch shook her head, frowning. "They should never mess with artifacts. It has never ended well for their kind."

"Yeah, kaboom!" The wizard puffed up his cheeks and rolled his eyes, blowing out the breath in one gasp.

"You should really get out with more adults," the witch told him. "Now, try again."

The wizard held out his wand and said the spell again, adding a twist. "Expandoria, infintinia!" The safe swung open with a whoosh, knocking the wizard back on his heels.

"Nicely done," said the witch. "I'll have to remember that one for the next time. Can you move back a little now?"

The witch stepped over the wizard and into the foyer of the vault. It was the next layer of defense and was disguised as an employee bathroom with a tall, thick door on steroids. Inside was just one stall and a small sink with an air dryer for hands. The dryer possessed the same decibel level as a small aircraft revving its engines.

It was a subtle alarm system in case the vault was ever left open and a tourist wandered into the facilities. The sound alerted nearby Griffins to come and get the lost human being back to their group and away from the vault. And then figure out how the thick door on the outside was opened.

It was an unlikely possibility, but every precaution was necessary. The vault was too dangerous to even ignore the ridiculous.

The witch bypassed the sink and dryer and stepped into the stall, removing the lid on the back of the toilet. The wizard had followed her into the vault behind her and was standing just behind her, peering over her shoulder. "Can you back up a little, Mark? You know it can't recognize two of us at once. It won't work."

Mark reluctantly stepped back and pocketed his wand, waiting impatiently for her to open the next door. Mabel rolled her eyes at him and turned back, looking into the back of the toilet at her own watery reflection as she flushed. "Silver Griffin number two hundred and eighty-five, Mabel Garner," she said quickly, before the flush was complete.

The water began to slowly swirl first in one direction and then counterclockwise as it refilled the tank, sparkling bright enough to illuminate Mabel Garner's face. It settled back again to a deep sea green. The recognition spell had worked. Mabel replaced the lid, stepping back, breathing a sigh of relief. "I don't know why you worry so much every time we get to this part," said Mark.

"You know why," she replied, without bothering to look back. A denial turned the water a bubbling red and sent tentacles with sharp barbs shooting out at the trespasser's face. She had seen one recipient, a witch from the Dark Families years ago who had dared to try to illegally enter. The image of the sliced and swollen face had never left her. A shudder passed across Mable's shoulders at the memory, once again.

"Every time," muttered Mark, folding his arms across his chest. He saw the rise in Mabel's shoulders. "What?"

The wall behind the toilet split in two with a whoosh that sounded like sand being released, opening just wide enough for Mabel and Mark to make their way into the next part of the vault.

They stepped out onto an iron balcony that ran around the top of a vast room.

This part of the vault stretched out underneath the pumping station and across the street under the nearby buildings.

Mabel walked across the ten foot wide platform till she was almost to the plate glass window. In front of the witch far below were different aisles circling in on themselves in an endless spiral that stretched up two stories, full of thousands of different boxes from small to the size of a large truck. Each one had a different charm on them to keep an artifact in and an intruder out.

Even the window in front of Mable was a charmed glass wall that acted as another line of protection for the oversized repository. The glass was an artifact found in Lebanon a thousand years ago when it was a green oasis surrounded by deserts. It was said to hold the magic of a powerful Phoenician. A sea captain who ruled peacefully for over a hundred years but was betrayed by his brother. At the last minute he created the glass as a protection that reflected his brother's evil back at him before sucking the life out of him.

The glass became a strange kind of reflection of true intentions, able to absorb spells and return them to their owner with often dire consequences. Every junior Silver Griffin agent knew about the rogue wizard in 1908 who tried to use a light spell to break the glass. The glass instantly turned into a mirror, refracting the light back at him, breaking him into six different versions of himself. Each one possessed only some of his abilities and left him looking permanently punch drunk, staggering around and wildly waving splintered wands.

The Griffins on duty found him and it took days to put some of him back together again before shipping all the versions off to Trevilsom Prison.

"Karma never loses your address," muttered Mabel, letting out a tired sign. "They should post it just above this thing as a reminder."

"What do you think the glass would say about me?" Mark slid his wand out of his pocket, tapping it against his leg.

"That you have too much time on your hands and not enough sense in your head." Mabel clutched the necklace a little closer, reaching out to touch the cool glass.

She took a step closer until her nose was practically pressed against the window and looked out over the vast shelving system that circled in on itself in an endless spiral that kept stretching the further an agent walked inside. "Come on, we can't dawdle. Let's get this thing filed away."

The witch grabbed one of the smaller velvet-lined boxes from a nearby shelf and set the necklace inside, snapping the case shut and twisting the lock.

In the center of the room were two pedestals, each with a large opaque glass ball on top of them. "Come on, it takes two to be able to search the archive."

"I get it. It's harder to come up with two traitors breaking in than it is just one." Mark put his hand on top of the left sphere.

Mable furrowed her brow and scrutinized him again, placing her hand on the other one. "Yeah... sure. That's one way to look at it." A virtual dashboard appeared between the two screens. "Silver Griffin number two hundred eighty-five, Mable Garner."

"Silver Griffin number three hundred forty-seven, Mark Johnson."

"Royal artifact from Oriceran, named for Prince Rolim."

The dashboard spun until it blurred, skimming over all the inventory till it came to rest in the R section, clicking just past Jack the Ripper.

"That's where we're headed," said Mable with a nod.

"That's three and a half miles away!"

"Yeah, that's what it says. Hope you've been getting your run on."

Mable removed her hand, causing the image to fade and went to the door that lead into the vault. It looked just like any other metal door except it lacked a doorknob and any visible way to open it without a crowbar.

Mable placed her hand flat against the door, pressing gently and waited for the spell to recognize her and allow them entry to the sanctuary below. The air shimmered around the door and there was a click as Mabel pressed a little harder, opening the door.

She stepped inside, instantly feeling the cooler temperature of the vault with a reverse air flow and a lower pressure. It lowered the risk of any magical artifact in a gaseous form escaping through a vent. Mark passed through, the doorway scanning his body, ready to deny him entry.

He went and stood next to Mabel as the door closed behind him with a firm click, locking them inside. Mabel waited till Mark was right next to her. "Ready? We have to do this together or we both get kicked out."

"I'm aware. Not my first entry. Why are you so jumpy?"

"There's been way too much unlicensed activity lately, some of it nearby! I don't like it. It feels like there's a plan in motion on the dark side of magic."

"What have you heard?"

"I haven't heard anything specific. Just a bad feeling."

"Relax. The Dark Families are always up to something and we always push them back to their side of things. An uneasy truce." He rubbed his hands together, smiling. "Let's do this." They each put their hands firmly on the metal railing in front of them, feeling it warm against their skin, making their hands glow an ocean blue as it read their individual biometrics. The stairs shifted with a loud creak from the center of the railing over to the left where Mabel and Mark stood. The railing in their hands vanished, finally giving the witch and wizard entry to the collection below.

"I have to get to Lincoln Square to see my kid's lacrosse game. Let's go, we have a few miles to go to get to the R's." Mabel hurried down the stairs, turning at the platform midway and picking up speed to get down to the bottom. Mark was close behind her. "We can use a spell to get us their quicker."

"I thought you said you had been down here before." Mabel turned around and took another, longer look at him. "Magic doesn't work the same way down here. With all the concentrated magic from thousands of artifacts, it throws off spells. Everyone knows that."

"I know, but it's far and you're in a hurry. One spell. It might work."

Mabel let out an irritated tsk and got to the floor of the room, hurrying toward the entrance of the spiral. "Quit joking around. Are you coming?"

Mark trotted along behind her, losing sight of Mabel at a few turns. He hesitated at the D's, glancing up at a black box with the name, Kenji Doihara printed on the front along with a brief description of the charmed box inside of it. The deadly Japanese general had used the box to bewitch thousands during WWII and became a drug kingpin over the opium trade before the Silver Griffins defeated him and seized the box.

"So much power in all these boxes," muttered Mark. "All going to waste." He raised his hand to feel the soft velvet, an aching throb passing through his fingers from the dark magic trapped within the box.

Mabel's head popped back from around the curve, startling him.

"Are you coming?" She waved, frowning and disappeared again. Mark started walking faster, catching up with her even as she was in mid-sentence about the sanctity of the archives.

"This place has only been breached a few times. The last one was in 1942, a tricky time and they got away with a few valuable items. One of them was Occam's Razor. Yeah, that's really a thing." She was talking with her hands, the box tucked under her arm. "Mussolini used it to confuse his enemies, but we got it back and well, you know how that ended up for him." They went deeper in the spiral the stacks rising far above their heads. Artificial lit orbs bounced along just above them, lighting the way as they turned round and round. "I feel like I've lost my sense of direction," said Mark, giving a shake to his head.

"That's the point. Every time someone has tried to break in, they've added another barrier to the entrance," said the witch. "If it happens again who knows what hoop they'll make us jump through."

"Probably a real hoop." Mark glanced at Mabel and tried to smile but he was already breathing hard from the long trek.

"We're here. The R's. It's fitting that it's under the dead Prince's name. It holds the last of his energy," she said, looking up at the markers for the Rs. "Ah, there we go. The vault has already made a sign for it. Rolim. Right between Jack the Ripper's razor artifact, now, that was a wicked piece of business," she said, sliding the box into place. "And snuggled nicely next to the running shoes. Remember that one? Ran a few people to their death back in the seventies! Worse than steroids!"

"I remember. Both of those wizards got sent back to Oriceran and Trevilsom Prison. Unsolved mysteries over here."

"Makes for a good TV show, doesn't it? Even when you know

the real ending. Fun to see what the humans come up with to explain these things."

"Never the same thing twice, either," Mark agreed, looking around at the shelves. "There has to be thousands of artifacts and relics in here by now, maybe hundreds of thousands."

"May no one outside of the Order ever find that out," Mabel replied with a shudder.

"Come on, let's get out of here. I have a junior high basketball game to referee. Make sure you put the glamour charm back in place to hide the building. Something darker than usual is searching for this necklace."

"I know, I know," said Mable. They marched out to the front of the vault and Mark noticed the far wall in the shadows and the large hangar door. "Funny, I don't remember seeing that before. What's in there?"

"I thought you had a game waiting for you."

Mark bit his lower lip and looked at his watch. "What's a few more minutes? You know how to get in there?"

"Really, Mark. It's like you never go to any Griffin meetings. If you can get into the sanctuary, you can get in there. They teach the charms all at once. Come on, I'll give you a quick look." Mable went and pressed her hand against the wall next to the overhead rolling door that stretched for three hundred and fifty feet.

"Looks like two football fields," said Mark, his mouth hanging open.

"Just over," said Mable, staring ahead at the blank wall.

"What are you doing?"

"Quiet, I have to concentrate for this part." A laser emerged from the wall, shining a pinpoint of light into her eye and to the back of her skull. Mable held perfectly still, holding her breath till it was finished and abruptly blinked off. She removed her hand and let out the breath as the giant door began to raise, pulled along by chains attached along each side and in the middle.

"What the fuck was that?" choked out Mark.

"It's a very old spell that's only used here for this vault. The light scans your memories for any sign that you've betrayed the Order and reports anything suspicious to the highest council. Relax, if you've got nothing to hide, you've got nothing to worry about."

"Everyone has things they don't want someone to know about." Mark's face reddened, even as he was starting to see a glimpse of something strange and wondrous under the rising door. The lights came on gradually, illuminating from the ground up.

"The scan doesn't care that you binge Netflix when you're on duty, Mark. It's specifically designed to look for betrayal."

The door finished lifting and standing in front of them was leather and metal battle armor that stretched half the size of the door. Mable looked pleased at the stunned expression on Mark's face. "I know, right! It's battle armor for a blue whale."

"Wouldn't that be heavy in water?"

"That's the part you're wondering about first? It's infused up the yin yang with magic. But that's just the start. See that right behind it?" She was pointing to a long submarine propped up on a display stand. "That's a Gato class submarine from World War II. It can be taken to the depths of the ocean or up into space." She nodded her head, smiling. "Yeah, that's right. Space." She waved her arms around before clamping them over her mouth in delight. "I love this place. Okay, that's enough. We need to get out of here."

"Just a little more," Mark said, breathlessly, already walking around the submarine.

"Hey, you can't just wander around back there. Some of this stuff is still dangerous." Mable took off at a trot to catch up to him. Mark had stopped in front of a large square stand with a circle in the middle of it and a bed attached on the front. "What is this? Is it a CAT scan?"

"Get away from that thing!" barked Mable. "Stand back!"

Mark startled, staggering backward, his eyes wide with fear. "Why? What just happened?"

"Nothing so far and I'd like to keep it that way. That thing is worse than almost everything else out there in the spiral."

"It looks like an old CAT scan machine." Mark crouched down to get a better look underneath it. "I don't see anything menacing. Where do you plug it in?"

"It's not what it looks like. It's what it can do. That machine was created by a Light Elf named Harkin about a hundred years ago. Way ahead of the technology on Earth."

"Hmmm, that's a good thing."

"Not this one. This scan can see down to a molecular level and then make changes." Another shudder passed down Mable's spine. "Harkin swore at his trial that his intentions were good, but that's not how things turned out."

"Trial? Did he end up in Trevilsom?" It was Mark's turn to feel a tremor pass through his body.

"That's what they say but no one will really talk about him. It's forbidden in the Order."

"What could he have changed that would cause that?"

"He made his best friend into a monster… a magical freak that lost its mind and killed a few Light Elves before it was stopped. I hear it took a battalion to bring him down."

"That is some serious shit," whispered Mark. He took a few more steps away from the machine. "Did it ever do any good?"

"It never got the chance. After that it was moved here and has never been turned on again." Mable looked down at her watch and gasped. "Oh geez, I'm gonna be late. Come on, my kid will mope the entire night if I don't get there soon. We have to hustle!"

The pair made their way out of the side warehouse, closing

the roller door and heading quickly back up the stairs, through the foyer, then the bathroom wall and passed through the enormous door.

"Make sure you shut it tight." Mark wiped the sweat off his forehead from the climb up the stairs.

"Now who's the worrier? Not that I don't approve," she said, pulling out her wand. "Compressoria, infintinia!"

The door groaned loudly, grinding against the concrete, and lumbered shut, the brass gears whirring and clicking as the mechanism locked into place. Built by the gnomes of Oriceran, known for their ability to not only keep secrets but create clever ways to guard them as well. Shipped over to Earth a piece at a time with a few gnomes to put it back together correctly.

"The vault has stood the test of time for well over a hundred years without a single successful break-in." The witch brushed a strand of hair out of her face, admiring the structure.

"I'm not one to get all weird about feelings, but I have a bad one about this necklace. Whatever's hunting it, I hope this vault can stand the test."

"It's seen the worst and been fine. Come on, you have a game to get to. We've been underground long enough."

Correk helped Leira carry the boxes from the car to the guesthouse. "Most of this is yours, anyway," she smirked.

"Not really. Most of this belongs to your family at the bar." Correk pulled down the knit hat covering his distinctly pointed ears. The spell had worn off and he was too low on stored energy to glamour his ears.

"So much that's wrong with that description. What about these?" Leira held up the large plastic jug of orange cheese puffs. "You planning to share these? Didn't think so."

"They're back!" yelled Paul. "You have my whiskey?"

Estelle gave a long, hard look at Paul. The ash on the cigarette dangling out of her mouth fell, landing on the bar. She took a damp bar towel and wiped it off, not taking her eyes off Paul.

"Don't take it that way, Estelle. I have to spend some time at home."

"Which is why he needs the home stash," said Craig.

Estelle squinted through the smoke and stepped off the stool she was standing on behind the bar. She turned and went to check on the early diners and the happy hour crowd inside.

"That tiny old lady is very scary," Mike said.

"Has she actually ever done anything?" asked Paul. "That we know of?"

"There are legends, dude." Craig shuddered.

Leira balanced a box on her knee while she unlocked the door of the guesthouse.

"You can play with your friends once you help me carry all of this into the kitchen," she said.

"Very funny."

"Leave the troll at home, please."

"I have probably a hundred years or more on you and have even seen my share of battle."

"Your point? I've seen my share of shootings, stabbings and other nastiness people can do to each other, if we're comparing notes."

"I'm past the need for parenting. Besides, I still know more magic than you do and can leave a fireball to hover above you if you keep it up."

"Point taken," Leira conceded, opening the door and dropping her purse on the red velvet chair. The wooden blinds were all closed. She wasn't going to mention his ebbing magic. "But the day is coming when I'll have a few magic tricks up my sleeve."

"We can only hope that a little wisdom will come with the newly found power." Correk followed her into the kitchen and put the box down on the kitchen table and started sorting.

Leira pulled out a new small blue cat bowl and put it on the counter. She grabbed the bag of Purina Cat Chow and poured some in. "What? It's what we feed our pets on this planet. It'll be good for him. Too much junk food. I get it. I don't know the biochemistry of a troll but seriously, old gum, Cheetos and pizza crust can't be good for any species. Look, it says right on the bag that it's a balanced diet." Leira laughed giddily. "This is ridiculous. I'm trying to feed cat chow to a troll from another planet."

Correk reached in and scooped out the troll who promptly bit his finger. "Moons of Oriceran!" Correk dropped the troll unceremoniously on the counter and watched the creature scramble over to the bowl, settling himself in the middle of the bowl, and shoveling the small triangles into his mouth.

"Well, that's one way to eat it," Leira said. "Does that pass as swearing on Oriceran? Moons of Oriceran! Don't you have anything with a nice hard sound like fuck or something that makes you think of something that stanks like shit? Nothing?"

"Yumfuck!" The troll looked up with a smile, his mouth overflowing with nuggets.

"He gets it, don't you Yumfuck."

Correk's eyes lit up as he focused on his finger, healing it. Leira watched with fascination and relief. He still had some energy left.

"Now, that's a magic trick that will come in handy. Does it work on humans too?"

"Not as consistently and sometimes with unforeseen consequences."

"Like what? Some weird polka-dotted rash? Pulsing lights coming out of them? They turn into a zombie?"

"Something like that."

Leira was surprised. "Oh, wow, I thought for sure you'd basically tell me to zip it, nothing like that. Good to know. No trying to fix humans with magic."

"A good idea, in general."

"What about half elves? What can we do for them?"

Correk stopped digging through the boxes in search of the socks for Craig. He looked up at Leira solemnly. "I suppose we are now talking about your mother. Are we talking about using magic to break her out?"

"That and to fix whatever that place may have broken inside of her."

Correk saw the pain in Leira's eyes and said nothing, letting her talk. He had already learned that she took her time trusting anyone and avoided ever showing there even was a vulnerable side to her. If she was choosing to trust him, even a little, he was going to be careful not to step on the moment.

"I want to go see her." Leira let the words hang in the air for a minute. The only sound was the troll plowing through the food in his bowl. He looked up at Leira, sensing her mild distress but she smiled at him and he rolled happily over onto his back, dropping food into his mouth.

"I've been avoiding the place. It wasn't my original intention. It just kind of happened. You let enough time go by and it gets harder to go at all. Besides, when I did go, at some point she always got around to talking about elves and a magical place…"

Correk interrupted her. "And you thought it was proof she was crazy."

"Yes," said Leira, softly. "I'm not proud of it but I've taught myself to avoid hopeless situations with people I care about."

"What if I went with you?"

"You're up for that?"

"My Costco adventure has gotten me just a little deeper in the bar family, the fan club otherwise known as the Leira Society. And yes, before you say anything, we have fan clubs on Oriceran. They're just for real accomplishments like winning at Gringleball or championing a battle. That will even earn you a spot in a child's hero book."

"Gringleball?"

"A wonderful game but to your point. You are also half Elf, that is very clear and you will learn that we don't divide ourselves up into smaller and smaller units of family. We are all part of one large family, and we show up for each other, good or bad."

"You have each other's backs."

"Yes, my dear Leira. We, we have each other's backs. I will go with you to see your mother."

Leira felt something settle into her chest. A feeling she hadn't experienced in way too many years. Gratitude.

"Oh crap, I don't do tears," she said, brushing away a tear on her cheek.

"Not to spoil the moment, but you're just intending a visit, right? Not breaking her out."

Leira turned away from Correk, surprised at how quickly her sadness was replaced with anger. She wasn't even sure exactly who she was angry with right in that moment. She realized her hands were balled into fists at her side and the troll had stood up in the dish, looking around for the danger.

"He's like an emotional weathervane. Can't be in denial about fucking anything with a pocket troll around."

"I'm not suggesting that we don't get your mother out of that institution. Not at all. I'm not even saying that we take our time."

"Then what are you saying?"

"That if we don't do this by the Earth rules, they'll just come after her again. It will sit on her record and if she gets stopped by one of your kind in traffic…"

"My kind… a cop."

"Yes, or ends up in an argument that normally would mean nothing…"

"Someone will see that she was in a hospital and broke out and put her back in under even tighter security."

"Yes, and best case your mother will live the rest of her life looking over her shoulder or worst case, die in a hospital under a diagnosis that isn't true."

"Not if we break her out and take her to Oriceran through a portal."

"That means your mother, who's had no say about her living conditions for fifteen years, will once again, even with better intentions, have to deal with what was decided for her."

Leira clenched her teeth, struggling not to get angrier. *This is why I don't talk about any of this. Too much pain, too many dead ends.*

"There is another way and you and I will find it. Soon. In the meantime, we'll go and see her. You know, your mother is a magical creature, and if your father's human, she's even more magical than you are."

"If?"

Correk ignored her question. "There's a chance she may have some valuable ideas of her own about how to get her out of there that we haven't thought of. You are her daughter, and I imagine, more alike than you may have been willing to admit in a lot of years."

The grief in Leira's chest surged forward, over the tipping point, and the sobs broke out before she could contain them. Correk didn't hesitate and wrapped his arms around her pulling her in tight as she let out the pain and frustration she had been carrying with her for most of her life.

Lois hurried down the hall, trying to get to the Paranormal Defense Force in enough time to warn Patsy the generals were on their way. She checked the cat-shaped watch that was pinned to her sweater, pulling it out on the retractable gold cord to get a better look. She was dressed in her fifties look, complete with poodle skirt and crinolines. It was something she liked to do to break up the monotony of the job. She pushed the sparkly cat-eye glasses back up her nose and looked at the time.

"She'll be watching those damn Housewives shows right about now." Lois did her best to pick up her pace, without breaking into a run. She didn't want to look back at the long, narrow hallway behind her to see who was at the other end, but she knew it wouldn't look good to the humans if she was in too big of a hurry.

She burst through the door of the PDF out of breath and sweating, startling Patsy who bit down hard on a piece of deep-dish pizza. The sauce squirted out, splashing Patsy in the face.

"Oh, for the love of all things magical! Moons of Oriceran! What has got you rushing in here like that? I told you I'd save you a good two pieces! I know how you love deep dish. Although, I have to tell you, they do it better in Chicago. Must be something in the water when they make the dough. All that good Chicago River water."

Lois took in a gulp of air, waving her hands around, rolling her eyes.

"Are you having a fit? It's hard to tell in that getup. Is that a dance? This whole act has really progressed. Next thing you know, you're going to be dragging a karaoke machine in here."

Lois finally caught her breath and whipped out her wand, tempted to first use it on Patsy to shut her up. She quickly thought better of that. "Brass is on their way and they look determined," she said, waving her wand to change over the virtual magic readout from the Housewives of Orange County to incoming data about magical activity.

"Huh, there's a little blip in Arizona. Wonder what that's about," said Patsy, wiping off her face. She licked each of her fingers, slid her paper plate into the box, and shoved the whole thing under a pile of papers.

She turned back toward the glowing green symbols flying across the room, and Patsy tucked away her wand, just as four men in full military dress came through the door.

"As you were," said the small man in the lead. He took off his hat, revealing a small tuft of dark hair on the very top of what was mostly a shiny, bald head.

Patsy gave Lois a look, rolling her eyes. She never took it well when humans told her what to do, even though she'd been in a government job for years.

"Can we help you?" asked Lois, doing her best to ignore Patsy. She adjusted her glasses, giving her a moment to take in the four men who were busy doing variations on the Wonder Woman stance, hands on hips, their heads back, looking around the room.

"Do I smell pizza?"

Lois heard Patsy quietly say, "Never was..." and moved in front of her, glaring at her. "What if we need that again in just a minute," she whispered, leaning over, pretending to pick something up so she could get closer to Patsy. "Save the big guns," she hissed. "We don't even know why they're here!"

"Ladies," said the diminutive General. "I trust all is well." He gestured at the symbols.

Patsy mumbled a spell under her breath, making the symbols suddenly spin apart and swirl around the general's arm, giving the distinct impression he had mucked up the system by getting too close.

Even Lois had a hard time not smiling. She ducked her chin down, pressing her glasses back up her nose, stealing glances at the general who looked flummoxed, even panicked. Lois gave Patsy another sharp look to get her to stop before the joke went on too long. *Humans. They don't have a very good sense of humor about themselves*, thought Lois. *Eventually they bring out weapons and these guys actually have access to an armory.*

"Brahawa," babbled the general, trying to get out words. He cleared his throat and squeezed his eyes shut. Patsy finally cut it out and let the feed restore itself, humming along over everyone's head. The general opened his eyes and saw the feed was restored. He looked relieved. Lois gave him a reassuring smile.

"Can we help you?" she asked again.

He cleared his throat, again. So far, they weren't making any progress. The men with him all shuffled their feet and looked around, not making eye contact with anyone. Patsy was smirking and saying nothing, letting them squirm. Meddling humans brought out the worst in her. She stuck her tongue out at Lois while no one was looking. Lois almost laughed but tried to cover it up, making a sound resembling a honk. Her face warmed as Patsy raised a few papers in front of her face, her shoulders shaking from holding in the giggles.

"Yes, yes," the general finally said. "We are here to see what you have on a particular magical woman. A Detective Leira Berens. We understand she's an unaffiliated magical person. Do you have a file?"

"A file?" asked Patsy, getting up from her chair.

"Oh great," Lois muttered under her breath.

"No, but I can make you one?" Her question was just for show. She was already in mid-spell, moving her wand theatrically through the air. Lois took note that she started with *alakazam*, which was not a spell, before finally performing actual magic.

The generals watched in awe as the screen split lengthwise and opened. Data poured from the opening, spiraling down, and into Patsy's wand. She walked to the copier shoved against the wall, though not plugged in, and tapped her wand against the top of it, causing it to shudder and shimmy and roar to life. It began spitting out pages into four collated piles, which Patsy was happy to snatch up and hand out to the men. All of them stood there slack-jawed, barely able to take the papers from her.

Lois wanted to applaud. None of it was really necessary. They had everything on a drive and could have just handed that over to the general and let him download it later the old-fashioned way. But where was the fun in that?

"Thank you, ladies," the general said nervously. Lois noticed the papers were shaking in his hand. The men all mumbled some form of thank you, and together they quickly shuffled back out of the room.

Lois waited a few seconds and then peeked out the door to make sure they were far enough away.

"You should be more careful! One of these days they're going to remember how fond they are of burning witches at the stake or dissecting aliens. We technically fit in both categories!"

"You and I were both born here. Calm down."

"They rewrite what makes you an alien every other day, to suit their fancy!"

"Besides, if they did try, we'd turn them into toads. Something old school. We were never in any danger. Bonus to all of this, they once again fear and respect us and will think long and hard before they ask for more information. I think we acted prudently."

"You going to tell your cousin in the Order about this?"

"Already texted her. Done and done. If the government is looking for Leira Berens, the Order needs to warn her. We watch out for our own."

"When we're not arresting them ourselves."

"Yeah, well, that's another story."

CHAPTER SIX

"We all need to get out tonight!" Craig was eating nachos and swilling a beer.

"We are out," Estelle croaked from the other end of the bar. She was busy giving a young couple at the other end of the bar two shots of tequila, telling them they didn't *really* want martinis. Smoke swirled around her head, making it difficult to see her face.

"I mean go hear some music," said Craig.

"You better slow down on those nachos, dude. Remember what happened the last time," said Paul.

"Yeah, you went home and passed out, had acid reflux in your sleep, stood up, had an asthma attack and passed clean out. Your dog had to wake you up!" Margaret ticked off all the maladies on the end of her fingers. "Death by nachos is not what you want Facebook to say."

"How would Facebook even find out?"

"I'd tell them," said Mike.

"Yeah, me too," said Mitzi. "That one would go viral, especially if we could get pictures."

"Fine! I'll slow down! Hey, Bert, you have my tube socks?"

Correk was carrying an old cardboard box stamped Del Monte Tomato Paste. It was overflowing with the tube socks balanced on the top. He was using his chin to keep everything inside of the box.

Leira followed him, carrying the Oreos.

"I see you have your priorities straight," Paul said, taking the cookies from her. "Was there any change?"

"Paul!" A chorus went up from the group.

"What? Okay, okay, carrying fees. But was there?"

"Don't answer him," Mike ordered. Correk put the change on the bar.

"Ah, good man. You do know us!" said Paul, lunging toward the money to count it out.

"He knows you," said Mitzi.

"Leira, we all want to go out tonight. You should come. We'll go hear a little music down on 6th Street," Craig said.

"Sure, why not."

"What? I can't believe it! You never say yes!"

"Unless you get Estelle involved. She's hard to turn down."

"Out of fear of the unknown."

"I heard that!" Estelle emerged on top of her stool at the other end of the bar. "What'll it be? Wait, don't tell me. I have just the other thing." She made a gin and tonic and plopped it down in front of the pretty blonde who looked down the bar like she needed help. "Anything else? You don't look hungry," Estelle informed her. "You got a friend needs a drink?"

"It's like being faced with a gremlin," Scott mused.

"She hears you, you disappear," Mike said.

"Fuck, you become barbeque," Margaret added.

"Dancing!" Craig said, changing the subject.

"I never agreed to that. I said I'd go along for the music. Does everyone have their supply of useless things from Costco?" Leira looked in the box to make sure it was completely empty.

"Tube socks are not useless. Even Bert wanted some."

"What's so great about them?"

Craig put a sock on his hand and demonstrated. "You get a hole on one side, you just turn it. Lasts four times longer than your ordinary sock."

"That's very sad, Craig. I feel for your wife and kids."

"Supporting a wife and kids is why I'm so practical."

Correk whispered to Leira. "How long does this usually go on?"

"Until someone makes them stop." Leira clapped her hands sharply twice and put her fingers to her lips and produced a high-pitched whistle. "Okay, who's riding with us, because we're out of here?"

"Hey, who whistled like that? Oh, Leira, well then," said Estelle, turning around to go back inside.

"I told you she was Estelle's favorite."

"You're just figuring that out? Do you have a card in your pocket that says where to send you home in case you're found alone? That might be a good idea."

Leira headed resolutely toward the gate with Correk right behind her. "I take it they eventually follow you."

"Most of the time. Some get left behind on occasion, but they learn."

Craig and Scott piled into the back of the Mustang. Craig asked Leira to run the lights just for a second every time the traffic slowed down. Leira mostly ignored the backseat and instead watched how Correk occasionally tried to chime in and be part of the group. That was the moment she realized all the time spent on Earth was taking him away from his own family somewhere on Oriceran. *He's trying to bloom where he's planted,* she thought, remembering something her grandmother used to say. *Haven't thought of her in a while either. Strange day.*

They took three cars and parked in a deck just off Congress Avenue on 8th Street and walked down Brazos Street, passing the Driskill Hotel, turning onto 6th Street. The hotel was built out of brick and limestone just after the Civil War. It was ornately decorated, with curved openings, and busts of the founder and his two sons on the peaks of the facades still watching over everything.

"They say this old hotel is haunted," Scott remarked, as they walked past the valet stand.

"That's just gossip," said Margaret.

Leira noticed Correk's slowing down and looking up at the Driskill with a growing interest.

They got to the corner and crossed at the light. Leira tugged at Correk's sleeve and asked, "You don't believe in ghosts, do you? They're just old stories."

Correk's face grew solemn. "Not ghosts, no. In Oriceran we call it something else. The world in between, and it's very real. It's the one thing that gives even the adults nightmares."

"I didn't know magical beings had nightmares," Leira said, glancing up at the hotel.

"I assure you, there are hideous things to be afraid of even where there is magic. Sometimes, because there is magic."

"I wonder if I should have taken my gun instead of relying on just a Light Elf by my side. Might be a dangerous hole in my plan."

"Your firearm would prove useless in this instance."

Leira glanced back at Correk and shuddered so hard it shook her shoulders. "Why is it ghost stories always creep people out?"

"Because sometimes they're real.

High above in a window on the third floor a figure watched the street below.

At first, the older woman didn't believe it could really be her. After four years, the memory of what the young woman looked like had faded and the woman below was some distance from her under a darkening sky. This wasn't even the first time she thought she was catching a glimpse of the detective.

She did her best to concentrate and study the woman walking within a group toward 6th Street.

"It is her!" she shouted, hearing the hollow echo the sound made in the dimension where she was trapped. The world in between.

Even here, in this place, the woman still felt the sharp pain of longing for something she couldn't touch. Especially for the touch of her granddaughter.

Mara Berens instinctively reached toward Leira to call to her, but her hand passed through the windowpane, dissolving into mist until Mara pulled it back. She was trapped in a place with only the other beings who were trapped, the living and the dead, to talk to. Some of them more dangerous than others.

There were consequences for mingling with the darker beings trapped in there with everyone else, and it could be difficult to tell one from the other in time.

Time was difficult to calculate in the world in between, but it wasn't long after she was trapped in there before Mara saw the darkness creep over a Wood Elf who had fallen in trying to use a portal. The same kind of accident that had trapped Mara. The Wood Elf begged for help as the darkness covered him like ebony liquid, engulfing him till he was absorbed. *There are even worse things than the world in between*, thought Mara.

She made a point to trust no one after that.

Leira looked up toward the windows and Mara saw the sharp pointed chin, just like her own and the familiar short, dark hair. She looked at the man standing next to her just as he tilted his head up toward the hotel.

"A Light Elf," she cried out in horror. "No!" Mara felt the

panic rising and fought it. It would make it more difficult for her to hold her energy still and stay in one place. She watched Leira look up one more time as they walked down the street and she focused all her energy, trying to send a warning to her granddaughter. *Stay away from the Oricerans. No good will come of it. I have to find a way to warn her before it's too late.* It felt like a scream in her chest that had nowhere to go, trapped in the world in between.

"Hey, you guys, keep up! We found the bar where we're going to start our great adventure."

Craig and Mike were frantically waving them on toward a bar that was completely open in the front. The only thing that separated the people inside from the sidewalk was an iron barrier painted black.

"Oh, pizza!" Correk pointed to the Due Forni sign down the block.

"You have good taste, but no..." said Craig. "Tonight, we show you the musical side of Austin! We start with the Dirty Dog Bar!"

"For once this will not be about the food," said Mike. "Whiskey, women and song."

Mitzi shook her head. "Come on King Kong, let's go in. Pay the doorman. No, he doesn't want to see your ID. That's how old you look to the world. No one doubts you're well over twenty-one."

"Hey, it's the Bourgeois Mystics!"

"Funk band!"

"Funk what?" Correk shouted over the trumpets and the bass guitar. The sound reverberated off the walls and made his ears hum. He looked around and quietly said, "Calmination," symbols briefly appearing under his skin.

A young man with a fade and a zigzag cut into the sides of his hair smiled and lifted his glass to Correk. "Cool tattoo!"

The sound of his voice traveled to Correk in a tube of air all its own, separated out from the other noise in the room. Correk gave him a smile and a nod and turned away.

Now he was free to focus on the different sounds of the band and regulate the volume, blending the music.

"You're really enjoying the music!" Leira looked at him with surprise.

"No need to shout," he said, a feeling of calm running through him.

"What?" she shouted.

He laughed and shook his head, taking a beer from Scott and lifting it to the group. "To family," he said, letting the spell push the sound out to only the people standing around him. They all lifted their beer and answered, "To family".

Leira cocked her head to one side and said, "You cast a spell, didn't you?" She lowered her voice even more. "And you can still hear me. Mister you had better not do magic, especially in public." She raised her eyebrows and smiled, taking a sip of her beer.

Correk shrugged and smiled back as he swayed to the music.

"Is that Elven dancing?" Leira laughed and said, "Show me the spell, Cousin, or I try to feel my way through one of my own invention."

He held up his hand, trying to look serious but his eyes gave him away. "I'll need to use some of your energy. Give me your hand."

She took his hand, and he inhaled and said the spell again, "Calmination," blowing out the breath toward Leira. The air swirled around her, expanding, glowing in a way that only she

87

could see, separating all the sounds and images, letting her choose what she wanted to hear or see in any given moment. A look of delight came over her face.

"Now, use the energy within you to mix the sounds you want to hear. This is a lot easier if you believe you can do it. Elven magic strengthens with belief."

Leira started, looking up to see who else had heard him say, 'Elven magic' and realized no one else could hear them. They weren't even interested.

Correk smiled and gave her an encouraging nod.

"The sound travels through its own tunnel, separate from what everyone else can hear," she said, watching the light swirl around her. "Am I the only one who can see this light?"

"I can see it too. Other magical creatures, all elves especially, can see it. Look around you. Open your mind and your heart to the energy around you."

Leira hesitated, unsure she even wanted to try. Correk smiled and nodded again. "You can turn it off any time you want to. Shut your eyes if it makes it easier to start."

"I'm a cop. I've got this," she said. *Come on Leira, you don't back down from a challenge.*

"What is there in this world that you trust? Who do you trust? Draw on that feeling."

"I trust Hagan to have my back."

Correk shrugged. "Start with that. Trust that feeling. This isn't something you do. It's more like you allow it to be."

Leira thought about Hagan and relaxed into the feeling, letting it spread through her.

One by one, first the people closest to her, and then spreading out through the room, different people took on the same ethereal light, swirling around them in a tunnel.

It looks like a hundred fireflies.

Leira turned in a circle, amazed, taking it in.

She stared at a tall, thin man with long hair. He seemed to feel her energy reaching out to his and he turned and smiled, before going back to watching the band.

"Leira Berens, you are at least half a Light Elf." Correk's voice floated to her. "That makes any of the people who you can now see surrounded by light your family. Wherever you go, you belong to them, they belong to you."

Leira felt the wave of energy cresting, threatening to overwhelm her. At the edges, she could also feel the pain of losing first her mother, and then her grandmother. Hell, not even knowing the name of her father. It drove straight through the center of the emotions coursing through her and punched her in the chest.

Instinctively, she pulled back, letting the energy subside.

Correk saw the pain in her eyes. "It's okay. That's enough for now. We're here to enjoy the music and be with the humans you've adopted, anyway."

"No, I want to know," Leira protested, taking a sip of her beer, resisting the urge to ball her hands into fists.

"You will know. Give it time. At least longer than five minutes. Start by enjoying what's happening around you," he said, pointing at the band. "They're not bad. You call this, what, funk? I might like this."

She smiled, still struggling with the different emotions pushing their way through her from the inside out.

"When you get better at this, I'll show you how to see the different colors in the light around everybody. It's like being able to read their minds. Right now, you're a swirl of purple and yellow, which by the way, does not exactly look good on you. Very conflicted. I think you puny humans call it, mixed emotions."

Leira laughed and gave Correk a gentle shove.

"Much better. You've blended into a nice green. On Oriceran it can be hard to have secrets. Everyone's always up inside your colors."

"I've said this before, you've been watching the puny humans way too much and it appears it's mostly been bad cable TV." Leira laughed again and felt the music move through her, making her want to dance. She started to move in time with the music. *What the hell? Dance? I don't do things like dance.*

"Magic is just as much a part of you as the human elements," said Correk. "Although, I'm not sure either world would actually call that dancing." He laughed this time. Leira smiled and did her best to ignore him.

"Tell me more about the magical community. About Enchanted Rock."

"Ah, the kemana."

"The what?"

"The kemana. It's a place on Earth where the Oricerans who were here thousands of years ago stored as much energy as they could. They created different places where they'd be able to gather energy later, just in case."

"Like an emergency battery. You mean in case they wanted to get home."

"Not necessarily. Some Oricerans have chosen to stay here and some have chosen to live in the kemana. Others go there so they can practice magic in the open and recharge their energy."

"Wow. So fucking weird. I suppose Oriceran is my home too, at least partly. It's like finding out you're part giraffe."

"Not really. I'm letting that one go. You're getting over-whelmed. Just enjoy the music. Let the spell work its way through you."

"This isn't like a drug thing, right?"

"You'd have a better time if you stopped thinking so much." Correk watched Leira fight against the calming spell, looking around, taking in her environment. "Alright, no, it's not. You're not becoming a magic junkie. It's a way of getting all your emotions, your energy to align but it only works for a little while. It's nothing permanent. For that, you'll have to learn to relax on your own. Apparently, it's been too long since you've arrested someone."

"Over twenty-four hours. That *does* feel like withdrawal."

"You wanted to come here. Any chance you can be present and enjoy it?"

"You know how much I love a fucking challenge. Fine, I'll be here, but I want a promise from you."

"Let's have it."

"Go back with me to Enchanted Rock and introduce me to everyone. Help me to get to know the family I didn't even know I had." Leira's voice cracked when she said the last words. She was surprised yet again that night, at the emotion inside of her. *Son of a bitch, if this is happiness...* "Okay, okay. I can do this," she said, shaking out her arms. "But promise me anyway."

"I promise. I'll take you to the local kemana. It will prove to be more interesting than you can imagine."

"A teaser. I like it."

"Come on, guys. How are you still standing over here like statues? Move to the music!" Mitzi was twirling around, her arms over her head, spinning between Correk and Leira. Scott was busy doing the twist with Margaret and Lucy, and Craig and Mike were jumping straight up and down. Leira joined Mitzi, throwing her arms up in the air and doing a bad rendition of the pony. She laughed harder than she could remember in a very long time.

I have more family than I realized. She spun around and felt the energy surge through her, lighting up all the magical people in the room. *Everywhere.*

CHAPTER SEVEN

"You look like something I scraped off my shoe this morning." Detective Hagan put a mug of hot coffee down in front of Leira, who was sitting upright at her desk in the precinct but resting her head to one side in the palm of her hand.

"Why so loud?" She lifted her head and looked at him.

"I could have sworn you never go out." He sat down at his desk directly across from her and chuckled. "Good! It's about time you acted your age, instead of mine. Believe me, you'll get here fast enough. No need to speed things up. Next thing you know, you'll need a good solid grunt to get out of a chair."

"It wasn't the drinking so much as the dancing. And I'm a damn runner!"

"Dancing! Now I've heard everything. You got your dance on! You must have strained something." He did a little dancing in his chair. "No? Okay. Well, well, well. You were actually letting loose. This may take me longer to get used to than the idea of magic and shit. What the hell!" He laughed and slammed his hand down hard on the top of his desk, startling her.

"Seriously?"

"Sorry, I get exuberant. Rose points that out to me all the time. Frankly, half the time I think she likes it."

"That's definitely TMI. How do people do this every weekend?" Leira rolled her chair closer to the column next to her desk and leaned against it.

"You went at it too hard your first time. You have to build up to it. You got the bends," Hagan said, chortling. "Boy, that takes me back to my community college days. Didn't even go out till eleven. Still woke up pretty early in the morning. Take an actual sip of your coffee."

"I don't have a hangover."

"Meh, can't hurt. Coffee cures a lot of early morning issues." Hagan wheeled his chair closer and put his hand up by his mouth to whisper, "Why don't you stir a little magic in your coffee. Huh? You must have something in your magic bag that would help something like this?"

"You know, when you hold your hand up like that everyone knows you're saying something they want to hear." Leira did her best to muster up a dead fish look.

"That's sad. Can't even look bored, much less menacing. I'm surprised you people can get laid low so easily."

"You people? We've already started with the you people? That's got to be racist, somehow. And I'm your people. Well, mostly."

"Try taking that one to IA. I insulted the people who live at the end of rainbows. Green stars, pink hearts," he said, doing a bad imitation of an Irish accent. "Blue moons."

"I think it's yellow moons. Who ever heard of a green star," Leira said, blowing on the coffee. The steam felt good on her face.

"Uh huh. See who they decide to *help*." He did air quotes when he said 'help', annoying Leira more.

"That's exactly why I'm not trying to magic my way out of this. If I got caught it won't end like a Disney movie."

"I don't know. It might. Seven dwarves. A witch out to get you."

Leira sipped the coffee. "This is not department issue coffee. It doesn't taste like burned leaves and it's not plastering the inside of my throat."

Hagan put his hand back up to the side of his mouth and whispered, "It's my private stash. Don't tell anyone."

"For such a great detective…"

"Thank you," he said, taking a bow.

"You're not very good at being subtle with your own secrets."

"Hey, no one's found my stash yet."

"Point taken."

"Hagan, Berens, you've caught a case." Captain Napora was standing in his doorway holding a file.

"Uh oh, this can't be good. The Captain is handing out cases." Hagan scratched the top of his head.

"Any day now," said the Captain.

Hagan gave a half-hearted smile. "Right away, sir."

"Someone important is dead." Leira stood up slowly and took another large swallow of coffee.

"Or somebody died in a particularly inventive way."

She put the mug down and followed Hagan across the room. The Captain handed Hagan the file, a grim look on his face.

"String of robberies with no suspects and until today, no real injuries to speak of. Today, a guard inside a jewelry store was fatally wounded. Gun shot. You're going to help Thomas and Leakes in Robbery. This could use a fresh set of eyes. The basics are that a gang of three have been holding up high-end retailers in the more rural parts of Travis County where there aren't as many witnesses or traffic."

"So, not the Domain. I can never find a parking place there. I have to haunt someone with my car and follow them slowly back to where they parked," Hagan said.

"They wear ski masks and say very little, preferring to let

their guns speak for them. Very smooth. This isn't even the first time a guard has tried to shoot it out with them. But every other time they were able to disarm the guard. No muss, no fuss. This time something went haywire. The guard got off a shot and may have winged one of them. One of the others reacted and shot the guard dead. They fled immediately and managed to leave no prints. Not even a drop of blood."

Hagan glanced at Leira but she kept her eyes on the Captain. She knew what Hagan was thinking. *Magic. Can't be true.*

"What kind of description did the witnesses give?" Leira took the file from Hagan and looked over the details. "It says there are ten robberies. That's a lot. These descriptions are pretty vague. Medium height, medium build. No real accent. Some witnesses say they're white and others swear they're black."

"Yeah, go figure. A crew of three finally figured out how to blend into the background in ski masks. They have the footage from the stores' cameras and sure enough, average height, average build. Hard to say much else." The Captain put his hands on his hips and smiled grimly. "I look forward to meeting these geniuses."

"Understood," said Hagan. "Come on Berens. Let's see what we can dig up to assist our colleagues."

The Captain went back into his office, shutting the door as Hagan and Berens walked away.

"Don't say anything. Not in here." Leira grabbed her leather jacket.

"I'm driving."

"Not today." Leira walked ahead of Hagan toward the door, the file under her arm. Hagan started to say something but Leira cut him off. "Not one word."

"We go talk to the witnesses in the last robbery. It's the best place to start." Leira turned onto Ben White Boulevard.

"Maybe your funny friend can conveniently stop by," Hagan suggested, waggling his fingers.

"That's not how anyone does a spell, ever. Put your hands down. You are a decorated detective," she said sternly.

"What? Did I embarrass you within the confines of the car? Nobody's watching us, are they?" Hagan turned around and shouted into the back of the car, "Hey, if you are listening, meet us at the Rollins Jewelry store on Ben White near the Trader Joe's. Can't miss it. Big sign with a diamond on it."

"It's like you think there are tiny little elves hiding down there."

"After everything I've seen lately that's not so hard to believe. Besides, elves are often shown as very small. That had to come from somewhere, right?"

"Yeah, an ad exec who wanted to keep his job. Focus, Hagan. If you still didn't believe in magic what would you see?"

"A very professional crew. Maybe former mercenaries. Disciplined. But..."

"No buts. We don't start seeing magic everywhere. We didn't wonder what weird shit was happening two weeks ago. No need to start doing that now."

A traffic light was out near the highway on-ramp. Leira ran the siren for a few seconds, making it easier to cross over the intersection.

"You gonna call that in?" asked Hagan, already pulling out his cell phone.

"We already have an assignment. Go ahead, you call 311 and be the good citizen."

"You can text it in. Much easier. Fine, have it your way. Not magic. I'm not convinced... hang on. These fat fingers, can't talk and type."

"The fact that they responded to gunfire with gunfire suggests ordinary humans who took a lot of precautions trying to make the robberies as smooth as possible."

Hagan leafed through the folder. "They also seem to have figured out what days each store has the most cash on hand. Inside man?"

"Would have to be."

"Hey, we've been partners for a while. We're even friends, maybe family, right?"

Leira pulled into the parking lot of the strip mall. The jewelry store was tucked into a corner on the far left side next to a store that sold different flavors of olive oil.

"Go on," she said, eyeing Hagan suspiciously.

"Well, I get the whole, *I can't do anything that will draw suspicion*, but what about something no one will notice? Okay, not work related. How about a robotic lawnmower for your old pal? Hear me out!"

Leira was shaking her head and rolling her eyes as she turned off the engine. "Why robotic? Wouldn't I just make a normal lawnmower do all the work? Skip the robotic part."

"That works!"

"Not doing it." Leira got out of the car, still shaking her head. "Besides, that's probably the only kind of exercise you get."

"Harassing me about my weight or my exercise is part of my marriage vows, reserved solely for Rose's pleasure."

Leira smiled. "Sorry, my bad."

Hagan stopped on the sidewalk in front of the Starbucks. "Coffee first?"

"Always."

"After you." He held the door open, still talking as Leira did her best to ignore him.

"It would be like a dream come true. Sit on my ass from the comfort of my lounger right by the big window in the back and watch that sucker fly! Hey, that's a good idea too."

"In what world would a flying lawnmower be a good idea?"

Leira moved up in the line with Hagan close behind her. "Two ventis, one with a shot of foam."

"I could see it," said the cashier.

"See, he gets it," said Hagan. Leira raised an eyebrow at the young man and slid her card to pay for the coffee. An older woman slid two coffees in front of them. "The one on the left has the foam," she said.

Leira took her cup and headed for the door. "Yeah, and the same guy thought piercing his nose was a good idea."

"Yeah, I saw that. Do girls like that kind of thing?"

"Not this one."

"What if it was just every other mow?"

"What if you just paid someone to do it for you? Mmmm, coffee."

"Rose handles the finances. She already said no. Much the same arguments, plus we're saving for a trip to Hawaii."

Leira stopped in front of the jewelry store. "Look, you realize this is all deadly serious, right? I have to be careful. People disappear forever for less. My mother, for one." She winced when she said those words.

"Hey, kid…"

"It's okay. We're going to get her out. The *funny fellow*, whose name is Correk by the way, Bert if you're around the crowd at Estelle's."

"What…"

"I panicked. Gave him another name so I wouldn't have to explain. He has that same high forehead like the Muppet? There's a steep adjustment curve with all this. Fuck! How did we get here?"

"From the looks of things, you were always here," he said. "Now, you have answers, maybe more."

"Other thing is, I don't know enough about what I can do or how to do it. I can't be sure of unforeseen consequences. What if the lawnmower kept going down the street and ran over someone?"

Hagan recoiled, squeezing one eye shut, trying not to picture what that would look like. "That would take a lot of explaining. Fine, I'll stick to my riding lawnmower."

"Riding? You were bitching about a riding lawnmower?"

"Hey, that still takes effort! Come on, let's get in here. Figure out what our average but clever felons have been doing and catch these sons of bitches."

A small group stood in a circle on the top of Shiprock, a rocky outcropping over fifteen hundred feet high situated all by itself in the open desert of San Juan County, New Mexico. The ground was considered sacred by the local Navajo and never open to the general public, but there was nothing *general* about this gathering.

It was a mixed lot of magical beings whose ancestors came from Oriceran thousands of years ago and stayed, mating with the local population of humans. Two were rogue witches who were briefly part of the Silver Griffins, a few more were half Light or Wood Elf but could pass for locals on Earth, and some were from the Crystal tribe, but without the magic from Oriceran had reverted from being covered in crystals to a more human appearance. Still, they preferred the coldest climates on Earth and the heat of New Mexico was making them surly.

A few were even said to have Atlantean blood in them from the only magical tribe that originated on Earth. They never tired of pointing that out. They came from different parts of the globe to pool the recesses of the magic they had stored in different relics and artifacts.

Even though they were all very different, they had one thing in common. They believed in the rise of Rhazdon and that his magic would unite the magical community again. And this time, they would win.

They were gathered on the top of a large kemana, holding hands around every artifact they had saved in their closets and attics, pulling them out of old boxes and drawers, waiting for a day like this.

The vibrations from the explosion in Chicago were felt as far away as Missouri and every magical being inside of the radius took note. Most brushed it off and went on about their day. These things happened and the Silver Griffins would get to the bottom of it. There was a proper and orderly system. Best to not get involved.

But there were others who had met in secret for generations who longed for a different ending. A rebirth of Rhazdon's movement and the purity of magic and the right beings to follow his teachings.

Recently, rumors were flying around their circles at dinner tables and card games and standing by the soccer fields at children's games, that there was a new high priest rising up to take Rhazdon's place. He believed everything Rhazdon had taught and even was said to have mad skills at dark magic.

A twisted hope sprang up, weaving itself through groups spread out over the Earth, bringing them together in ever closer circles. Then the explosion happened and those closest to it knew it was all true.

An artifact from Oriceran that carried great powers, both light and dark, was brought to Chicago. The most powerful kind of artifact that could be used for something magnificent and dangerous.

They wanted to open a gate, between the two worlds centuries early. It would stay open but be hidden from everyone but their own kind. Those who believed in the teachings of Rhazdon.

This time it would be possible to find their new leader, this high priest, and join forces. A new darkness would begin and this time, on both worlds.

They joined hands around the pile of artifacts and relics that were purposefully arranged so that the energy would continue to combine and connect outward toward the circle.

Each hand grasped the one next to it, and the energy began to flow faster around the circle, building in intensity, flooding the members of the new cult. Their faces glowed, first pale gold, building to a dark royal purple. A feeling of bliss came over them, a few even giggled, unable to contain themselves.

But everyone held even tighter, determined not to break the ring of energy. Slowly, small embers appeared around the pile, racing around it in the sand. A blue light expanded upward, throwing off a hot wind powerful enough to knock someone off the rock formation if they got too close.

The heat intensified as the artifacts and relics were picked up by the wind, swirling into the blue haze, melting into pure energy. Rivulets of glowing, metallic blue liquid flowed out toward each member of the circle, seeking them out. A young half elf cried out, trying to pull her hands away and run but the others held on tighter. The energy seeped into their feet, crawling through their veins and settling into their bones.

A vision appeared in each of their minds. The same vision.

"The necklace is in Chicago," said the young elf, wonder in her voice. She could feel the surge of power. The blue fire subsided, gradually disappearing back into the ground. The artifacts and relics were gone and in their place the rock beneath their feet was cold to the touch, scattered with small crystals littering the ground. Everyone in the circle let go at the same moment and went to fill their pockets with the crystals. Small pieces of energy they could use later that worked like an energy balm. The user only needed to be magical and hold it tightly in their hands for a burst of temporary energy, enough to pull off one good spell.

"We should get going," said an older male Light Elf. His face was aglow with a blue inner light, much like everyone else. A younger Light Elf stared at him in wonder. "The glow wears off in a few hours," he said. "The energy will too after a few days. There isn't a lot of time. We'll need to gather together again and hit the road."

"Not everyone," said a half-Crystal man. "We should ring the city with followers. That way if the Order manages to escape with the necklace, there will be others waiting to stop them. Besides, it will be easier for us to slip through unnoticed by the humans if we don't march in there like a brigade."

"Then we have a plan."

"And a mission." The Light Elf's eyes glowed blue and he smiled as he looked out over the dark vista.

CHAPTER EIGHT

"Thank God! A day off! Why does this feel like the first day of school?" Leira was driving the green Mustang toward Enchanted Rock. "You didn't need to bring snacks this time. Twenty miles doesn't count as a road trip."

She looked over at Correk, happily using a Twizzler as a straw in a Dr. Pepper.

"That can't be good."

"I imagine just as good as all that coffee you're constantly drinking." He slurped the bottom of the can.

"Coffee is a national treasure."

"Mine!" chirped the troll, sitting on Correk's leg. Its little hands reached out, tiny claws digging into the Twizzler. Correk let him drag it away. He looked up in time to see Leira glare.

"I'm not fighting a troll over a licorice stick. I have my limits," he said.

"I was beginning to wonder."

"Besides, I bought the big box at Costco. I have hundreds left."

"You keep this up you're going to need a bigger portal to get back home."

"Light Elves have amazing metabolisms. Like hummingbirds. We burn fuel at a very high rate."

"Twizzlers and Dr. Peppers are not fuel but that does explain a lot about my own ability to eat and stay in shape."

She turned onto the gravel road into McKinney State Park. The road wound back to the right till it reached an oversized lavender-colored crystal spread over three acres. Enchanted Rock.

The sides jutted out, making a natural staircase to the top that was flat and fairly smooth, and big enough to lay out a blanket and relax or hang out with friends. Leira pulled into the small lot parking the Mustang off by itself.

"Are we planning for a quick getaway?"

"I'm still not used to this whole idea of magical people everywhere. I'm not sure how I feel about being surrounded by them."

"You've been surrounded by them your entire existence. That would be true if you were completely human. Oricerans stayed behind after the gates closed thousands of years ago. They made a home here and their descendants do their best to blend in most of the time. Your dentist could be part dwarf, or the lady who bags your groceries could be part Dark Elf. Humans have a hard time with the smallest of differences amongst themselves. We find it's better to stay hidden when on this planet."

"But the gates are going to start to open in my lifetime."

"Your lifetime, I predict, will turn out to be longer than you imagined, and then some. But yes, there are only twenty years or so till the gates start to gradually open again and Earth will be introduced to a rise in magic, whether they like it or not. Eventually, nothing will keep the two worlds from becoming enmeshed."

"Wouldn't it be better if there was some planning going on now?" Leira asked, scooping up the troll and sliding him into her pocket. She was getting used to having him along. She got out of the car and adjusted her jacket and noticed Correk was watching her.

"What?" She looked around, turning in a circle, trying to figure out what Correk was looking at so intently.

"Are you wearing your gun?"

"They call it *carrying*. Are you carrying your gun," Leira said. "And yeah, I am. I'm still an officer of the law."

"Now who sounds like bad cable TV?" Correk narrowed his eyes at her. A thought occurred to him and he hoped he was wrong.

"You're unhappy that you're Elven, aren't you? This is some kind of self-hate thing!"

Leira was taken aback, her face warming as she stammered, "It's not that... I don't trust, well, anyone." The words hit her square in the chest and knocked the wind out of her. She put the thought away and pushed past Correk, marching toward the large rock.

"I'm also not afraid of anything," she said over her shoulder.

"That first part, that not trusting anyone. It's not even true," Correk declared. He was taking long strides to catch up with her. "Craig, Mitzi, Mike, Scott, Estelle..."

"Okay, I get it. I have a tribe. That's what the Huffington Post calls it these days, right? They're more of a team than a tribe. I take care of myself. It's been that way, more or less, since I was ten years old. I'm an independent spirit who kicks ass, mother-fuckers!" She spit the words out, feeling the anger growing inside of her.

She felt it before she saw it. The magic was taking over her body.

She looked down and saw the symbols blossoming under her skin, crawling up her arm. She clenched her fists but that only made the color deepen and the symbols spread to her neck. The tall grass around them bent away from her and a nearby tree rattled as a flock of starlings shook loose and rose to the sky, turning north and flying away. The troll stirred in her pocket.

Correk thought about saying something but instead held out his hand and waited.

"I can take care of myself."

"No doubt of that at all. You are very independent. That doesn't mean you have to be alone. It just means you get to choose to let people help you. It's a choice." His hand was still extended. "It takes courage to ask people for help, even when you can do it yourself." He looked into her eyes, lit from within, and the angry set of her jaw, and he waited.

Leira slowly opened her hands. It was taking all her willpower to harness the magic flowing through her. Part of her wanted to let it have its way and flow out from her, just to see what it could do. What she could do.

The troll trembled in her pocket and burrowed deeper, curling up in a ball.

"You have a choice right now," Correk said gently. His hair was flowing out behind him from the blast of energy coming from Leira. The nearby pines were starting to bend in the direction of the flow of magic.

He was using his own magic to steady his heart rate and center the energy within himself. The harder she pushed, the calmer he became. A calm in the middle of a storm.

Leira felt like she could hold the pulse forever. It was like a runner's high. Just there, and endless. She pulled her shoulders back, standing up straighter, lifting her chin. A familiar defiance came back to her. *It's easier to just do it alone.*

Thin streams of lightning within the energy flow crackled and popped and suddenly started to reverse themselves. Correk watched with some concern but he did nothing to interrupt the flow. The sharp blue tendrils of magic continued to find their way through Leira's wide open surge, traveling back to the source. To Leira.

The opposing energy was now pulsing blue and white,

climbing up the outside of Leira's body until it reached her chest and disappeared into her body in tiny spirals.

An ache appeared inside of her as she felt the connection of the other energy meeting hers. Something familiar that she recognized, but it had been too long. She did her best to ignore it, wanting to hold on to the feeling of power, but it kept spiraling inside of her, tapping away at her consciousness.

"Mom," she whispered, shocked. Her mother was making contact, again. The energy surged forward, doubling its strength and weaving in on itself. Leira could hear the sounds within the energy. Like the singing speech of Light Elves on Oriceran. Her eyes widened as she realized their music were small pulses of magic energy. She opened her mouth and the same stream flowed out of her. She knew how to do it without anyone teaching her. It was a part of her.

The energy from her mother wrapped itself around her, searching for answers.

Leira let go of the pulse she created, and the energy abruptly reversed itself, flowing back into Leira with a *whomp* that made her stagger backward a few steps. Leira reached out for Correk's hand, still open in front of her. He closed his fingers around hers and held tight, pulling until he could wrap his arms around her. Leira held on as a shudder moved through her.

Her knees buckled and she felt her legs give way but Correk held her up until she could find her feet again. There were tears streaming down her face

The air around them settled and the grass stopped moving. Leira pushed away from Correk and turned away as her stomach lurched.

"What the hell was that?" she asked. The world seemed to be spinning in front of her. Correk reached out to grab hold of her again but she took a step back. He looked pained but dropped his arms and stepped away.

"That was an amazing display of magic, Cousin. You are a natural channel of energy. A rare being. I have never seen a display of magic like that. I've only heard about something like this from hundreds of years ago at the time of the defeat of Rhazdon."

"My mother..." Leira gasped, trying to catch her breath. Another wave of nausea threatened to overtake her. She pressed her palm into her stomach.

This time Correk insisted and steadied her, holding her arm. His eyes glowed dimly for just a minute and he sang in a low voice, letting the small pulses of magic vibrate around her, steadying the stream. Slowly, Leira began to feel normal again. She held her hands out in front of her to check, but they were rock steady.

"One more time. What the fuck was that?"

"Basically, a pure stream of energy, of magic. You were able to channel the energy coming off the nearby rock, straight through you. You were a part of the kemana for a little while."

"But my mother. She was here! I could feel her!"

"Yes, I saw what happened. Your magic is so strong it reached out to her. She felt your pulse of energy and responded to you. That doesn't entirely surprise me. After all, you share the same DNA. But I can clearly see from the varying strength of your energy flow not all your powers came from your mother. Your father must have had some magic as well."

"Yes, well, he's a big question mark. My mother would never talk about him." Leira shook out her arms and blinked a few times. "I don't feel tired or worn out from that," she said, surprised. "I would have thought that would take something from you. You said you have to recharge when you perform magic."

"It can and I do. That's what I mean. You are a very special being. A natural channel. You can use the magic flowing through you and pull in even more. We'll look into that, but for now, we should go introduce ourselves."

"What about my mother?"

"It's good news. Her ability to control her emotions is still strong enough for her to send a pulse this far, and to basically check on you. Your mother was making sure you're alright."

"We have to go see her." Leira turned to head back to the car. Correk pulled her back and rested his hands on her shoulders.

"Every magical being within ten miles felt the hum of that surge. It's a lot like the bomb blast in Chicago but in the opposite, positive way," he said sternly. "They'll be coming off the rock to see who it was. Best we just go say hello. We'll go to see your mother, just like we talked about. We'll even get her out. Did you just see what you could do? What in this world or the next could stop you? But we do it right. For now, let's go let everyone know that nothing other than the usual weirdness happened. Stop them from making up their own stories."

"So, it's a good thing I brought my gun."

"You put out that kind of magical energy and still think you even need a gun." He shook his head and trudged ahead of her, up the hill toward the rock, mumbling about missing the obvious and newbies.

"This all still feels like an episode of Oprah during sweeps week," Leira called, taking off at a run and passing him easily. It felt good to use her muscles and feel her legs move up the rough terrain. She leapt over a small boulder and felt more of the fragments of energy still clinging to her burn away, the energy rising in waves through the air. "Last one there eats too much junk food!"

"First one there has to introduce herself!" Correk called out. Leira stopped and looked back at him.

I can choose to be with others. She waited until he caught up with her and changed her mind, running ahead. *And I can choose to do it my way.* A smile spread across her face. *My mother came to check on me. She's okay. I will bring her home.* Leira ran as fast as she could, leaping up the first few steps of Enchanted Rock.

She stopped, a thin sheen of sweat on her face and looked back at Correk who was walking up the path at a fast clip. She looked up toward the top of the rock and realized there was a small crowd, all peering over the edge, staring at her with varying degrees of curiosity and worry.

Leira waved just as the troll popped his head out of her jacket pocket. He gave a small wave of his own. She froze, not sure what to do next.

"First the magic quake and now Oriceran trolls," she said quietly. Correk caught up to her and saw what had made her stop in her tracks.

She looked at him, and asked, "Is this good or bad?"

"I'm learning, Leira Berens, that with you there will have to be entirely new definitions. It's not a great way to walk into this world but it could be worse. At least we won't have to explain who we are."

"I thought they could all do that little thing we did the other night and tell who's magical and who's not."

"It's not like we do that all the time, but yes, they could. That only goes so far. It reads the magic but doesn't give you any history and it can tell you how powerful the being is, but only up to a point.

"Well, are you coming up or not?" A woman with a large, bouncy afro was shouting down to them, a welcoming smile on her face.

"So far, so good."

"I told you, even Oricerans who have been on Earth for generations don't separate themselves out like human beings are so fond of doing. That woman is elven. She's happy to meet more family."

"Now, that's a concept. Like fast food family."

"Yes!" Correk smiled at her but Leira only shook her head.

"Dude, I'm going to introduce you to some Texas barbeque. That's the real fast food. And fingers crossed, these people are more like that. Substance along with being wonderfully delicious, rooted in tradition. Not false hopes that just make your ass fat and your face break out."

"Welcome, I'm Toni," said the woman, as she held out her hand and helped pull Leira up onto the mesa. Correk followed behind her and stopped for a moment to take in the view.

"Earth is really very beautiful." He turned around and around to get a better look at the rolling green landscape topped with groves of pine trees and the distant limestone cliffs.

"This part of Texas is called hill country. I take it you're a recent immigrant? A real alien?" Toni offered an easy laugh, her hair bobbing gently in the breeze.

"So peaceful up here." Leira felt her worries fall away. Leira felt the same hum that had run through her on her last visit, but this time it was steadier. She was learning to control it, at least a little.

"That's a combination of the view and the energy that leaks out of this big ol' rock," said Toni, tapping it with her foot. "And maybe the wine we brought with us. Want a glass? It's a Riesling. I thought it went with the view."

Leira wasn't sure if she should introduce herself. She wasn't used to people jumping into the middle of conversations and taking her in like they'd been waiting for her to arrive.

"Sure, very good idea." She cleared her throat, mentally kicking her butt for feeling so awkward. *So much to learn. So much to get used to.* "Leira Berens," she said, pointing to herself like Toni might be confused. That just made Toni laugh again as she handed Leira a paper cup half full of wine.

"Sorry about the paper cup. No glass allowed on the rock. Safety hazard." She pulled another cup out of a canvas backpack and poured, handing the wine to Correk.

"Now," she said. "Let's see if we can introduce you to a few more people. Leira, right? And?"

"Correk." He said his name quickly before Leira had a chance to say *Bert.*

"Oh, Light Elf, of course. You too, I suppose. That was a groovy energy pulse you had going down there. A little intense but the backdraft was amazing! Come on," she said, waving for them to follow her.

CHAPTER NINE

Folding canvas chairs were scattered in the middle of the plateau, and people were playing guitars or talking loudly, laughing and telling each other long stories. There was food in plastic containers and straight out of boxes.

Toni watched Leira taking it all in. "It's our own small, weekly family reunion that helps to center our energy and remind us of who we are as a whole being. Not just human. This is how we stay connected."

"And get recharged," Leira added, feeling the hum through her feet.

"And stay recharged, as much as that's possible." The woman gave Leira a puzzled look. "Although, that doesn't seem to be an issue for you." She looked Leira up and down. "There's something rarefied about you. Okay, enough of me pecking away at you," said Toni, grabbing Leira by the arm. "You're coming with me. Time to meet the local magnificent magical beings."

Leira looked back at Correk, who was standing there, looking amused, sipping his wine. He shrugged at her, arching an eyebrow. She was getting used to that look.

"Jim, this is Leira, one of our kind," she said, smiling and giving an exaggerated wink.

"I kind of gathered that," he said, pointing with his cup at the troll poking out of Leira's pocket. The troll trilled and jumped out, running toward the food.

"Yumfuck!" Leira gasped and lunged for him, still not sure if this was a good idea but everyone else just laughed.

"Love the name!" exclaimed Jim.

"You've been to Oriceran and you rescued the little thing, didn't you," said a small woman with long auburn hair wearing a long peasant dress and sandals. "Been there, did that. I'm Mary Ellen. Most people just call me Molly." She stretched out her arm making the long line of silver bracelets on her arm slide down toward her hand with a tinkling sound.

"That's Perry, and over there is Lucy, and the twins are Fran and Fern. And there's more of us," Toni explained.

"A lot more," agreed a middle-aged man with a bushy mustache that was only outdone by the bushy hair on his head.

"That's Eric. The philosopher of the group. He'll help enlighten you."

"So, you finally see things my way," he said, smiling as he sat down. He pulled off a small chunk of the cheddar cheese and fed it to the troll.

"Mmmmm, mine. Yumfuck."

"Aw, he knows his name!"

"He kind of named himself," said Leira.

There was a chorus of laughter and Eric broke off another piece to see if the troll would do it again.

"Yumfuck! Yumfuck, mmmmm." The troll chewed the cheese heartily, even going back to lick Eric's fingers.

"I take it you swear a lot." He smiled at Leira.

"Only when I'm awake."

"You're going to fit right in!" yelled Molly. "Sit by me!"

"Who's the big one hanging back over there?" Jim pointed at Correk.

"Come on, don't make me pull you over too!" Toni waved at Correk. "Entire group, Correk. Correk, your home away from home." She looked at him slyly. "You don't usually hang in these parts, do you?"

Correk said nothing but gave her a half smile and turned back to the view.

"No worries. No one here is a member of the Order and we're not rats. We don't need to do their job for them. What happens on the rock, or down in the parking lot," she said, raising her cup, "stays in the parking lot!"

"Here, here!"

Leira settled into the chair next to Molly and sat back, watching everyone, absorbing it. *Another tribe. It's a lot to take in but I think I like this.*

———

Mara Berens moved as quickly as she could through the thick, gelatinous ether that made up the world in between. The substance was there, and then it wasn't, impeding movement and making it harder to reach out toward the living world just beyond.

There were malevolent forces living in the world in between who were using darker magic they brought with them to slice through the filmy substance and move rapidly, showing up in different places in only a heartbeat. Even though most of them no longer had a heartbeat.

The dead existed alongside the living on this side of the thin veil.

The world in between permeated the world of the living where time still passed in a linear progression, even if it didn't in the void where Mara was trapped. The world in between stretched around and through and mingled with both Earth and Oriceran, giving a peculiar view to the myriad of inhabitants trapped there, watching time pass. Wanting it to pass for them again, or at least stop forever.

That was the misery of the world in between. Trapped beings could watch for centuries, millennia even, not aging if they fell in while still alive, or never going on to the afterlife if they were dead. But they couldn't participate, and communication was rare with anyone on the other side.

All they could do was watch, and hide when necessary, from the evil that coursed through the world in between.

Mara knew that after years trapped in the middle of nowhere and everywhere all at once. It took her well over a year to locate her daughter, Eireka in the psych ward but she still wasn't sure how to get a message to her. Leira moved not long after Mara was trapped, and Mara lost track of her altogether. Until she saw her on the street, walking with a Light Elf.

The fear clutched at her again. Oriceran had brought nothing but pain to her family from the start. Now, they had found her granddaughter. Mara was determined to find a way to warn her.

That meant dealing with the minions who moved throughout the world in between, mingling with the darker forces. The dead the humans called poltergeists that had learned just enough about how the world in between worked to cause trouble and dispense nightmares, but not enough to really harm anyone.

They were the nasty bullies of the world in between.

I can do this. I can do this for my granddaughter. Even if it's the last thing I get to do.

It wasn't unusual to barter with the poltergeists to reach the other side of the veil but every once in a while, the darkness was attracted to what was happening and intervened, taking over the mind of someone trapped in there. The living in the world in between were their favorite targets.

Mara knew she was risking madness.

I can do this. I know enough magic to at least glamour myself for an hour. Hide from everything, living or dead. Long enough.

The poltergeists were easy to spot. The energy surrounding them was erratic and tended to throw off sparks into the ether, creating popping bursts of light.

Mara saw what looked like a storm cloud in the distance and focused on it, pulling herself closer. Distances in the world in between were relative. They could be a few feet, a few miles or another world. It took the same amount of focus to pull a being from Sacramento, California to Rome, Italy as it did to roam over a square city block. The world in between didn't follow time *or* space.

She pulled close enough that the sparks were flashing in her face. She knew the poltergeist was aware of her presence and it was best to wait for it to choose to pay attention to her. The negotiations would be easier that way. Mara made a point of spending the past four years wisely, gathering information, making allies when she could. It wasn't easy. None of it was.

You must want something. The poltergeist turned and fixed glowing eyes on Mara. It was dressed in a brown suit, still wearing a woolen winter coat and leather Florsheims. A dead human man, killed on a workday. Part of his head was smashed in. Mara wondered if he realized he was dead.

She made a point of looking right back at him.

I want to barter.

What could you have that I want?

Time.

The dead man smiled, his broken teeth giving him the appearance of a jack o'lantern.

Car crash? Mara pushed for information, if only to show she wasn't afraid. If only to convince herself. Fear was something everyone trapped in the world in between could feel. Strong enough and it could even be seen, radiating off someone for miles. That kind never lasted long.

Something like that. What has time got to do with this place?

I can give you some. Mara focused on remaining calm, serene, giving nothing away. The poltergeist's energy swirled around her, probing for a sense of what she was up to.

Nothing. Impressive. You're not a witch. I can tell you don't play in the darkness. They often twist early, and into something permanently ugly. Let's say you can give me time. What do you want in return?

Knowledge. I want to know how to send messages to the living.

Oh darling, that is going to cost you. Tell me what time is in this place and I'll tell you if I want to teach you anything.

The energy swirled closer. A bitter, acrid smell filled her nose, surprising her. She didn't know if it was possible to still use the sense of smell.

Of course it is. The dead man sensed what she was feeling. *All your senses are still there. They just turn on and turn off differently and you have to know what you're doing. You won't figure a lot of this out accidentally. So, tell me, what is time?*

A space where you can hide from the darkness to pull off one trick without being seen.

You know how to glamour in here? I am impressed. You've been saving that one. Light Elf aren't you.

The energy pulled back, sizing her up. *And something more.* He came in closer, again. *Okay, deal. You first.*

No. You teach me, I hide you, or we go watch the universe's largest reality show for a billion more years, ducking and hiding. Mara let go of wanting this to work and centered her energy. Indifference, as much as she could manage it, was going to help her win.

Deal. But I choose the trick.

Deal. Show me how to leave a message. She did her best not to think about what the dead man might want to do and paid close attention to his instructions. She was determined to warn Leira.

CHAPTER TEN

Leira and Hagan sat outside the jewelry store, waiting for something, anything, to happen. They had a tip from an informant they both trusted, Pink Harry, that this was the next target. The store was known to have a lot of cash and diamonds on hand. They had a guard and a safe but details like that hadn't stopped the burglars so far.

The Captain decided it would be less conspicuous to put his two detectives nearby rather than regular patrol cars.

Hours had already passed. Hagan was getting antsy.

"Are you telling me that you can't ding dong something up and tell if the bad guys are on their way?" He was fluttering his fingers again, in front of his chest. It had become his signal for all things magical.

"What's with the old man jazz hands?"

"Oh, that hurts, Berens. I could have taken the jazz hands part. You had to throw in old man. That wounds. Ah, and now the dead fish face. We're going for broke."

"You deserved it. We've talked about this. No magic."

"They ain't coming. I can feel it. I have a kind of magic all my own. A magical gut. Sometimes I even have a singing ass." Hagan chortled at his own joke. "That one is really Rose's joke. I should give her credit since she suffers through the consequences."

Leira almost spit out her coffee, coughing for a few seconds. "We aren't this familiar, are we? By the way, I already knew. We've been on a few stakeouts together. It's why you're banned from anything spicy for twelve hours before you get in the car. You did follow the rule this time, I so hope."

Hagan made a small cross over his heart and gave the Boy Scout salute. "I swear. No singing asses tonight. By the looks of things, no nothing. Geez, we're gonna end up here till that store closes."

"Which is not too long from now. They don't know we're out here, right?"

"No, I have the same suspicion you do. Inside help. But how they would know at more than one store...I don't know." Hagan threw up his hands and shrugged. "Any doughnuts left?" He dove for the pink box on the floor.

"You're the only one eating them. You tell me." Leira picked up the small binoculars and watched an older woman scan the street before entering the store. "That was weird."

"What?" Hagan took a bite of a cake doughnut, made a face and dropped the box. "Cake. Why bother. What's happening," he asked, picking up his pair of binoculars. "I don't see anything."

"Woman looked around before she walked in the store. It looked like she expected to see something or hoped she didn't see it. You think we've been made?"

"She look in our direction?" He brushed off the front of his shirt.

"Hey, watch the crumbs. That's not a trash can down there. And, no, she didn't look directly at us, but I got the impression she knew we were here somewhere. Someone tipped them off."

"That's not good. That leaves us with less than nothing *and* a leak." Hagan tilted his head expectantly at Leira, raising his eyebrows.

"No. Not gonna do it. We are damn good detectives. We've figured out harder cases the old fashioned way for some time now. We don't take fucking shortcuts!" Leira ran her hand through her dark hair and lifted up the glasses again. The woman came back out, stopped just outside the door to check her phone, and took another look around before she texted someone.

"There she is, doing the same damn thing. She's the lookout. Maybe she gave them the all clear."

"Well, we'll know soon enough. Not too much time before they close and take all that money with them to deposit. Now or never."

The woman held up her arm for a car service that pulled up right next to her. She opened the back door and got in, and the car drove off. Hagan took pictures of the license plate and the car. "If she's in on it, they won't have her real name. But at least we'll have a good picture of her."

"If they're smart, they use different lookouts every time and they've been smart so far."

Just then, a balding man ran out of the front of the store, waving his arms, calling for help. A call came over the police radio at the same time reporting a robbery at the same address they had been watching for hours.

"Dispatch, we are at this location," said Hagan, doing his best not to sound embarrassed.

"Already?" said the startled operator. They both ignored the question and pushed opened their doors.

"What the fuck!" Leira barreled out, pulling her gun from the holster as she sprinted for the store. Hagan was right behind her.

"Goddamn motherfuckers! Make me look like a goddamn fool!" Hagan swore with every step he took, his face beet red. "Fucking amateur hour but it turns out we're the fucking amateurs!" He spit out the last words as they reached the man, still frantically waving on the sidewalk.

"They came in the back!" he sputtered. "Three of them! Bing, bam, boom! Just like that!"

"You get a look at them?" Leira asked.

"No, not really. Ski masks. I couldn't see much of anything. They took everything! How did this happen?"

"Good question," Leira said grimly, pulling open the door to the store. "Very good question." She felt the small traces of magic still in the room and a shiver went down her back. *Something's not right here.*

"You look funny. What is it?" Hagan narrowed his eyes. "I know that look. You already found a fucking clue! Spidey senses?" He fluttered his hands again.

"There was nothing radioactive about my upbringing. At least, I don't think so," Leira replied, trying to ignore Hagan long enough to let herself feel the fading bits of magic still present. "Don't do the fucking jazz hands again." She turned away from him so she could concentrate. *It's there. I can feel it. Not smart thieves. Magical ones.*

"We may have a problem."

"You mean, besides sitting in front of a robbery in progress? There aren't enough doughnuts in the world to live this one down. What else could make this worse?"

"Magic."

"Fuck me. Well, there you go," said Hagan, doing his jazz hands again but with a sour expression.

The crime scene didn't take long to investigate. There wasn't much to find. Just like the other robberies the victims were confused about what they saw, if anything, and there were no fibers, no fingerprints and no real clues. Except for the unexpected one Leira found. Magical traces.

"What do we do now?" Hagan watched Leira as if he expected her to do something immediately.

They were sitting back in the Mustang as Leira finished explaining what she found.

"I'm not going to pull out a spell. I don't even know more than one or two. Don't ask if I have a wand. I'm not that kind of magical."

"There are kinds? Fuck me again. How many kinds?"

"You're losing focus here. The game has changed. If magic is involved, we need to come at this from a different angle. But I'm going to need to do some research."

"You're gonna talk to the big guy with the pointy ears. Spock man."

"I have an idea how we can catch these guys without anyone getting hurt."

"I'm all for that."

"We use magic to find the gun that shot that guard and then find a reason to go get it."

"Works for me! You think it still exists?"

"I don't know. But a spell to find something can't be that hard. Not if you can believe every Lucasfilm movie ever made."

"Call your friend. Do you need a phone for that, or do we just say his name three times?"

"I'm starting to see why we get on his nerves. We'll have to go find him. He doesn't have a phone. Okay, yes, there is a way to talk to him using magic. I haven't learned that one yet."

"It's like riding with someone from the Justice League. You should have a superhero name."

"Do it and I will fill your drawer with cotton balls. Remember, I know how they secretly creep you out. Come up with a name and I swear you will find cotton balls when you least expect it for an entire month. I'll even use magic to make sure it happens."

Hagan held up his hands. "Fine. No nicknames. Kill all the fun."

"Let's go get that gun."

"I can settle for that," Hagan agreed. "Our clearance rate is going to skyrocket. Loving this new thing we've got going here."

Leira glared at him but wondered. *Have things changed forever?*

"Okay, try again." Correk waited patiently for Leira to move her hands through the intricate movements.

"This isn't easy with everyone watching me."

Hagan rolled his eyes and turned around so his back was to her. "This better?"

Leira looked at his sagging pants. "Not really."

"Hardy har, Berens. Come on, try again," he said, turning back around. "What? I don't want to miss the show."

"Not a show. I'm not doing sleight of hand on South Congress for the tourists."

They were standing in the center of Leira's small living room in the guesthouse behind Estelle's bar. The only place they could be certain no one would bother them. Correk preferred a confined space anyway, where it would be easier to contain her magic while she was learning. He had already put a charm around the cottage, ensuring no one would see any light or hear suspicious noises from the patio.

The bar was humming with patrons, including Leira's tribe of regulars, but Estelle had made it very clear early on that just because Leira lived nearby and someone had a few drinks didn't mean they could waltz over and knock on her door. It was up to Leira when she wanted to come out.

Everyone respected the rule, for the most part. Estelle was small but scary and no one wanted to be on her bad side. Mitzi and Margaret were known to do drive-bys but even they would only do that during the daylight, most of the time. They said that was normal girlfriend behavior.

"Oh, come on, this is like a show! And for an old homicide detective it's like Christmas Day and hearing the words, *we find the defendant guilty*, all rolled into one. You move your hands around and have all the feelings and boom, there's your murder weapon. Didn't even leave home. It's a fucking show!"

"You're doing the magic hands again. It's distracting. Okay, okay, I can do this." Leira took a deep breath and shook out her hands. "Attempt number five. I thought you said this was one of the easy ones."

"I said this was a simple one. None of them are necessarily easy. Let me show you again." Correk raised his hands, making circles with his thumb and forefingers.

"Why can't you just do it and tell us where the gun is?" There was a sheen of sweat on Leira's forehead.

"You need to embrace this side of you. If I do it for you what will you do when there's some kind of danger and you have to find something or someone with just moments to spare?"

"You can find people this way, too? Holy crap, this changes everything!" Hagan slapped his forehead, smiling as he hitched his pants back up over his belly.

"Not always. Even human beings have the ability to hide themselves from us with their intentions or feelings. Even when they don't realize they're doing it. That's why the late Bill Somers was impossible for us to find. Now, try again. I thought you said you never back down from a challenge."

"Oh, okay, fuck me," she grumbled. "He threw down a challenge. Alright, okay." She cocked her head to one side then the other, stretching her neck and flexing her fingers.

"Oh, now she's ready. Now you got her." Hagan licked his lips nervously. "You can feel it, right?"

"I haven't even started! Okay, everyone take a step back."

Correk stepped back and folded his arms across his chest. "The floor is yours."

"Okay."

"Try shutting your eyes. It can help." Correk gave her an encouraging look. "Remember how it felt at Enchanted Rock. That wasn't something you created. It was something you allowed. Like turning on one of your light switches. You flip up the switch and the electricity just flows."

Leira closed her eyes and started moving her hands. She felt the first small surge of energy, boosting her confidence.

Hagan and Correk watched as her skin started to glow and the symbols appeared. Hagan's mouth opened, forming a perfect O. He started to say something but Correk put a heavy hand on his arm and gave him a stern shake of his head. Hagan nodded, whispering, "Right, right," earning another withering look from Correk. "Okay," he whispered, holding a finger to his lips. "Shhhhhh."

Leira was already lost in the spell, mesmerized by the images passing through her head and feeling the surge of power that was becoming familiar.

Correk read the symbols as they appeared and saw that she was getting close. "Remember what you know about the robbery, the gun and the store. Recall the traces of magic left behind in the last robbery. Let all that flow through you and focus on what you desire. To know where the gun is that was used to shoot the guard."

His voice was deep and soothing, reaching her like an echo inside of her head. She saw images of the different stores, at first like snapshots in her mind.

"Think about slapping the cuffs on someone. That always helps you focus." Hagan's voice came through like a sharp, tinny song, but he was right. The feeling she got when she finally put all the pieces together and knew she had the right person.

"The gun," she whispered, pushing the magic out from her.

Correk watched the symbols on her, reading them. "That's right, you're very close."

"You can read those? I'll be damned." Hagan was bent over at the waist, his hands on his hips, squinting at the symbols. "No, nothing. Don't get a thing."

Correk did his best to ignore Hagan and focused on Leira. "What do you see?"

The snapshots started to come faster, pulling her along until a stream of images flashed in her mind. "Lake Anna. The bottom of Lake Anna toward the interstate on the south side of the lake." Her eyes popped open and the symbols started to fade. "I did it! Lake Anna! For a bunch of magical beings, they're as dumb as a bag of rocks. Old school throw the gun in a lake." She began to realize what she had done. *She was a magical creature.*

"The good news is we don't need a warrant to search a lake. The bad news is we need a damn good reason to use the resources."

Leira felt the energy subside, clearing her head. "What about Pink Harry?"

"You mean get him to lie for us and call in a tip?" Hagan made a face, but the idea seemed to grow on him. "That could work. I have to tell you, Berens, you mix in this magical stuff and it gets harder to know the rules, exactly."

"I have a better idea," said Correk. "It involves magical sugges-tion, so the person believes the story they're telling. We can charm this Pink Harry. It'll make him sound more believable."

"Not that I'm against this," said Hagan, "but how is this not a lie, too?"

"Do it," Leira decided. "We can figure out magical ethics later. We're not creating the evidence, Hagan. We're using the tools at our disposal to find the evidence."

"Good enough for me, I guess. Okay, big guy, do your thing."

"It's already done," said Correk, looking smug.

"That is not a good look on you," Leira said.

"What just happened?" Hagan blinked, looking around with his hands held out like he expected something to jump out at him.

"You two should go. Pink Harry is about to call in a tip."

"Yeah, good idea, right," said a flustered Hagan. "Like we're in a sci-fi cop movie. The older guy always lives till the end, right?"

"You really already pulled that off?" whispered Leira. Correk smiled and did a good imitation of Hagan's magic hands.

"No, but it was fun watching his face. But by the time you get to the precinct, Pink Harry will have said enough to convince your captain it's worth his while." Correk winked. "Fun with humans."

"Hey," she said, swatting him on the chest with the back of her hand, "I'm partially human. Man, that's still weird to say out loud."

"You'll get used to it, now go!"

It didn't take long for the divers to find the gun. Pink Harry's information was remarkably accurate. The gun was in the exact spot Leira had seen. There were no fingerprints on the outside of the gun but one of the bullets in the chamber had enough of a partial to give up a name.

They found the three men holed up in an apartment complex off St. Edwards Drive. They looked confused when the police came barreling through the door, heavily armed, wearing vests. Leira made a point to stay in the background while the lead detectives from robbery read them their rights. She had pointed out to Hagan that it was their case anyway, and besides, no one needed angry magical felons recognizing Leira's newly discovered status.

That didn't stop tongues from wagging in the precinct, though. Some of the other detectives took note of how two big cases, both with almost no leads, suddenly broke wide open and were solved in no time at all.

"Ignore them," Hagan said. "Jealous of age and beauty. My beauty, your age."

Leira smiled but she was growing wary. "We need to be more careful. At least make it look more difficult or someone will start to ask questions we can't answer. For all we know, there are other magical beings nearby."

"You mean in here?" Hagan's eyebrows shot up as he looked around the room suspiciously.

"I don't think you're going to see anything, Hagan. I just mean, this could go south on us, quickly."

"At least the Captain is happy. Look at him."

Captain Napora was standing behind his desk on the phone, smiling from ear to ear, talking away.

"That's good, I suppose, but it just makes the bitches among us even more aware of our every move."

"Well," said Hagan, getting up and putting on his coat, "I'm going home to Rose. My corner in the world of sanity. Especially these days. Thank whatever there is that Rose is predictable, even if that means yelling at me for something at least once a week."

"Completely deserved."

"Completely," said Hagan, scooping up his keys. "Frankly, she keeps me alive. Don't stay too much longer. There'll be another case before we know it and a new set of problems. Enjoy whatever time we've got right now. At least go hang out with those people you call neighbors." Hagan laughed. "Only you could have mobile neighbors who don't live near you so much as drink near you. Ah, the dead fish look I have come to love. Don't ever change that."

"Enough. Go home. I'm leaving right behind you." *Before something else goes wrong and so I can finally corner Correk on how to get my mother home.*

CHAPTER ELEVEN

The ground shook slightly and everyone walking along Michigan Avenue looked up from their phones, mildly surprised, looking back down again to check on Facebook for reports of an earthquake. But a plume of smoke rising from the Pumping Station struck a note of fear. The tourists in particular started walking quickly in the other direction while some turned and held up their phones to record the event. A few turned around to make sure and get a selfie with the smoke in the background, making their best duck faces and holding up the peace sign.

The media descended after the first explosion, bringing their satellite trucks close before the police could arrive to push them back. It helped that it was all happening so close to their studios.

Still, there were others who kept one eye on the old stone building that looked more like a castle but kept on moving down the street anyway, determined not to have their day interrupted. Most of them were locals and native Chicagoans weren't easily shaken, and some of them had roots that wove their way back to Oriceran. They had seen stranger things in Chi-town under a full moon. Among that crowd there was a general consensus that this too would pass.

Not everyone took it so calmly.

It was Chicago and normally any spate of violence might have taken some time for anyone to notice, but this was the Magnificent Mile, the heart of the Gold Coast. People were up in arms from the first billow of ash, calling their aldermen, demanding they do something. The mayor was informed and there was a brief mention of marshaling the forces.

But then, just like that, there was an explanation. An old gas pipe under the pumping station on Michigan Avenue had exploded. An accident. A fluke. No injuries. The news coverage quickly melted away and regular programming resumed. There were a few grumblings and tweets about how these sorts of things aren't supposed to happen, and what if someone was hurt. Stores reopened and in the nearby Water Tower, wine was being offered to any shoppers shaken by the interruption to their day.

The Order of the Silver Griffin was using their extensive network of connections to change the story.

They had a guy.

Members of the Order stepped out onto the street and like a chorus of band leaders held up their wands, almost as one and chanted, "Never was, never will be." The humans on the street froze for a minute or two and when they came to, shook their heads, tried to remember what they were doing, *why was their phone in their hand*, and let it go. *Back to their day.*

Other members sat in front of their computer screens, sending out a virus that sought out coverage of the explosion or posts in social media, eating the pixels like a magical Pac-Man and replacing them with cat videos.

Witches and wizards who were going about their day, sitting in meetings, picking up kids, looking at apples in Trader Joe's suddenly felt their phones buzzing and twitching with an emergency chirp, a chime too pleasant for anyone outside of the Order to take notice.

A wizard at the gym looked up at another wizard running on the treadmill and gave him a nod. Both of their phones were jumping and chirping.

The worst was happening. The vault was under attack. The text was short and simple and was prepared years ago, ready to go if it ever became necessary.

Report at once to your primary battle station. Stop the offenders. Defend by any means necessary. Use lethal force as required.

They both got up as if they were finished working out, even smiling and waving as they left.

"Best of everything," said the taller of the two as they met at the door.

"All the best in the world," said the other, as they parted ways to go to their stations. It was an old saying from Oriceran used when preparing to go to war, not heard much in hundreds of years on Oriceran but whispered on many a battlefield on Earth.

At ground level, everything appeared quiet. Beneath the streets, the fighting raged on as the Order of the Silver Griffins fought against the onslaught of magical beings trying to get to the safe.

The rebirth of Rhazdon's cult. His followers had come for the necklace.

Two witches from the Order stood at the top of the stairs, their wands drawn, determined looks on their faces. They both looked more like mothers getting ready to pick up their kids from school than combat veterans. But they were trained by the Order to fight till the end to keep the vault from all comers. They weren't backing down.

Behind them the stairs were partially destroyed, rubble every-where with dust floating up and clinging to everything. An injured wizard lay on the first landing, pressing on his broken leg with one hand while still managing to hold out his wand with the other. His casual corporate attire was singed in places with a long, ragged tear in the slacks where he took a direct hit from a half human, half dwarf male.

The spell sent out a cloud of glittering black dust that coalesced into an arrow, aimed straight at the wizard, vanishing after it hit its mark. Old magic, forbidden for eons. The wound was already festering and bubbling.

The witches at the top of the stairs looked ashen. They knew they were outnumbered but stood firm, wands at the ready.

A female half Wood Elf produced green sprouts from her hands that quickly grew into thorny vines, wrapping around the closest witch's ankles, rapidly spreading up her legs, pricking her skin. The other witch swirled her wand, yelling, "Expedia," turning the vine to rot. The witch in front held her ground, ignoring the stinging pain and focused, sending blinding sparks from her wand, hitting the elf square in the chest knocking the Rhazdon follower out cold as her head connected with the far wall making a satisfying thud.

An older couple walking by darted inside, pulling out their wands. A witch and wizard who had joined Rhazdon's cult and were being called in as reinforcements. The witches in the Order looked momentarily surprised but they immediately recovered and aimed a spray of gold sparks at the couple.

"Betrayer of your own kind!" shouted the witch whose legs were covered in a rash from the poisonous vine.

The Rhazdon wizard held out his wand, sending a silver shower while a black cloud swirled around his wand. A sure sign of dark magic and a poisoned heart. His companion joined in, sending out more sparks that pushed back against the Order's stream of magic fire.

The streams met, curling around each other, pushing back and forth as both sides held their positions. The injured wizard from below crawled up the steps, dragging his leg, his face caught in a grimace, his teeth clenched. He got close enough to aim and whispered, "Tabula rasa."

A pulse of magic sought out the couple, wrapping around their heads, searching for any recent memories, erasing them for all time. They dropped their wands, the silver streams of magic faded and the gold hit them, knocking them back. Both of them sat down hard, looking around, confused.

The witch closest to the wizard turned around, surprised. "That's forbidden. Always!"

"By any means necessary," he grunted, resting his head on the step.

"That is a line we don't cross!"

The other witch snapped at her, "And then they take whatever they want from the vault! Hundreds of dangerous artifacts and relics! And chaos reigns on this world! He was right! We defend the vault!"

There was no time to say anything further. They could see a double-decker bus stopping at the corner and a stream of people getting off. They looked like tourists, smiling and chatting with each other. But the two witches knew they were a wall of intruders about to invade their sanctuary. They were going to be overrun.

The witch hurriedly spoke into the device on her shoulder, a walkie talkie that was infused with a charm. "We can't hold them much longer. Stand ready below. It was a privilege to serve."

But just as they breached the door, auxiliary members of the Order came from stores, the nearby subway stop, and from the beach a few blocks away. They poured into the Pumping Station from the opposite door, pulling out their wands, already firing at the onslaught coming from the other direction.

The spells on the doors made them impenetrable and no sound or light escaped the room. The humans passing by had no idea what raged on just yards from them. Some looked with curiosity at the number of tourists suddenly interested in the building, wondering if a play was about to start, but kept moving on to their destinations.

The waves of energy crossed each other in lines that made a checkerboard of light, starting small magical fires that would burn until someone deliberately put them out.

There were casualties on both sides. The Order used hidden charms in the walls to help them climb as if they were weightless, shooting down from above. More members of the Order flooded up the stairs from the vault, aiming low, knocking the cultists over like bowling pins.

In the middle of the chaos, no one noticed the young witch whisper a glamour spell, cloaking herself. She had worked her way deep into the spiral of the archives and hid there, waiting till the arranged time.

She slipped up the stairs from the vault and moved along the wall, avoiding the fighting and reached an exit door in the back. She ran for the red line subway stop two blocks west, taking the stairs down two at a time, not making eye contact with anyone. More members of the Order flowed up the stairs. The glamour spell held, they ignored her.

Most of them knew who she was and would have wondered why she was leaving. On a more normal day they would have even noticed the telltale trail of magic that would have given away her cloaking spell. But today was no ordinary day. The wizard that brushed up against her outside on the sidewalk thought he saw a young college student intent on her phone. He didn't give it a second thought as he hurried on to his destination.

When she got to the concrete platform below it was mostly empty, just a few people waiting for the next train. At the far end there was an old man sitting on a bench who looked like he might be homeless. Most people were avoiding him, standing at the other end. The girl walked as quickly as she could without drawing attention. He looked up at her as she drew closer, giving her a quick shake of his head.

She stopped where she was in front of a nearby bench and sat down, trying not to cry. She reached into her pocket and pulled out the velvet box she had taken from the vault and slid it under the bench when no one was looking in her direction. She knew she was betraying the Order she had sworn an oath to, just like her mother and grandmother before her. But it was this or let them breach the vault. Much worse things could happen. At least that's what she told herself as she got up and headed back to the stairs.

The old man grunted as he stood up and smacked his lips, picking his nose. People moved further away from him, turning their backs. No one wanted to see what he might do next. He sat down on the bench and pulled out the case, opening it to make sure. Inside was a heavy gold necklace with a diamond-shaped lavender colored jewel hanging from the end.

Rhazdon's new followers had their prize.

He held open his worn puffy coat, releasing a nauseating wave of old sweat and bile that could be smelled yards away from him. He chuckled to himself, knowing no one would want anything to do with him.

"Retreat," he whispered, his eyes glowing for a moment as he held a clear fireball inside of his jacket, breathing the word into it. It looked like a bubble as it floated up the stairs to the surface. Once it was clear of the subway it rose higher, taking off like a shot toward the Pumping Station, sliding through a door.

The old man's voice blared out over the crowd. His whisper had become a shout. "Retreat!"

All of the Rhazdon cult members looked up, still brandishing their wands but they stepped back. No one tried to make any further progress toward the stairs and the vault.

"This can't be good," said a witch. "Why are they giving up?"

Once the cult got outside they folded up their wands, putting them back into their pockets. Those with older models made out of wood slid them into purses or inner pockets specially made for a long wand. Most went back to the double decker bus, chatting away about the Chicago scenery, as if it was just another day.

"It's gone! The necklace is gone!" A young wizard tore up the stairs, stepping over fallen comrades, searching the faces around him for someone to tell him what he should do next. Two older witches barreled down the stairs past the young wizard and into the vault. They ran down the aisles to the left, looking up till they hit the R's.

There it was. An empty space right next to Jack the Ripper's razor. The necklace was gone. Someone had betrayed them. Worse, they knew it had to be one of their own.

"You stay here and make sure nothing else was taken. Get help and check every other piece in here," said the witch with a short grey bob. She had a black streak across her cable knit sweater where a blast had come a little too close.

Hundreds of items, all carefully catalogued. It would take a while to be certain.

"Consider it done, Eloise," said a short, round witch with a twisted braid pinned into a bun on the back of her head.

Eloise ran back up the stairs, already yelling, "Secure the wounded enemies. Don't let any of them go! Get help for our own!" Someone would pay for this betrayal, even if it meant opening a portal to Trevilsom Prison, or death.

Leira felt the tremors from the magical earthquake all the way across the country. She was sitting at her desk in the precinct looking at a new case file, another dead body, when the rolling energy passed through her. She looked up at Hagan, half expecting him to look startled too, but then she realized it wasn't the ground shaking. It was passing through the air. She saw the wavy opaque lines spreading out, and just as quickly dissipating.

"I gotta go." She stood up, pulling her jacket off the back of her chair.

"What? What just happened?" Hagan looked up from the report he was typing. There were always reports to do for someone about something. "What'd I miss?"

"Nothing, we're good. I just remembered something. I'll be back. Forgot an errand."

"Don't lie to me, Berens. I know that look. What just happened?"

Leira looked around to make sure no one else was in earshot. It was between a shift change and the main rooms were mostly empty. Everyone was out on the streets except a few who were working on reports from their desk.

"Something I don't understand but feels like it's important. This feeling's bullshit," she said, patting her chest, "it's like having someone tied to you who won't shut the fuck up."

"Berens, you're just not used to feeling much of anything except determined, angry, bored and victorious. Anything else, you dismissed," he said, brushing his hands together. "You're building an internal dial to regulate all of that so-called bullshit. It'll come together and then it'll be like one of those old-fashioned meters Johnny Carson used to have."

Leira looked confused, making Hagan roll his eyes at her.

"Carson? Aw, come on Berens. Greatest late-night TV host ever! Fine, you're building this internal dial that will get better at recognizing the more touchy-feelie variety that doesn't involve a takedown. Like actual happiness."

"Well, my gut is saying this is important, but I don't know what to do with it. I gotta go!"

"I get it. You need to ask your magical guru, the big alien. Go! Go! I'll cover for you here. No chance you'd... alright! Don't give me that look! I'm almost done, anyway. I'm outta here soon enough. I want to try and mow the yard before the sun sets."

"On your riding lawn mower." Leira turned to go without waiting for an answer.

"A lot more effort than the ads let on," yelled Hagan. Leira was already halfway down the hall, heading for the door.

She drove home, tapping the steering wheel, her nerves on edge. The magic had left a dark feeling that jangled her nerves.

She pulled into a spot in front of Estelle's and got out, heading for the gate. She noticed Craig standing on the front porch with Mitzi and her schnauzer, Lemon and picked up her pace, shutting the gate behind her. She gave a short wave in the direction of the bar, in anticipation of all the shouted greetings.

"Leira!"

"We'll save you a seat!"

They were used to getting a short nod or a wave most of the time and she secretly liked knowing she could count on the invitation, even if she only took them up on it occasionally. *Want to be invited, don't want to go. Got to find out if something bad has happened.*

Leira was worried it was her mother but couldn't bring herself to call the hospital. Not yet. She wanted to find Correk first.

She burst through the door to find Correk sitting on the couch watching her small TV, wearing some of the sweatpants he bought at Costco, the troll balanced on his knee eating popcorn. Startled, she stopped on the threshold trying to take in the scene. The troll opened his mouth wide, letting out a high-pitched whine.

"You're letting in the sunlight. It's glaring off the TV." Correk looked sheepish as he pressed the pause button on the remote.

"I see you figured out how to work Netflix."

"It wasn't hard, and it's HBO. *Game of Thrones* is actually quite accurate at times, although we're not nearly so violent. At least not in the last thousand years. Yes, Queen Saria when left to her own devices can destroy a room…"

"When did I get HBO? You didn't cast some spell to get that, did you? Never mind!" She held up her hand to stop him from answering. Her face was tight with worry as she shut the door behind her.

The troll frowned, shaking all over, his fur settling back down. He smiled and trilled, turning back to the large bowl of popcorn on the couch next to them. He dove headfirst into it, mouth open, chewing his way toward the bottom.

"I stopped eating it after the first few times he did that."

"First few?" Leira dropped her purse on the red velvet chair and went to lock her gun away in the metal lockbox in her bedroom.

Correk got up to follow her. The troll barked sharply.

"Okay, okay, my apologies." Correk hit play again and the troll settled back into the bowl, his legs crossed, one arm behind his head, throwing popcorn into his mouth. "Don't get too comfortable," Correk said, as he followed Leira into her bedroom.

"You're anxious."

"Can you feel what I'm feeling? There is no fucking privacy anymore." The lingering residue of magic was making her cranky.

"I went old school and used a human trick on you. Observation. Your face looks very determined and you're home early, already pacing. You usually reserve that for later."

"Funny." Leira stopped and marshaled her thoughts. "Didn't you feel that? Come on! Less than an hour ago. Big wave? Felt like…like…" She was clasping her hands, twisting them, trying to find the right words, afraid to say them. "Like something was dying."

Correk's expression immediately changed and he stepped closer to her, touching her arm. The remnants of the tremor passed through Leira and into Correk. His face grew serious as he pulled in just enough energy to push out the last traces of darkness.

"Thank God!" Leira finally took in a deep breath, letting it out with a shudder. "I could not shake that. What was it? Was it my mother?" She blurted out the words before she could stop herself.

He took a good look at her. "How long ago did this happen? When did you first notice it?"

"Why do you suddenly look so concerned? What the hell has happened?" Leira studied his face, feeling herself shift into detective mode, grateful for a familiar feeling. "Tell me what you know."

It was a moment before Correk replied. "There was a surge of energy that I've felt before but *only* when there is a battle nearby."

"Impossible," she shook her head. "I'm with the Austin PD, remember? They would have called everyone in."

"You're thinking like a *human* detective. That's going to get in your way with this. Combine the two sides of who you are. A magical detective. Use both skills together."

She eyed him. "You're magical. Why wouldn't you have felt it?"

He barely moved his head left, then right. "It's what I felt when we were at Enchanted Rock. You're far more powerful than almost any other magical being. There's something different about your DNA."

"How is that possible?" she continued her questioning. "How could I not have known all these years?"

"The short answer is that magic relies on feelings, like I've told you. You chose to put your feelings away. And I suspect there were clues that you were able to ignore."

"Like being very lucky," she drew the last word out.

"Exactly." He pointed to her. "You were pulling in magic energy against all the odds. But that's as far as it went. It's difficult to really advance in magic without a mentor of some kind who can show you how to harness it, direct the flow. You pushed back against it, suppressing your powers. You have to invite magic into whatever you're doing. Otherwise it waits patiently on the sidelines."

"Magic's not douchie. That's what you're saying."

"I refuse to respond to that."

"Do beings on Oriceran not cuss?"

There was the slightest tug at the corner of his mouth towards a smirk. "No, we prefer to send out fireballs. Makes the point much more efficiently."

Leira sat back on her bed. "I can feel this power from someplace deep inside. It feels like it comes up through my feet from somewhere else. Somewhere bigger." She looked up at him. "But where?"

"Where this power is coming from is for another day. I can't determine that just by transferring some of what you were feeling through me. Besides, that can wait. What matters right now is that what I felt pass through me was not only from a battle, it was laced with very powerful *dark* magic. Magic that is supposed to not only be outlawed but under lock and key."

"Protected in the Light Castle."

"And yet, here it is, being used on Earth, but for what?" He started pacing back and forth. "That pulse you felt was stronger than what you did at Enchanted Rock. It may have traveled a great distance."

"No reports about any disaster, natural or otherwise. They covered it up. Fighting in front of humans is undesirable even for the darker side."

He stopped pacing and looked over at her. "There you go. *Now*, you're using all of your abilities. Two forces went at each other, but both had their own reasons for not wanting to be detected."

"What matters here is the reason why. What would magical beings think was worth the risk of being exposed using dark magic? Even death. I felt death inside of it when it first hit me. I could feel the pain of beings dying." Leira pushed her fist into her stomach, the memory of the feeling washing over her again.

"I've never seen abilities like these," Correk said, looking at her from top to bottom, shaking his head. The troll barked and laughed from the other room. "He can still feel your emotions, but he thinks the flying dragons are funny. Ignore him."

She drew a breath in, and then blew it out. "I'm not sure what to do next."

"Focus. Allow the feelings to come to the surface and the information it wants to tell you will just be there. It's like reading. You feel a lot of impressions, or symbols and you interpret their meaning. Focus. Shut your eyes if you need to."

Leira closed her eyes. *Just let it be. Let it come through me. Lean into it.*

"So far, all I've got are clichés running through my head." She opened her eyes in time to see Correk roll his. He looked exasperated. "Stop judging everything. Clichés are fine. Let loose of the controls a little."

Leira shut her eyes again.

"Relax your shoulders. You're too tense. It's not like chasing a criminal. It's the opposite, in fact. Let the magic do the work. It leads, you follow. Not the other way around."

"Wait, there's something familiar here. I can't quite place it."

"Let it come to you. Confidence plays a big part in magic, too. The more you believe, the more you're able to let things happen. The magic knows what to do if you get out of the way."

"Then why are spells necessary?" Leira opened her eyes again.

"Stop resisting. It's not your mother, I'm sure of it. We can call the hospital to be sure, if that's what it takes." He held up a hand to stop the next question. "Because I was there when your mother reached out. A very distinctive magic trail, similar to yours. I would have recognized it instantly when I pulled the last of the battle energy from you. It's not your mother."

"Then who is it?"

"Stop asking so many questions. Find out who it is. We need information. Focus," he admonished.

Leira lay back against the padded headboard and closed her eyes again. She started counting backwards from one hundred, tricking herself into not thinking quite so much. The energy started to gather around her legs, churning slowly as it spread up her body. *Relax into it. Let the magic do its work. Seventy-seven, seventy-six, seventy-five...*

Then it happened. It felt like it was flowing through her veins and up her neck, behind her eyes, filling her skull. "The necklace. The necklace is in play." She sat up, swinging her legs over the side of the bed. "I recognize the magic. You're right! It came to me!" She stood up, excited. "I could feel it. It was like hearing a familiar voice. You just know it."

"The necklace. That can't be good for anyone." Correk's forehead wrinkled and concern spread across his face.

The importance of what she had just said came to Leira as she let the excitement of mastering a little more of her magical abilities subside. "The necklace," she said in a low voice. "Prince Rolim's powers encased in a crystal."

"That damnable necklace." Correk drove his fist into the palm of his hand.

"So, you do get angry." Leira instantly regretted saying it. "Sorry, I know he was your friend. How do we figure out where this all happened?"

"We'll need more help."

"Back to the rock."

"Correct. But we'll have to be careful. We're dealing with something malevolent and large..."

"Which means a group with bad intentions and we don't know how many or who it is yet. I get it. Trust but verify."

"There's a full moon tonight. They'll be gathering to celebrate it. Magic comes up from the center of the Earth more easily during a full moon. It's a reason to come together..."

"And party. I heard Toni talking about it. We'll need to bring a dish. It's something humans call a potluck. No, Cheetos don't count. We'll actually have to make something. Or make Whole Foods make it."

"Jim said they meet at a place called the Jackalope."

"Know it well. It's on 6th Street."

"He said the owner is a wizard who retired from the Order."

"Didn't know that was a thing. I thought once you were in something like that, you were in. You know, Masons for life."

"He's still a member but at some point, everyone is allowed to stop serving and go have a life, even if not many take them up on it."

"You have to change before we go. That's not a good look on you. Or anyone."

"I see your kind wearing these everywhere."

"Which should have been enough of a visual to clue you in why you're changing before we go out in public. Your pants have to have a zipper, or your olden days pants that lace up. No elastic band. Slippery slope to fatdom, my friend."

"We take Yumfuck."

"We take Yumfuck."

"Someone will have to peel him away from Game of Thrones. He's only on the second season."

"You started him on that drug. You break the news to him."

"It may take a spell to pull him away."

"You mean me."

"You rescued him. Still your troll."

"Hurry up and show me. We need to figure out this puzzle and none of the pieces are coming together fast enough to suit me. That damn necklace is in play again, but we don't know who has it, or where it is now, or if that's good or bad news. And I want to see if an idea comes up for how to rescue my mother. She can't be the first magical being trapped in a psych ward."

"Okay, let's get the troll and get out of here."

MARTHA CARR & MICHAEL ANDERLE

"You're going to love Whole Foods, but you can't buy anything in there. I can't afford it. The place should be called whole paycheck."

"What's a paycheck?"

"Never mind. Come on."

"You don't cook at all, do you?"

"I microwave with the best of them."

"Nice to see you're not bringing your gun."

"It's a potluck and I'm off duty."

"And you have magic."

"That crossed my mind. Next thing I want you to show me how to do is make a mean fireball."

"Of course you do."

Hagan sat on his old red Troy-Bilt riding lawnmower in his backyard on the north side of Austin, firing it up to mow his quarter acre, made smaller by his wife's flower beds in the back, still blooming in the warm winter sun. He was wearing his favorite old blue jeans that were soft with age and his worn Sperry boat shoes from his canoeing phase years ago. Rose was not fond of the look but tolerated it if he was doing chores around the house.

He pulled his Cubs baseball hat down, securing it firmly on his head and prepared to mow, hurrying to finish before it was dark. His old black poodle watched him from the back porch, his eyes closing despite the noise from the mower.

The sky was purple with ribbons of red in between the clouds.

"Not much longer, better hurry old girl," he said, steering the tractor into the first pass around the yard.

He mowed a nice straight line, and came back the other way, glancing back at the perfectly straight lines. *There's a certain satis-*

faction to doing a job right. Leira was right. I don't need magic. I got this.

He turned and made another pass, working his way toward the back fence, careful to turn before he got to the flowerbeds, leaving a small margin for error that he could cut later with the weed whacker. Back and forth he went, falling into the routine, daydreaming about what he would eat when he was through with the mowing. *Maybe make a sandwich. I earned it. This is still physical labor. I had to start the mower. All this vibrating.* He could hear Rose telling him no in his head. *Maybe just a pickle.*

A rabbit poked its head under the fence near the gate, not seeing the large poodle at first. The poodle lifted its head, spotted the rabbit and jumped up, barking madly as it took off for a chase. The rabbit streaked across the yard in front of the mower, pursued by the dog.

Startled out of his daydream, Hagan gripped the steering wheel of the Troy-Bilt, his foot hitting the gas as he jerked the wheel, turning the mower straight into the flower beds. It was over in seconds.

He turned the mower away as quickly as he could, steering back onto the grass, and shut it off, turning in his seat to get a look at what was left of the flowers.

A large U-shaped swath was cut into the flowers, mowed down to green stubs with a colorful band of chopped confetti spread out around them.

"Fuck me," Hagan groaned. He was already trying to figure out how to buy himself enough time to go get more plants and hide this from Rose. He looked at his watch and realized the local Lowe's was closing in just a few minutes. The poodle trotted up, panting, a smile on his face.

"I'm glad you're happy. Make room for me, will ya? I'm going to be in the doghouse for sure."

He started up the mower again, shooing the poodle away, so he could finish the lawn and buy himself some time. There was a chance Rose wouldn't notice the flowers that night, but she'd see it through the back door in the morning. A half-finished job would make her come out and take a closer look. Better to calm down enough to finish. He figured it would give him more time to think of a plan or plausible denial, anyway.

Hagan pursed his lips as he carefully turned the mower again, determined not to mow over any more of the flowers. *I'll have to ask Leira to get me out of this one,* he thought. *Do some of that hocus pocus.*

"Or they will be investigating my homicide next. Woo boy," he said, making another turn. "Leira's got to understand this one."

Outside the Chicago Avenue Pumping Station there was a sign on the sidewalk that said, 'Closed for Renovations. Check back soon.'

The run of the play, Peter Pan was quietly moved to the Broadway Playhouse at the nearby Water Tower with the explanation that there was an unfortunate gas leak, mimicking the story in the press. The crew of the play scrambled to figure out sets and lighting and quickly forgot about the explosion at the Pumping Station, except to complain about their bad luck.

Inside the Pumping Station, the elders of the Order of the Silver Griffins picked through the rubble, occasionally stopping to turn over fallen debris and examine the burn patterns from a fireball. The dead and wounded had all been removed and the enemy combatants identified. The bodies were returned quietly to their families who came up with alternative stories about dying from an illness or in a car accident. A witch in the coroner's office agreed to help with the cover up, according to previously approved protocol for this extreme situation.

This was the first time in recent memory that anyone had to pull the protocols out and give them a read through.

"I think we have enough," said a witch, straightening up, placing her hand in the small of her back and stretching. "Let's convene in the theater."

The other five witches and wizards followed her without comment, walking toward the theater that sat over the northern side of the vault. They sat in the folding chairs in a tight circle on the stage and waited for the witch to begin speaking. Nothing about her gave the impression that she was in charge of an Order hundreds of years old that kept human beings from finding out about magic and looked out for everyone's well-being.

She wore her usual outfit of jeans and a t-shirt with a puffy coat and thick socks tucked into Crocs. If it was snowing or icy, she would have changed into Uggs.

"Where to start," she said solemnly, licking her lips. The whole thing gave her pause and made her feel older than her years. "Well, has anyone found Hannah yet? No?" The young witch had disappeared during the fighting and her mother and grand-mother were frantic, wondering if she had been dragged off by the darkness that had invaded the Pumping Station.

The witch knew better. She pulled out her wand and uttered a short incantation, swirling the wand, drawing up images from the fight. The others recoiled. No one wanted to see the fighting again and watch friends struck down.

The witch waved her wand again, enlarging just a portion of the image, pouring light into the background. There was Hannah, sliding along the wall, doing her best not to attract attention.

The witch waved her wand one more time, helping everyone to see what she had spotted the first time she watched this, enlarging Hannah's pocket. The corner of a black velvet box was sticking out.

There was a chorus of gasps and one witch put a hand to her mouth, gasping, "No!" A wizard sat back hard in his chair, exclaiming, "Bullshit!" Others shook their heads and leaned in closer, trying to be sure, not wanting to believe what they could clearly see.

Hannah was a traitor.

"We were done in by a third-generation member who handed over the prize. No, we don't believe she went so far as to lead them here. She still has some integrity intact and perhaps it's possible she had a reason for what she did, but there it is. I haven't told her family yet. We need to know more, first."

"You saw the traces upstairs. The marks on the rubble," said a wizard with short silver hair, slicked straight back. "We all know whose old magic they were using. Rhazdon."

"They've improved on it, if that's what you'd call it. Added tracking to it. Did you see how some of those bolts turned when we ducked?" asked another wizard, still wearing his woolen topcoat over his suit. His face was ashen. "I've known Hannah since she was a little girl," he said quietly.

"She's not little anymore, and she chose to betray us," the other wizard said angrily. "She knew every one of us and chose her path anyway."

"Hannah will be dealt with, like any other member who works with the dark side," the witch said tersely. "There is already a team out searching for her and no matter what charm she's placed on herself to hide her whereabouts, it won't work. She'll be found."

"Unless they're hiding her."

The witch glared at the silver-haired wizard. "Let's hope it didn't go that far. But to your point, we will find them, as well. They have dispersed, back into their communities spread out across the United States but we all know that magic leaves a trail as singular as a fingerprint."

"Are they followers of Rhazdon's?"

"It would appear so, and there was yet another cache of powerful, dark magic books and spells hidden by the original cult, just waiting for a rebirth. We don't seem to be able to completely rid ourselves of that damnable Atlantean," the witch spat. "But dark magic leaves its own trail, even if they have yet another artifact from Rhazdon's collection to hide them." The witch turned toward the far exit and called, "You can come in now!"

A young woman pushed open the heavy door and stepped into the theater. She stopped at the top of the stairs that led down to the circular stage-in-the-round.

"Come down here and meet everyone." When she reached the stage, the older witch said, "Meet Katie Toler, our new secret weapon. She's been appointed as a special agent to find the new uprising of the cult."

She was a young woman with blonde hair to her shoulders and striking blue eyes behind brown square glasses, wearing tights and a long puffy coat, with boots up to her knees. Nothing about her seemed formidable.

Everyone looked skeptical, but no one said anything.

"Good evening, everyone. I know there's a full moon tonight and most families like to celebrate so I'll keep this short. I have a small demonstration that will explain why I was chosen as a special agent for the Order of the Silver Griffins."

Katie pulled out a retractable wand, letting it unfold and snap into place automatically.

"Transformalia." She waved the wand above her head, the shooting sparks flowing down around her. As they fell her hair transformed into long, thin tentacles and her eyes took on distinctive slits instead of round pupils. "Beautiful, aren't they?" She ran her fingers through the tentacles as they wound around her fingers, the small suction cups clinging to her. "As you can see, I'm half Atlantean and half witch. Not human at all. My great grandfather was even in the original cult. Not to worry," she said, holding out her wand to stop anyone from getting up from their seat. She was used to this reaction and found it best to push back right away. Let everyone get to know her later. Make a stand first.

"We aren't all arrogant bitches. Oh, I'm a bitch alright. Fortunately, I'm on your side this time. I know normally this much Atlantean blood would disqualify me for the Order…"

"Which is why she's been appointed as a special liaison to the Order as an agent to be used on assignment as needed."

"And dear ones, it looks like there's an assignment. I'm not fond of what my ancestor started and not happy that some whack jobs have picked up where he left off. Just when people were starting to get over what my kind had done. Well, half of me at least," she said, winking at one of the wizards, who gave her a cold, stony look in return.

"My usual reception. Don't worry, I grow on you. In the meantime, I know a little about these artifacts. Family lore passed down through the generations and I have contacts and access you don't have and can't get. Even better, a skill set that combines your powers," she said, waving her wand to transform herself back into the pretty young blonde, "with theirs. Pretty sick, right? They won't see me coming." She pulled out a strand of her hair and waved a wand over it, turning it back into a coiled tentacle. She moved her wand above it, whispering into it, swirling the air around it faster and faster, until it disappeared into the stream. She meticulously folded up her wand and put it away.

"I should have something for you later tonight. You bitches stay up that late?" She smiled broadly. "Don't worry. I'm mostly harmless." She dropped the smile. "Unless you cross one of mine. And the wizard who got his leg broken last night and lost a lot of blood? That was my father. Cold reckoning is coming for some foolish elves out there."

"This isn't about revenge," said a witch.

Katie leveled an icy stare at the witch. "I don't get even, honey. I just get it done."

CHAPTER TWELVE

C orrek and Leira walked into the Jackalope Bar and stopped, staring at the loud party already underway.

"Come on," said Leira, "Let's find the food table so I can put this down." They veered around the three-foot high statue of an antlered brown rabbit sitting square in the middle of the entrance to the bar. Hanging from its neck was a sign that read, 'closed for a private function.'

Leira was carrying a large plastic container full of three-bean salad she had bought at Whole Foods. In the car, she poured it into the container she brought from home while Correk watched her with a bemused smile. "It's a thing, trust me," she said. "Don't judge."

They found the food table along a back wall, loaded down with casseroles, fried chicken and salads. At the far end were open bags of chips and jars of salsa. Leira tugged Correk's sleeve until he looked at her. She shook her head firmly. *No.* Correk sighed and waited till she turned her back, grabbing one chip and stuffing it into his mouth with a loud crunch. Leira turned back to see what he'd done but he stood there, waiting patiently till she turned around again and melted into the crowd before he finished chewing.

"Vinegar and salt. Not bad."

Leira went in search of new people to mingle with so she could mine them for information and get to know people who were like her. One foot firmly planted in two different realities. Average human mixed with a little magic, and a distant world cut off from them for the most part, but only for a while longer.

"Leira! You made it!" Toni shouted over the music and the buzz of everyone talking and laughing. She held out her arms and pulled Leira into a hug. "I'm so glad you came! Oh good, you brought your friend, too." Leira looked back to see Correk sliding another chip into his mouth. She smiled despite herself.

"It's a full moon, isn't it wonderful? Can't you feel the buzz? My mother used to say, make a wish! They come true when you make them on the night of a full moon. I think that's because all that childlike belief gave them an added boost. You get a beer yet? Go tell the bartender. It's an open bar. Crazy Jack, yeah, that's his name, he lets crazy magical people drink for free at these parties. We always take up a collection at the end anyway."

"How did all of you find each other?" Leira turned around, looking at all the people packed into the bar. "I had no idea..." Her voice trailed off and she felt a pang in her chest. Kind of family, kind of not.

"This didn't happen overnight. It was hundreds of years in the making. Generations of people. Now, you're here and we've grown a little more. That's how it happens. We're everywhere, all over the world, doing amazing things, impressing the hell out of humans. Even inspiring them to try harder because they think it's one of them doing that flippin' feat!" Toni let out a deep-throated laugh. "All those YouTube videos! We're certainly not a shy lot. Where's the troll? You brought him, didn't you? He probably needs to get out around people who won't try and squash him first chance they get."

Leira reached into her pocket and brought out the troll. He was curled into a ball, his eyes wide open, calmly looking around at everyone. "If you're sure..."

Toni nodded.

Leira whispered over him, releasing him from the spell and he sat up in a flash, bounded off her hand, and landed easily on the floor, bouncing to the music. The people right around him smiled and cheered as he spun on his green head, neatly jumping back to his feet.

"Trolls can dance!"

"They're basically showoffs," shouted Toni. "Come on, I'll introduce you to some more people. Jeff, come here, I want you to meet someone! This is Leira. Jeff works for Google in Round Rock. He's been helping the humans get ready for our arrival, even if they don't know it."

"I slide things into the search engine about ancient so-called myths," said Jeff, smiling as he took a sip of his beer. "Go on, you can ask. I can tell you want to. New people, especially the ones who just found out they're not entirely human, always want to ask. I'm a wizard, full blooded, born here. You?"

Leira hesitated. It was the first time she said the words out loud. "I'm half human, half Light Elf, I think."

"There, that wasn't so hard. Although I think you got that human percentage wrong. That buzz I feel when I get near you is not just the beer. There's something else there, something powerful but I can't quite put my finger on it. Oh look!"

The troll was popping and locking as a chant went up from the crowd. "Go troll! Go troll!"

Second time someone has said that to me.

"Hey, Stacey, have you met Leira yet? Stacey's family has been a part of this group for at least a century. Nice family. Light Elves and Southern Baptists."

"We started the fire dancing night," Stacey laughed. "We go

155

out to Ryland's ranch where we can really carry on and take turns with flaming hula hoops and flaming ropes."

"The men love to joust with flaming swords," Toni said.

"Of course they do!" The women hooted with laughter, clinking their bottles together.

I really like them, thought Leira, tempted to hold off on asking any questions. *That's not who I am. Detective down to my bones.* She steadied herself, remembering what Correk had told her and pulled in energy through her feet, mixing it with the skills she had learned as a detective.

"Anyone else feel that ginormous magic wave earlier today?"

The two women stopped laughing, trying to hide their surprise, not doing a very good job of it. They glanced meaningfully at each other and Stacey took a long sip from her beer, looking away.

Leira stayed in detective mode, waiting for someone to figure out an answer. Hagan was always telling her, he who speaks first, loses. She had time, she could wait patiently. She fixed Toni with her best dead fish look and felt a hum of energy at her feet. Mixing the two skills was getting easier every time.

"You're a hard one to ignore," Toni said with a nervous smile. "Look, I don't know how you so called *felt it*, this far away but no one outside of the Order of Silver Griffins is supposed to know anything. That includes the magical community at large. We only know because Brian over there is a wizard with a cousin in the Order and neither one of them is the best at keeping a secret."

Leira turned to look at Stacey who was still sucking on the end of her beer bottle. Leira focused even more, waiting, pulling the energy up from the ground, her eyes starting to shimmer. Stacey caught a glimpse, started and put her arm down.

"You do not fool around. How do you do that on this planet? Only Oricerans can pull that off and that's if they go back to recharge. Fine, fine. It was in Chicago, some kind of explosion at a facility the Order maintains. Right in the heart of the Gold Coast where all the fancy people live. The one percenters."

Correk walked up next to Leira, holding a plate of food. "This salad made of potatoes is amazing! Hello."

Leira focused on Stacey. She wasn't sure if she was exactly playing fair, but she didn't care. She needed information and was in no mood to wait till someone felt like telling her.

"The Order had something that this cult wanted. Some kind of jewelry."

Correk choked as a bite went down the wrong way. Toni pounded on his back. "I'm alright. I'm fine. Thank you, that's enough pounding."

Leira continued to focus on the energy within, waiting patiently for Stacey to finish. "Brian's cousin said they used dark magic, really old stuff. Hundreds of years old at least. Left over from that scary Atlantean they try to teach us about at Saturday magical school. When you grow up inside the community on this planet, they give you a basic overview, teach you some magic, and all the rules. Then there's the history lesson."

"With a lot of time spent on that fellow, Rhazdon," Toni explained. "Stacey's forever forgetting his name. It's Rhazdon. Geez, Stacey, it's not like there weren't enough Saturdays talking about him."

"Right, Rhazdon. It was some of his old artifacts. Somehow, they used ones no one knew about. The Order thinks it's a bunch of misguided magical beings in this world who've started up the cult again after all these years!"

"Our own kind," Toni wailed. "Can you believe it? Like we're not misfits enough to the humans. If they ever found out, we'd be toast!"

Correk was listening intently, looking for a place to put down his plate. "How did the battle end?"

"Well, that's the weird part," said Stacey, leaning in so no one else could hear them. "And Brian made us swear not to tell anyone else. Oh hell, after a few beers this whole place will know."

"And he'll make every person he tells, swear not to tell anyone else. It's the way he is. Makes you wonder if there's a bit of Willen in him," snickered Toni. She was getting tipsy.

"One of their own, an Order witch betrayed them and slipped out with the necklace and handed it over to the damn fools. The marauders got some kind of signal after that and just put down their wands and left. The Order captured the wounded ones but so far no one is talking."

"Who betrayed them?" Leira asked.

Toni put out her hand to stop Stacey from answering.

"I know you're more powerful than we are, that's very obvious, and you can probably get us to tell you," she admitted. "But before we do all the giving, there's something we want from you. It's only fair, especially seeing as how we're all family."

Leira glanced at Correk who looked more annoyed than worried, arching an eyebrow.

"What is it?"

"To be named later. You'd have to trust us that we won't ask you to do anything unethical."

"Well, not too unethical," Stacey laughed. She was past tipsy, well on her way to drunk.

"And we have to trust that you won't get us into hot water with the Order, or worse. Plus, I'll throw in a bonus for you."

"Oh yeah, that message we were supposed to give her. Totally forgot," Stacey slapped her forehead with her palm.

"Ignore her. I didn't forget. I was just feeling you out a little first. You've popped up on the government radar. Something about an explosion in Chicago?" Toni gave her a knowing look. "Yeah, I already knew you were somehow mixed up in all of that. As you might imagine, we have an amazing grapevine."

"Don't even need the two cans and a string," Stacey chirped.

"Be careful," warned Toni, growing serious. "The humans who work in politics are very tricky to deal with. We'll all watch your back, but those sneaky bastards can be at your door when you least expect it."

Leira was stunned.

"Nothing to worry about, yet," Toni reassured her, putting a smile back on her face. "But be aware. Some of our kind work for the government. It's better that way. We find out what they're up to a lot more easily and they feel better keeping us close. That's good advice without any strings. We have a deal on the rest?" Toni spit into her hand and held it out for Leira to shake. "That's not an Oriceran thing. It's just something I saw in a movie, but it kind of works, right?"

Correk rolled his eyes and looked over to see where the troll had gotten to. He was dancing on the large boot of a man with short hair and a long red beard. "A carnival," said Correk.

"I have one other condition," said Leira, growing serious. "You tell me right now the name of the witch, and anything you know about breaking a magical person out of a psych ward."

"Oh, that happens a lot to our kind. I would have told you that anyway. A crime, what they do to us. We have a deal?" Toni's hand was still out, waiting.

"Deal," Leira agreed, shaking Toni's hand and ignoring the cold slime in her palm from the spit.

"The witch's name is Hannah, Hannah Beecham. She comes from a long line of women who served in the Order. They had no idea. I hear they're crushed, humiliated," said Stacey.

"I'll bet she had a reason."

"You mean blackmail," said Leira.

"Well, you don't betray the Order without a really good reason. The consequences are a little steep. As for that other question you had, find someone who's got enough power in the human world and trade them something they want in exchange for vouching for your loved one. In most cases, that's not an easy trick to pull off, but with the power coming off you, it should be a snap!" Toni snapped her fingers. "You could even use a spell or two to make them think it was their idea all along."

CHAPTER THIRTEEN

"This is bad." Correk stood in the middle of the dance floor, his hands on his hips.

"Let's at least get out of the way. You look like a weathervane standing still in the middle of everyone having fun." Leira found an empty pocket of space near the jackalope statue. "The Order grabbed the necklace. They lied to us after the explosion. I suppose that was their call."

"And now they've lost it."

"Because of one of their own. This keeps getting worse. What do we do now?"

"Not much we can do tonight. We enjoy the party. Patience is just as much a part of magic as the spells and feeling the energy."

"Detective work is a lot like that too. Wait, have you seen Yumfuck?" Leira peered around dancers and got down lower trying to see if he was dancing on shoes again or ducked under a table.

No troll.

"Not good! I can't see him."

"He's magically attached to you, like a bungee cord. He may

stray but he'll be back." Correk picked his plate back up again and started eating.

"How can you eat with everything that's going wrong?" Leira was still trying to spot the troll. "You don't think he left, do you? Those streets at night are full of drunk twenty-somethings with big feet. He could get smooshed."

"To your first question, Light Elves live for hundreds of years, so take that news in slowly, *Cousin*. You had better learn to take the long view and be present wherever you are, or life's events will grind you down. Things are always happening around you, it doesn't mean you have to see them as happening to you."

"A regular fucking philosopher. That does make sense, though. I know, don't even need to ask this one. Just allow."

"Wash on, wash off," said Correk, taking a big bite of potato salad.

"You were watching my Netflix."

"Your technology is often very entertaining. To your second query, the trolls on Oriceran have to escape near death on a daily basis from great beasts with large teeth and horns and they do so, admirably. He can handle a few intoxicated human beings. Relax, dance a little, eat something. He'll be back. He'll even sense if you try to leave and come running. You can't shake a troll once they're attached.

Hagan stood in line at Voodoo doughnuts trying to decide what he wanted. He did this every time and then ordered the Maple Bars and the Mexican Hot Chocolate doughnuts. Sometimes he got a Grape Ape if he thought he'd be able to hold off and keep some for the next day.

The line was long, stretching down the narrow section penned in by a low wall down the far right side of the store. It was already full of drinkers coming in for a sugar hit. The three cashiers behind the counter were used to it and the line moved along steadily. Hagan waited, next in line, trying to decide who'd get done with their order first. It was a way to keep his patience with idiots too drunk to be able to make up their minds or pull out a ten dollar bill. He was tempted to flash his badge but that would just slow things down.

It's gonna be the girl ordering the glazed doughnuts. Stepped right up, knew what she wanted, pulled out her cash. Not her first doughnut run. Excellent.

"Next!" yelled the short stocky man with wild, curly hair that seemed to be trying to escape his head, barely hiding his irritation with everything about his job. He was Hagan's favorite.

"Two Maple Bars, two Mexican Hot Chocolate and two Grape Apes," he blurted. The cashier was already grabbing a pink box, heading to the back. Hagan was a regular and inevitably ordered the same thing. Even the fight with himself was part of the routine. *I can do it. Just eat two now, save the others. I'm a grown man. I can resist a...* "What the hell?" Hagan thought he was seeing things.

Creeping along the back of the store was a familiar furry creature with bright green hair.

"Fuck me!" Hagan looked around, biting his lip, trying to decide what to do, momentarily resting his hand on his gun, throwing away that idea, slapping the counter, followed by a slap to the top of his head.

The troll spotted Hagan and waved, yelling, "Yumfuck!" He was grabbing doughnuts off trays and throwing them into a box a cashier left on the back counter, while she went to fetch another tray of Homers, a strawberry iced doughnut with sprinkles. A couple sitting at a table nearby spotted the troll and laughed, waving back at him.

"Thank God for alcohol," said Hagan, rolling his eyes as he watched the troll lift the box over his head and jump to the floor. Two doughnuts bounced out of the box on the way down, but the troll quickly retrieved them, tossing them neatly upwards into the box. Hagan held his breath, waiting to see what might happen next. He had seen the five-inch creature grow to the size of a tree when angered.

"I do not want to shoot Leira's pet." He watched everyone around him, waiting to see how badly this would go. The troll was unconcerned, scurrying right by Hagan's feet with the box, smiling at people as he went.

"Look at the cute little dog!"

"Is that a Chihuahua?"

"Wish I could train my pet to do that."

"Even the rats like these doughnuts!"

The troll slid through the open door as a group of tourists came in, and he turned the corner, running away. All Hagan could see out the front window was the bobbing pink box, before it disappeared from view altogether.

Hagan shook his head, looking around at everyone in the place laughing and going back to what they were doing. "Why do I worry? Keep Austin weird. Here dude, keep the change." He put two twenties down on the counter to pay for his, and the troll's, doughnuts, and took his box. "I do not even want to know what that was about," he muttered, as he headed for the door. "A troll getting his own doughnuts." When he got to the street, the troll was nowhere to be seen.

"Fast little fucker, I'll give him that. Strong, too." Hagan had a Maple Bar out of the box, biting down hard, before he even made it all the way to his car. All part of the routine.

The Jackalope was hopping. "Last call to leave before we start the night's festivities." Jack was standing on a chair, wand in hand.

"I thought these were the festivities," Leira said.

Toni smiled and replied, "You ain't seen nothin' yet. The fun's just starting."

No one moved toward the exit. Leira noticed everyone was smiling with anticipation, watching Jack.

"Okay, last chance. Three, two..."

A loud chorus of "One!" went up from the crowd. But before Jack could move, a pink box appeared to float around the corner, scooting into the bar.

"That has to be one of us," yelled a man in the middle of the crowd.

The box weaved in and out of the crowd toward the food table and stopped in front of a woman looking over the desserts. Loud trilling erupted from under the box.

"Yumfuck!" Leira pushed her way through the crowd, grabbing the box as the woman stared, wondering what to do. The troll looked up and waved at everyone, heartily announcing, "Yumfuck!" He pointed at the box, waving his arms and pointing at the table until Leira put it down.

"It appears the troll wanted to contribute something," Correk observed, peeking into the box. "Don't eat any of them. I think he licked every last one."

"Do you think he actually paid for them?" Leira narrowed her eyes, watching the troll. "No pockets in that fur."

"Okay, nothing like a full moon party, motherfuckers!" Jack held up his wand, a toothy grin on his face. The crowd cheered. "One more time with gusto!" he said. "Three, two..."

The crowd yelled "One, motherfuckers!" Jack waved his wand and said, "Extemporius," bringing down a continuous silver waterfall, complete with noise. Leira started to shout over it but quickly realized she could easily be heard. It was as if the background noise wasn't there.

The crowd started laughing and someone yelled, "A newbie! Put her on the list!"

"Someone always falls for that," said Stacey, swaying from side to side, still drinking.

"What list?"

"You'll see. Jack put a glamour on the front of the bar. A pretty good one," Toni told her. "He can only pull it off on the night of a full moon and only for a couple of hours. That's why we wait until the party really gets going. From the other side it looks like the bar is closed. Can't hear a thing, either."

"I want to learn this trick," said Leira, dazzled.

"Who doesn't?" Toni squeezed Leira's hand. She surprised herself by squeezing back, looking up at Correk.

"This is what a good time with your kin looks like, at least on Earth," he whispered to her.

"But once he does it, you can't leave until he pulls it down. It surrounds the building. Kind of a fire hazard but pretty much everyone in here knows the water hose trick, anyway." Stacey leaned on Correk, who gently steered her into a chair, pulling himself out of her arms.

"It's not just the beer," said Toni, smiling at Correk. "You're a nice big Pop-Tart of a man."

"Big old blueberry one!" Stacey crowed.

Toni laughed. "I don't know about that part, but you got a little somethin', somethin' going on." She gave him a gentle elbow to the ribs as his face reddened. Leira smiled and shrugged, holding up her hands.

"All right ladies and gentlemen, species of every kind!" Jack hopped off the chair, still holding out his wand. "Who wants to go first?"

"Let the newbie! Rules are rules!"

"No," Leira shouted, smiling. "I don't know any yet. I'd be a flop!"

"Think of this like karaoke." It was Jim from Enchanted Rock. "You may not even know the words, but you'll have a good time trying." He put his hand in the small of her back and pushed her out into the center.

"Magic! Magic! Magic!" The crowd chanted as Leira looked at Correk helplessly. He smiled and shrugged, holding up his hands. "Touché, Cousin," she yelled. "Okay, free form magic. I can do this." Leira shut her eyes. *What did Correk tell me? Lesson number one. Imagine what you want to happen and believe in it. Got it.*

Leira focused, steadied her breathing and opened herself up to the possibilities, allowing the energy to flow up through her feet. *Don't think, just be.*

The image was firmly in her head. She embraced it in her mind, felt the joy come over her as the magic filled her, spreading throughout her body.

"Woooowwwww."

"How's she…"

"Whoa."

Leira heard the gasps but they were far away, and she let them slip past her, observing the stream of feelings passing her. She slowly opened her eyes, looking around, her arms outstretched, the symbols glowing in gold and silver all the way up her neck and face and down to the fingers, her eyes glowing. She smiled gently and looked down, knowing what she would see. She was floating just above the floor, inches off the ground and her entire being was glowing. She looked at the faces around her, taking in their surprise. *Time to land.*

Instead of trying to think her way through coming back to the ground, she opened herself up to the magic doing it for her, leading the way, as her feet gently touched down. There was a general silence throughout the room as she let the magic seep out of her and back into the ground.

"Uh, okay, ladies and gentlemen," Jack finally sputtered. "Who would like to follow that?"

For a moment, no one moved but then a burly man with blond curls yelled, "Well, that was fucking awesome! I will! This party is on!" A roar went up from the crowd and everyone broke into applause as Leira smiled, taking a bow. Correk handed her a beer, his usual look of exasperation and amusement on his face.

"What now? They loved it!"

"That trick is not in the usual tool kit. We don't usually fly on this planet when the gates are closed. Takes a lot more energy."

"I didn't fly. I levitated. Big difference. You did it when I first met you."

"Not really a difference. And you did all of this without wings or even a wand. I did it after years of mastering magic and with the energy from Oriceran."

"I followed your rules. Imagine, believe, allow."

"You're picking this up much faster than I expected and in ways I didn't imagine." He gave her another long look, wondering yet again what made up her DNA.

"Wait a minute, are all those Disney movies messing with us? Don't witches fly?"

"Not until the magic returns."

"Oooh, he's doing a fireball!" exclaimed Leira, moving closer to get a better look at how he did it.

"The girl floats above the Earth and is amazed by a fireball," muttered Correk. "The surprises have no end."

CHAPTER FOURTEEN

They were in the lobby of the movie theater, waiting for her mother's friend Ralph to arrive.

"That was a good call leaving Yumfuck at home," said Correk, holding onto a tub of popcorn with one hand and throwing some into his mouth.

"So you wouldn't have to share. I get it."

"Amusing and somewhat true. The aroma in this lobby. I'm not sure even a spell could have kept him from diving into that glass popcorn box."

Leira shifted her weight from one foot to the other, trying not to look anxious, but Correk noticed anyway.

"It was good of you to invite him."

"Just keeping my word. I should have done it years ago." Leira let out the breath she was holding. It was getting easier to talk to Correk. Working with the magic was having the unexpected side effect of helping her to open up and just talk. "I didn't like reminders of her. One, it was too hard to see other girls with their mothers and go home alone, and two, I always had this worry in the back of my mind that crazy is contagious. Someday I would end up just like her."

"Prophetic."

"Just not in the way I expected." Leira shook her head, pain crossing her face. "It makes me wonder if I had fought harder years ago, would I have figured all of this out sooner."

"Perhaps, or something worse could have happened, or a thousand other outcomes. There's no way to know and no point in torturing yourself with the shinier, better options. You did the best you could. After all, you're only partly human." He tossed a handful of popcorn into his mouth, satisfied, chewing away.

"You've been saving that one for a while." Leira rolled her eyes.

"Worth the wait."

"There he is! Act normal, please."

"I take it you mean *human normal.* All of that TV watching is about to pay off. Kidding, don't give me that look. As long as you explain that I go by Correk now, I will do whatever you want."

"Bert's a great name."

"Not doing it. It's a yellow puppet with a unibrow."

"Leira!" Ralph wrapped his arms around her, squeezing tight, not letting go for a few seconds. He was tall and wiry but Leira knew from watching him work on cars when she was little that he was freakishly strong.

I don't remember being hugged by so many people in just a couple of days, well, ever, Leira thought. *What is happening to me?*

"Ralph, you're cutting off my air." Her voice was muffled, pressed tightly into his shoulder. The smell of Lava soap clung to him, pulling her back into her childhood.

With one move, she could have wrapped a heel behind his foot and leveled him, sending him straight to the floor. No magic required.

But he was an old family friend. She waited for him to let go.

"Sorry. Just glad to see you. Hi again, Bert, right?"

Leira looked away, trying not to let out a snort.

"I've changed it actually. Bert didn't really suit me. It's Correk, from my father's side of the family."

"How do you say it?" Ralph screwed up his face, cupping a hand over his ear. Leira's shoulders started shaking as she held in the laughter, turning to face the concession stand.

"Core-eck. Correk. Simple."

"Right, well nice to see you again. What are we seeing?"

Leira turned back around, biting her lip, determined not to laugh. Ralph looked at both of them.

"Ask Leira," said Correk. "She said it's a timeless classic."

Leira said it quickly. "Lord of the Rings. Fellowship of the Rings." She doubled over, laughing again.

Ralph smiled, putting his hand on her back. "What? Nerves? I get it. Great movie, loved all of them. Have you seen it?"

"No, what's it about?" Correk rolled his eyes, still eating the popcorn.

"A quest by a hobbit named Frodo to get a magical ring back to the fire. There's elves, dwarves, all kinds of creatures."

Correk lowered his chin, looking at Leira with narrowed eyes. "Really."

"You'll love it. You want popcorn?" she said quickly, "He's not the best at sharing. You better get your own."

Ralph laughed, putting his arm around Leira, smiling at Correk. "Nah, I'm good. I try to eat healthy these days. Not getting any younger. Let's go get seats. High in the back, just in the middle work?"

"Perfect!" Leira found herself struggling to embrace what she felt. Part of her wanted to just observe all of this, feel less. *Maybe not this time, maybe.* "You still do the thumbs up, thumbs down at the previews?"

"Of course! We'll show you how it's done, Correk. Don't you work at that medieval theme park? I'd have thought they'd insist you see this movie. You guys are into that sort of thing. That's what I hear." Ralph chattered happily, filling up the space. Leira enjoyed his arm around her shoulders, watching Correk eat popcorn and make faces at her on the way to their seats. *Normal.*

The door of the Paranormal Defense Force was always kept ajar, mostly so that Lois was spared the trouble of magically opening it just to get something from the snack machine to fly down the hall and into her hands. She did her best to not leave her chair. She moved her government issue ID badge to the side and swiveled her chair around to face the door.

"Yummina." She gestured with her wand, focusing on what she wanted. A loud rattle and shake down the hall and in no time, the peanut M&Ms were in her hand.

"Good catch," Patsy said, pushing her bangs out of her face.

"Thanks. It doesn't always work so well with the chips. Sometimes the little door at the bottom of the machine slams on 'em and they're nothing but crumbs."

"I thought you didn't really like these."

"We're almost empty. They'll do in a pinch."

The sound of birds twittering suddenly echoed throughout the nondescript building.

"What the hell is that?" Lois pushed her brown frames back up her nose, squinching her face.

"You like it? That's the alarm system we installed. Very pleasant."

"That is nice. What is that, a wren? Even if the humans hear it from the parking lot…"

"Which they won't."

"Even if they do, they'll think it's for mood."

"It is. Ours." Patsy swirled her wand at the virtual screen, putting the show General Hospital in a small square in the corner. Images from the parking lot appeared. A small cadre of military were approaching the building, the short-statured general leading the way.

"They're baaaaacccck," Lois sang. She let out a laugh and hiccupped.

"Has to be about that second explosion in Chicago." Patsy looked up at the screen and raised her government issue wand, getting the information to scroll back to the right moment. "First time I've ever seen so many whirlygigs in a row! An actual magical battle!"

"That was a bad day. The Beechams are still reeling. The Order has put the whole family on administrative leave. I can't remember that ever happening, either!"

"Hannah still hasn't surfaced."

"I wonder if she's with the fishes."

"Oh, don't say that."

"You think that Berens woman had anything to do with that one, too?"

"Hard to say. From the looks of things, she's still tucked away in Austin. Pulled off some pretty good magic by Enchanted Rock. More than she should have been able to with the gates closed. Then, she did it again last night during the full moon. Keeps drawing in energy."

"You put both of those in a report?"

"Like I had a choice. Too many people saw it both times. We're a big bunch of gossips. G-men would have found out eventually and then wondered what else we didn't tell them."

"A lot," said Lois.

"Exactly. If the detective wants to be reckless, there's not much we can do about that. But wooohooo what a pull she has on the magic!"

"Imagine what she could do if the gates were open!"

"Put the bo-backslappyass on someone, that's what! The BBSA!" The two women cackled just as the birds chirped louder. Patsy looked up at the screen.

"Getting closer. Look at them," she laughed. "Looking everywhere like they expect something to pop out at them! It's not a haunted house," she yelled at the screen.

Lois gave her a look. "Don't even mention the world in between. Gives me the willies." She shuddered. "Pass me an M&M. A green one. They're the diet ones," she said, popping one into her mouth.

"Not unless you put a charm on them yourself."

"Not a bad idea."

"You hear the Order brought in an outsider?" Patsy nodded her head. "It's true. An Atlantean," she whispered, fluttering her fingers around her head. "Tentacles and a bitchy attitude to go with them. Glamours them most of the time."

"Will wonders never cease," said Lois, her mouth open in surprise.

"Probably not. We'd be out of a job if they did." Patsy gave another laugh and a hiccup, and waved her wand again, just in time.

The door flew open hard enough for the large silver knob to hit the wall and bounce back on the small general standing in front of the group, legs spread, arms behind his back. The four men behind him took a similar stance. The general caught the door and pushed back more gently this time. He paused, his mouth in a determined frown. He meant business today.

The small cadre of military marched in, keeping close ranks, doing their best to look like they were in charge. Patsy and Lois were happy to play along. It was better for everyone. Lois gave them a reassuring smile and Patsy slid her wand into her pocket.

"Hello ladies!" he said, a little too loudly, clearing his throat. He blinked a few times, gathering his thoughts before barreling into his speech. "We've come to ask for your advice! We want to find Leira Berens and offer her a position with the United States government." He was practically shouting, trying to put a smile on his face. It wasn't working. A sheen of sweat showed on his forehead and upper lip.

Patsy jerked in her chair, almost dropping her M&Ms, and grabbed one of the arms to steady herself.

"It's about time," said Patsy, smiling triumphantly. "We thought you'd never ask. What do you want to know?"

The general looked relieved, his shoulders relaxing. He seemed to be melting into his uniform.

"What?" Patsy gave Lois a look, but Lois was firmly focused on the general.

"Will the detective be joining us here?"

"Oh no, you ladies are doing a fine job," the general said nervously, waving his hands in front of him. The men behind him didn't move. "We have been reading your reports with interest. We have a special consultant job for Detective Berens. Her unique skills could be of great use to us... and, well, everyone." He gestured at Patsy and Lois as if they represented all of the magical community. Patsy made a face, barely hiding her exasperation.

"Oy vey," she mumbled under her breath.

"What do you need from us?" asked Lois patiently, doing her best to ignore Patsy.

"What's the best way to contact such a powerful being?"

"I hear the telephone works really well," said Lois, smiling, her eyebrows raised.

The general looked startled and someone behind him made a note. Lois slipped her wand out of her pocket, quietly mumbling a spell to send Patsy a sharp poke.

"Ya!" Patsy yelped, grabbing her side and looking at Lois, hurt and offended. Lois frowned at her. The group of men looked confused, glancing back and forth at each other but none of them said anything.

"You were saying?" Lois asked innocently.

"The phone works but we were wondering if there was another way… a kind of back channel?"

"You mean something magical that she'll recognize came from one of her kind?"

"We're not all the same species, you know," said Patsy, giving Lois a warning look. "We're not like human beings who separate themselves out by all kinds of things."

The general looked stymied and turned to look at his entourage, as if he was thinking of leaving.

"That doesn't mean you don't have a good idea." Lois pushed her glasses back up her nose. "Or that we can't help. Patsy's right, you know. Leira Berens is not a witch. She's part Light Elf, most likely. No D&D players? It's like a bigger, taller magical pixie. Like a giant Tinkerbell."

The group of men nodded their heads solemnly.

"But we can send her a message. We're well trained, highly qualified at what we do." Lois was constantly offering reasons to be given another raise. "What do you want us to tell her?"

"This letter we prepared has an outline of the job." The general handed Lois a folder with a single sheet in it.

Lois opened the folder and looked at the paper. One sentence. She rolled her eyes at all the pomp and circumstance for nineteen words. But the last part still made her let out a short gasp.

Act as a liaison between the human beings and the magical world at large, including other worlds or dimensions.

"Other worlds?" she squeaked.

"That's classified," the general said, holding up his hand. "We can only discuss that with Detective Berens. Can you get her the message?"

"It doesn't say anything in here about pay, or how to call you back, or where she'd work." Patsy looked over Lois' shoulder, flipping it over to see if anything might be on the back.

"All negotiable. Let Berens know that," he said firmly.

Patsy's eyebrows shot up.

"Here's my card," said the general, taking a step forward, finally separating himself from the rest of his group, looking even smaller as he held out the small square ivory-colored card. "My private number is on there. She can contact me there, and only there. I'll need the file back," he said, holding out his hand. "You have the message committed to memory?"

Lois shut the folder, handing it back. Patsy went back to frowning. "It's just the one sentence. I think we've got it."

"Send as soon as possible?"

"Right away, sir," Lois said, a look coming over her face. Patsy saw it and looked back at the general.

"Thank you for your service, ladies," he said, clicking his heels together and nodding his head. The men turned and waited, peeling out after the general. The sounds of the birds tweeting followed the men out, growing fainter as they got to the parking lot.

"We added that feature to let us know where they were when they're here," said Patsy. "Those are mourning doves. Very soothing." She waved her wand and put General Hospital back up, front and center. "Now, what was that look all about? You looked like you were sucking a lemon!"

"Didn't you get it? They know more than we told them."

"So? They're not obligated to tell us anything. We tell them. That's the gig."

Lois looked annoyed. "No shit, Sherlock. But if we didn't tell them, and they're hinting at other worlds, *other dimensions*, then who did and what do they know? What are they so worried about that they're looking for someone powerful to help them? And mark my words, Ms. Berens is very powerful. They seem to know it too."

"Ours is not to reason why. Ours is to do our job and get our paycheck." Patsy popped an M&M into her mouth.

"You're not at all worried? When has more information about our world in the hands of humans ever been a good idea?"

"Things are changing. The gates opening is getting closer, you know that. It's coming whether we like it or not. Besides, from the looks of the reports we got, Leira Berens can handle herself. She may be just what we need in there with them. Send the message."

"Like I had a choice," said Lois, pulling out her phone. "If they only knew. We use *their* technology half the time. Hello, Herman? Yeah, I need a favor. Can you send a ball of light with a message to that Light Elf, Leira Berens? Yeah, I know you saw her at Jackalope! Why do you think I'm calling you? She needs to call me at this number, right away. Tell her it's about a case."

"Oh, that's good." Patsy gave her the thumbs up. "What if she doesn't call back?"

"Then *we* send a ball of light."

CHAPTER FIFTEEN

Leira hung up the phone.

"Well?" Correk stood next to her, impatiently leaning over the kitchen counter, his hands on his hips.

The troll was hanging from the handle of the refrigerator, grunting and pulling, trying to get it open.

"They offered me a job." Leira shook her head. Everything in her life was changing. "That was a General Anderson. He said I can name my salary, name my hours and can even have a fancy title if I need one."

"What would you do for them that would rate all of that?"

The troll finally got the door of the fridge open, with a triumphant, "Aha!" He swung backward, still hanging on. He let go and dropped down, scurrying for the opening. Correk reached out and shut it swiftly with his foot, leaving the troll standing in front of the closed door. "Motherfuckers!" he squeaked.

"That's a new one. Your vocabulary is growing, four syllables," Leira said, looking down at the frustrated troll. "Why doesn't he just grow a little and push you aside?"

"There's a fortunate loophole to all of that. Once attached to another being, he can't grow or shrink on his own. He needs your emotions to do it. What's the job?"

"They want me to act as a kind of consultant between human beings and magical beings. They said there's more, but we would have to have a face to face meeting, and they need to know right away."

"Where are you meeting them?" Correk look concerned.

"Here, in Austin. They're coming here. I'm to go alone, which is a good idea. I don't want the U.S. government getting a good look at you. We still have black sites and I have no idea how advanced our technology really is. What if they have something that can block magic? Besides, you're running low. That last spell you tried at the party kinda fizzled. Sorry bro, that was a flop."

"It was a perfectly acceptable full-size unicorn made out of light from a fireball that ran around the room. Twice."

"Before mooing. Don't even say that was on purpose. It's okay, I get it. You need a recharge."

"Smug doesn't look good on you. At least tell me where you're going."

"In case you have to rally the troops?" Leira cocked her head to one side and gave him a crooked smile. "At an old warehouse on Ben White Boulevard. You didn't think they'd talk about all of this in a public place, did you?"

"Why are you even considering it? I thought you loved your job."

"Did and do, very much. But, my ability to hide what I can do is getting harder every day. Time is going to run out on me. The meeting's in a couple hours. Apparently, they're already in town. You'll have to go to the basketball game with Toni and her friends without me. Go, you'll have fun. You liked them, you know you did."

"I do need to visit home again, and soon."

"I figured."

The troll had managed to open the refrigerator again and this time, scrambled up to the top shelf where he was peeling American cheese slices as fast as he could, stuffing them into his mouth.

"Let him. Those have been in there forever. Look how happy he is. Is he even chewing?" Leira winced and looked away as the troll opened his mouth to shove in another piece, exposing the wet glob of cheese already in his craw.

Correk picked up the troll by the scruff of his neck, grabbing the cheese at the same time, and deposited both in the new round blue plastic toy box Leira had gotten for the tiny beast.

"You're in more danger around the ladies than I will be meeting the general today. It's clear they need me. They won't want to harm me."

"It's also clear they know a lot about you."

"It's a complicated world. Between human technology and magic, that was inevitable. Besides, magic leaves a trail and I left a couple of good ones lately. Somebody talked." She shrugged. "It was bound to happen."

"You look too unconcerned for my taste."

"I'm still bringing my gun and my spidey senses, along with my magic. I'm ready."

"I hope so."

"Believe so. I'm still a damn good detective, just enhanced. It'll be okay. Thanks for caring." She patted his arm, trying to reassure him.

Correk shook his head. "No, it's not the job. You think you've got a way to help your mother."

"That took you long enough. Of course I do, but it's still true that this could turn into a good move for me... if they're willing to play things my way. They should be a big enough bully to clear my mother's name and erase any record of her ever being diagnosed as crazy."

The troll belched cheese, giving his belly a satisfied rub.

"Maybe I'll bring the troll," she said.

181

"Much better plan."

Correk worked his way through the crowds in the stands at the Erwin Center, up to the rows near the top that held all the people from the Jackalope. The game was already underway, and everyone was yelling and cheering for the Longhorns men's basketball team.

People were on their feet shouting and Jack and Larry waved to him to sit with them.

"Sorry about the nosebleed section," said Jack. "It was the best we could do. The Longhorns have some devoted fans. Glad you could make it! Where's Leira?"

"She had a pressing matter come up and sends her regrets," said Correk, taking a seat. "What are those men down on that court doing? Trying to put that orange ball in the net over there?"

"Where could you have possibly been all these years that you don't recognize basketball? Don't you guys watch our sports from over there?" Larry jumped to his feet, yelling, "Go! Go! Go!"

Correk stood back up to get a better view and saw a player wearing a Longhorns jersey run down the court, throw the ball to someone else, who threw the ball from the far corner by the basket. It swished in, making a satisfying circle at the top of the net before dropping straight down.

"Three points!" Jack, yelled, holding up his fist for Correk to bump.

"This one I've seen," said Correk, smiling as he held up his fist.

"Hey, Correk." A row of women sitting in front of them turned, almost as one, smiling at him. Some of them waved.

"Loved your unicorn!"

"The mooing was the best part!"

Correk could feel his face warming up.

"You were apparently a big hit at the party. The women have

been jawing about you ever since." Jack's smile quickly turned to frustration and he jumped to his feet again. "That was traveling! I can see it from here!"

The women frowned at Jack before turning the charm offensive back on, asking Correk if he was enjoying the game.

"Can I get you anything?" asked an older brunette who had juggled fireballs at the Jackalope while doing the limbo.

"Watch out for those witches. They're man eaters." Larry gave him a friendly elbow.

Correk settled back into his seat and started twisting his fingers together in his lap, creating a small fireball. He cupped it in the palms of his hands, leaned down and whispered a spell.

The line of women in front of him abruptly looked around as if they had forgotten something and turned back to the game, chatting with each other about who hooked up with who at the party.

"Very clever," Jack gave him a wink. "Very wise, too. You'll have to teach me that one."

"Yeah, you need a spell to get the women to notice you first." Larry laughed. "Now, can we finally focus on the game?"

There was a makeshift meeting room set up on one side of the empty warehouse that consisted of a card table and chairs. The only people present were the general, one aide and Leira. The general's hat sat in front of him, neatly lined up next to his phone.

Leira sat up straight, her badge clearly visible on her belt, right next to her gun.

"I realize this looks fairly unremarkable." The general looked at the surroundings. "But it's for the best. The less attention we attract the better. I'm told this building is secure, so nothing we say can be heard. You can speak freely, and so can I. That's all we really need. There's not even any phone service. We own this building."

"Tell me why I'm here." Leira sat forward, her face set in a fierce stare. *When in a corner of any kind, get out of it as quickly as you can. Leave the fear behind.* Hagan taught her that the first week on the job as a detective.

"I was told you're good at what you do and are not easily intimidated. I can see that's true. That's good." He sat back in his chair. "I'll keep it short. There's not really much to say at this point, anyway. The U.S. government has become aware of an event that is going to happen about twenty years in the future. Ah, good, you already know what I'm talking about." He held up his hand. "It's alright, I was hoping you'd know. I have to be back in Washington very shortly and the less I have to explain, the better. Now, there's a lot of anxiety and confusion, as you might imagine, about what it means to have gates opening up between two worlds that neither side can control."

"It's not the first time this has happened," said Leira.

"So I've been told. But as a people, human beings have short memories and we tend to rewrite what we don't like, making it even harder to learn from history." He smiled at Leira. "I have several daughters, you know. Your determination reminds me of them."

"What is it you want me to do?"

"Right, good, keeping me on track. Eye on the prize. Of course. You have a unique combination of being both human and well, alien. Magical, from the other side. Your abilities have been noticed right up the chain of command within a very small, but high-ranking group. You are gifted at pulling pure power from the Earth, straight through you and channeling it. I've read about others like you but only from thousands of years ago."

That can't be true, thought Leira. "You still haven't gotten to what it is you want me to do." She drew her brows together, studying his face. *Friend or foe?* she wondered. *Still can't tell.*

"Humor me for one more minute. A little background so you can see we've done our homework. You are already a peace officer, used to working as part of a chain of command, and doing it very successfully. That gives certain people, myself included, a higher comfort level."

"I won't go off on my own agenda."

"Precisely. I like your rigorous honesty. Now is not the time for hidden agendas or polite truths. We've known about the magical beings among us for decades."

"Not always with the best results for the magical beings." Leira clenched her fists, thinking of the stories she had already heard from others at the Jackalope. And her mother.

"Unfortunately true. But we've all evolved to a different place. We want the Golden Age, that's what it's called I believe, to go as smoothly as possible. If that's to happen we need someone to bridge the gap between human beings and this other world. Between Earth and Oriceran."

"You know the name of the world."

"We know a lot, which we will share with you as soon as you accept the position of liaison, working for Earth on our behalf to set ground rules that everyone can live with."

"You're hoping to use my abilities to help you get your way."

"We only want to ensure the quality of life here on Earth is not threatened. We are not interested in being an aggressor."

"Fair enough. I have a few conditions."

"Name them."

"I stay here in Austin, I name my own salary, and you take care of a personal problem I'm having with the bureaucracy of a hospital."

"You're referring to your mother, Eireka Berens. I told you, we have done all our homework. What is it you want? For her to be released? Done. We can have her out this afternoon." He waved for his aide.

Leira was stunned, the breath knocked out of her. She sat still for a moment. There had to be more to this deal.

"I want more than that. I want any record of her ever being declared insane, erased. I want any mention, anywhere that she made of Oriceran or elves or magic erased for good. No trace anywhere. I want a new history in place that says she's been living a quiet life, here in Austin the entire fifteen years."

"That scenario would actually be better for all of us. Consider it done. Was that it?"

"One last thing. I retain the right to say no to any directive I find unethical or that crosses the line, and I decide where the line is."

The general looked momentarily angry but just as quickly, let it go. "We may not have the ability to speak a few words into the air and make something appear, but as a race, we rise to the occasion quite brilliantly, more times than not. And, you are still part human, along with your mother. Somewhere inside of you, you know this to be true."

Leira waited patiently for him to answer. *He who speaks first loses.*

"Fine, agreed. As if we could make you, anyway. As the gates open your power will only increase. Better we learn to trust each other now. Have we reached an agreement?"

"Free my mother. I'll come to work for you under the terms and conditions we discussed. I assume I'll be reporting directly to you."

"And only me. There are only a handful of people who will know of our arrangement. For now, that's best for everyone."

"I'll get you the name of the director at the hospital."

"No need, we already have it. I took the initiative to start the paperwork before you came in the door. It was going to be my bargaining chip, but you made things easy for both of us. I'll have your mother out of the psychiatric hospital by the morning at the latest, free and clear. You'll start on Monday. We can have someone speak to your Captain Napora."

"There's one other matter. It won't be quite as easy," Leira added, pulling out her phone. It was an idea so big she didn't share it with Correk so he couldn't talk her out of it. The general was about to find out what determined really looked like. "I'm texting you a file. It's a carefully curated list of other magical beings that are being held in mental hospitals as well, all over the country. They'll all need to be freed, given a clean slate. Then," she nodded solemnly, "we'll have a deal. You see, in my community, we don't make the same divisions you make. All of them are my family. All of them need to be freed."

CHAPTER SIXTEEN

There was only a three-quarter moon hanging over the hill country of Central Texas. Even that was covered in clouds, making the stars shine brightly above Enchanted Rock. The Park had been closed for hours, and the last stragglers had gotten down and driven home after the park ranger herded them all toward the exit.

He knew to always check the rock last. It was one of the first things he was told when he got the job.

The small group waited hours before hiking into the park, leaving their cars behind in a subdivision a mile up the road. They used only small penlights to guide their way, to ensure that no one would come and check because they saw a beam of light moving through the woods.

Even in the darkness, Enchanted Rock was easy to see among the trees. The pale lavender color sparkled under the stars and the kemana glowed from deep within the rock. The six people who stopped at the base stared up, taking in the sight before them, single file, before they started the long climb, using the natural stairs the fragmented rock provided.

They were a faction of the new followers of Rhazdon, chosen

to deliver the necklace to the new priest in Oriceran. The leaders of the movement who had planned and executed the theft were still in hiding from the Order. Their children and younger members were to finish the mission.

Once the group was on the flat shelf at the top they gathered in a circle and the leader, a half-Light Elf, pulled off his backpack, searching for a plastic container of blue crystals.

"Show me the crystals you have left. You couldn't have used them all. Don't hold back any of them. It'll take every last one for us to get a message across the veil. Even here." As he spoke, they could see that his tongue was still a sparkling blue, but the color was fading and with it, the energy they had gathered into themselves from the last ritual.

"I used some to pass an exam. Just... just a couple," said a nervous female who was part Wood Elf. She pulled out an HEB plastic grocery bag and went to the center of the circle, pouring out the contents.

"That's alright Rachel. I told you we could use some of them. We all have needs. We've been waiting so long for this. I just asked you to try and be conservative. You're fine."

"Why can't we use the necklace to send a message? It has more than enough power," said a brash, spirited young man, who was part Atlantean, with a little gnome mixed in to temper his personality. It wasn't helping much.

The leader stood up and walked to the center, adding his pile of crystals to the girl's. "You just explained why we can't do that. It's far more powerful than anything else we've ever seen. We'd be more likely to blow ourselves up and drill a hole right through Enchanted Rock than get a message to our redeemer in Oriceran. We've been tasked with getting the necklace, not using the necklace." He turned to the rest of the group. "Now, pony up. We don't know how long we have up here."

One by one they stood up and went to the center of the circle pouring out blue crystals.

A young man with spiky purple hair and some Arpak blood opened his hand to let out the five crystals he still possessed. "Sorry," he said, sheepishly. "Had a rager. Things got out of hand."

Once the remaining crystals were gathered, everyone joined hands, forming a tight circle around them.

"Now, focus. Let the energy flow through you. No resistance."

"Dude, don't say that. Now, that's all I can think about," said the part-Arpak. The girl next to him slapped the back of his head and took his hand again. "Think about that instead," she snapped.

They closed their eyes and gradually, the crystals began to glow.

"Focus," commanded the half Light Elf.

The crystals turned to a blue metallic liquid yet again, droplets racing around until they came together as a pool, turning into a window, rising into the air, and giving a glimpse to the other side. To Oriceran.

On the other side stood an old gnome in a cloak with the hood up, his face hidden in the shadows.

"Did you get it?" he demanded. "Show it to me. Prove it!"

The leader hesitated, not sure if he should break the circle.

"Prove it! Now! I will hold it open from here. Do it quickly!"

The half-Light Elf let go and grabbed his backpack, digging quickly through the contents, berating himself for not having it ready. "There it is," he said, relieved. He held up the heavy gold chain and let the diamond-shaped crystal dangle.

"Closer," the gnome demanded.

The man stepped closer to the small opening, peering into the darkness, wanting a glimpse of a world he had never seen before. It was hard to see anything but a large, stone arch. He held the necklace up closer and was about to shine his penlight on it when the gnome reached through the portal and grabbed the necklace, snatching it from his hand.

The startled man stepped back, not sure what to do next. "What?"

"You've done well," said the gnome, smiling as he looked at the artifact in his hands. "You have taken us so much closer, and we will rise again."

The half-Light Elf felt a sense of relief flood him. He opened his mouth to ask, what next, but the portal zipped shut without warning. The group was left standing on Enchanted Rock in the middle of the night with no idea of a plan.

"That was harsh."

"We should get going."

"Yeah, I have an exam tomorrow."

"My mom's expecting me home soon. You do not want to leave her waiting for news."

"Fine," said the young leader. "I suppose we did what we came here to do," he added sullenly.

"It's not our last mission, Jake," Rachel said, putting on her backpack. "This is just the beginning. It was a success. That's a good thing. The rise of Rhazdon's message. We were a part of the beginning!"

"I'm here to see Detective Berens? I have some information for her about a case?" Everything the pretty young blonde woman said sounded more like a question than a statement. "No, I can only tell her?"

The desk sergeant tried arguing with her. He was used to coaxing at least the basics from people before they got to go any further. Too many crackpots showed up at his desk. But after a few minutes he admitted defeat and called Leira.

"Who should I say is here?" he asked, looking up at the determined woman.

"Tell her my name is Katie Toler? I'm a friend of the Griffins? She should be expecting me?"

"Hello Detective? This is Sergeant Williams? Dammit, now

she has me doing it. There's a Katie Toler to see you. Said to tell you she's a friend of the Griffins."

Katie mouthed the name along with him to make sure he got it right, giving him a big, toothy smile when he did. He scowled back.

"Says you're expecting her. Great, happy to send her back as soon as you come get her. I'm not an escort service. No unescorted civilians, Detective." He hung up the phone and leaned out of the window to point to the plastic chairs against the back wall. "She'll be right out. Till then, you can have a seat. Soda machine's right there, too."

"Thank you?"

The sergeant stared at her for a second, waiting to see if there was sarcasm involved. He hated sarcasm. But she smiled and turned to the seats.

"Millennials. Not one good brain between them." He went back to his laptop, monitoring the police calls.

"Ms. Toler?" Leira looked at the young woman waiting patiently.

The sergeant grumbled, "Not you too," from his perch but didn't say anything else. Leira looked at the window and back at Katie Toler but Katie wasn't giving anything away.

"Would you follow me?"

"Oh, for the love of Pete," the sergeant exclaimed. A passing detective asked Leira, "What's that all about?"

"No idea," she replied, leading the way back to her desk. She knew what Katie meant when she said she was a friend of the Griffins. They got to her desk in the mostly empty room and Leira pulled the extra chair closer, patting the seat. Katie carefully sat down, still smiling and perched herself on the front, sitting up stick straight.

"You're a friend of the Silver Griffins. Why are you looking for me? I'm not a witch," Leira whispered. It felt like everyone could hear them, but when she looked around no one was paying any attention.

"I've been retained by them as a kind of consultant." Katie put her hand by her mouth and whispered, "Special Agent is the title they gave me."

Why do people do that? thought Leira.

She patted Leira's arm. "My first assignment was to keep tabs on you and help out when I could. Boy, you do not make that easy! Levitating at a party," she continued in a low voice. "That took a bit of doing and even some old school cashola to get the larger magical community to look the other way. Some I just outright, you know, never was..." She made a face, rolling her eyes. "Don't like to do that to your own kind and it takes a little added something to the spell, but some gossips, you know."

Leira rested her chin in her hand and her elbow on her desk and leaned in toward Katie. "I don't need a babysitter. You can stand down." Her face was hard.

"I'm not a babysitter. More like a guardian angel, and no. I don't take orders from you. I'm here in the background for the long haul." She made little circles with her finger, still smiling that smile that was starting to get on Leira's nerves.

"Is there any way I can make you go away?" *A regular bitch.*

Katie took off her glasses and leaned as close as she could to Leira, relaxing just enough that pupils of her eyes turned into slits, mesmerizing Leira.

Leira was drawn into them and in her mind she could see Katie transform, her hair becoming tentacles. Katie blinked, ending the connection as her pupils rounded.

"Not even a small one," she whispered back. "I can be just as determined as the gossip says you are. Two of a kind. Well, sort of. My people actually originated here on Earth. The only aboriginal magical people that did. Your kind wiped them out." She sat back, the smile still in place. "Ancient history, of course. Neither one of us was there. But for now, you can either have me find out what you're up to the hard way, meaning I dig into your business. Or you can see me as an asset and clue me in once in a while. Your choice."

Katie stood up, putting out her hand, the constant question back in her voice. "So nice to meet you? Everyone was right? I hope to see you at the next potluck?" With that she turned and headed for the exit, not waiting for the required escort. No one stopped her and Leira didn't bother to follow. *Not so regular after all, but still a bitch.*

CHAPTER SEVENTEEN

L eira was trying to make sense of what just happened. The vision she saw was of a species she had never seen before but remembered all too well how Correk had described them. A very determined race of people. Well, at least she had that in common with her.

That is one formidable woman. I suppose I should be glad she's on my side.

Captain Napora opened his door and motioned to Leira to come to his office without saying a word. He didn't look very happy. She got up and made her way through the desks, working out in her head what she could say to him.

"You finally messed something up, huh?" A detective leaned back in his chair, satisfied.

"Whatever." Even though Leira knew she wasn't in trouble, at least not technically, she wasn't looking forward to facing the Captain. He was responsible for giving her a chance and helping her become a homicide detective.

She wasn't even sure what excuse the General had given the Captain. The truth wasn't an option.

"Captain," she said, knocking gently on the frame of the door.

He gave a small wave, his lips pressed firmly together into a straight line. He pointed to the chair in front of his desk and came around to shut the door before sitting on the edge of his desk right in front of her. He started to speak more than once, stopping himself, and trying again.

Finally, he put his hands on his hips and looked her square in the eye. "This is not a surprise at all. Of course the Feds noticed you. Twenty-five years old and already going to be working on terrorist cases! I'm so damn proud I could bust! Come here, can I hug you? Maybe not. How about a handshake, no, let's go for the hug." He enveloped her in a hug, surprising her, giving her a hearty slap on the back.

Terrorism, okay, not too far off the truth. Well played, General.

"I…uh…I… thank you. Sir, it's been an honor and a privilege to serve under you. I hope I've contributed in some way to the team."

The Captain sat back down on the edge of his desk, a smile on his face. "You've been a pain in my ass of the first order. And I wouldn't have it any other way. You are relentless, Berens, which is why I know you're gonna tear it up for the Feds. I understand they're stationing you here. Still keeping an eye on Austin. Who knows, maybe we'll still get to work together from time to time. You'll still need us locals."

"Always, sir," she said, doing her best not to choke up.

"You told Hagan, yet?"

"He's my next stop. Today's his day off. I'm meeting him for a drink later."

"He's not going to be surprised either. He won't like losing you as his partner, but these things happen. You get a good one and they're young and the world comes calling!"

Two worlds, sometimes.

"Okay, well, they asked if they could have you right away, and just like the Feds they went over my head before they even asked so your last day is coming up this week! Maybe we can throw you a little party or at least meet for drinks."

"Sounds good, sir. I'd like that."

"Think of us as family, Berens. You can always come back if you need to." He laughed and waved at her. "That'll never happen. You're on your way to the top. Go on, get out of here. Start closing out your cases and hand them off. So proud of you."

Leira walked out of his office feeling like she was just starting to see what she'd had all along. *So much family all around me. I was never alone.*

Correk was standing in the middle of Leira's living room, trying to find the right words.

"You have to go back to recharge. I get it, I'll be fine," said Leira. "I took care of myself for years without a lot of assistance from anyone, you know. This whole, it takes a village to train a detective to just be herself is fairly new to me. Besides, you'll be back before I've had a chance to settle down on the couch with Yumfuck."

"Not quite that fast, but soon enough." He struggled to find the right words. "I know you can take care of yourself, probably better than anyone else on this planet. The powers you possess, to say nothing of a sidearm."

"Then go! Let me get a little peace before you're back with a thousand new stories!"

"I wanted to say, I'm proud of you." He nodded firmly. "Yes, there it is. You've faced up to having the way you see even the most basic of things flipped upside down and didn't back down once."

"Yeah, didn't run away, break a heel, wait for someone to rescue me."

"It's not a small thing. Every being has to have a few things they can take for granted in order to get through a day. The two moons will be there in the sky, a set of stairs will appear when I say the right words, the plants will sway and grow whenever they hear music..."

"Not what I'd have said, but I see where you're going."

"Magic introduces a truth that if you haven't known about it since birth can be hard to handle. Anything is possible."

"There are still rules. Someday I want to learn the basics of them."

"Yes, there are always rules, and then someone comes along who's just a little more clever, like yourself or powerful or evil and they find a way to break those rules, and we get reminded. Anything is possible. But you didn't back up once. You ran toward all of it." He reached out to hug her and gave her a pat on the back instead.

Leira raised an eyebrow and gave him a crooked smile. "We'll have to work on your social skills when you get back. I take it Light Elves aren't big huggers. Felt like you were helping me shake something loose. That explains a lot about me, too. Go, say hello to the King and Queen for me. Bring me back a souvenir. A t-shirt or a bobblehead. Or a postcard where all of the things in it actually move and can wave at you."

Correk was already conjuring a bright fireball in his hands, using the last of the energy he had held in reserve so he'd still be able to open a portal. "They would all fall out before I was halfway through the portal. All you'd get would be a blank piece of paper."

"Fine. Then just get back here safely."

The air in the middle of the room shimmered and grew wavy as an opening appeared. The red velvet chair disappeared and Leira found herself looking at the green forest of Oriceran. She looked up at him, still smiling but her expression changed, and her eyes grew wider. "Wait!" she yelled. "Your ears!"

Correk stepped through and took a last look back at her, a puzzled expression on his face as the portal closed behind him.

Strange way to say goodbye.

Correk shook his head and looked around. It felt good to be standing on Oriceran soil again. It was the longest he had ever been away and now that he was home, he realized how much he had missed it.

He stepped out of the brush and onto the path in the direction of the Light Castle and felt the familiar hum of the energy coming up from the ground and through his feet. He never really took note of it before.

"I never took you for the sentimental type. You have a foolish smile on your face."

Correk smiled, finally able to make out eyes watching him, blending in with the foliage behind him. The two pupils in each eye moving independently, keeping watch.

"Perrom, good to finally see you." He grabbed his old friend by the shoulders and pulled him into a hug, slapping him on the back.

"This is new." Perrom studied his friend, a smirk on his face, still blending perfectly with his surroundings. "Your time on Earth appears to have been instructive. You've come back as a sensitive human.

Correk gave him a good-natured frown. "It's called evolution and it's a good thing!" He started walking toward the castle. Perrom moved away from all the greenery. The scales of his skin flipped over in a rippling wave, changing him back to a Wood Elf, his long brown hair hanging down his back.

"That's not the only evolution going on." He caught up to Correk and flicked one of his rounded ears. "You really are becoming a squishy human!"

Correk slapped his hands over his ears. "Damn the moons! I forgot the spell!" He hurriedly moved his hands, creating a shortcut to remove the spell, botching it on the first try in his rush.

"Rusty. Like a schoolboy again." Perrom laughed, crossing his arms as he watched his friend struggle.

"Blast it. Fuck!"

Perrom laughed harder, bending over, holding his sides. "You've even learned to swear like the humans!"

Correk shoved him, but he kept laughing, even as he patiently waited for Correk to get it together.

Correk took a deep breath and looked at the plants around him. He let it out as a song, speaking in his native tongue, watching all the growing things rooted in the Oriceran soil bend toward him.

He tried the spell again, and finally his ears took on their more natural point. He raised an eyebrow and looked at Perrom. "Well?"

"Much better. Good you caught that before Queen Saria saw you. Her feelings about humans haven't changed." Perrom looked in the direction of the castle and in the distance Correk could see the Queen walking toward the gardens. A swarm of purple grieving fireflies clung to her, protecting her, blinking their lights. A sign of deep grief.

"She is no better," said Correk.

"Her son had hundreds of years left. A few weeks of mourning will not take away that pain. Although, the death of Bill Somers helped. The Willens say she has stopped trying to blow them apart."

"I'm sure they rewarded that with pinching a few of her things."

"And then selling them back to her. Commerce."

"I even missed the Willens."

Perrom laughed. "Go, see everyone. Find me later. This is where I leave you," he said, stopping at the edge of the woods.

"Tired of being seen with me?"

"Not at all. Things have gotten a little darker since you were here last. The dark bazaar has grown bigger and trades more Earthly technology every day. It influences everything. Someone must be behind all their success. You may have been right, my old friend. I hear there is a prophet who visits the tents."

"Do they know who it is?"

"No one will talk. Everyone is afraid of him, which is saying something. That kind doesn't scare easily. Watch your back. Sorry to put a damper on your return. You are staying, aren't you? I know Ossonia has missed you."

"You are weaving stories out of thin air. Ossonia is just a friend, and no, this is a visit to recharge. There are still things to do back on Earth."

"*Back* on Earth? This is your home, don't forget that. Go, there are people who will be happy to see you, no matter what you say." Perrom faded into the scenery until only his smile could be seen and even that disappeared when he turned and became one with the forest, taking a different path toward home.

Correk wasted no time hiking up the short hill and through the formal gardens toward the castle. Pixies fluttered across the path, their wings stirring the air by his ankles. A chorus of "Hello, Correk," piped up in high voices as they flew into the tall reeds. He smiled and waved. At last he arrived where he knew the castle was hovering, unseen by most.

"Altrea Extendia!" he shouted with joy. Sparks flew and a staircase curled around, down to the ground, appearing to hang in the air.

He climbed the stairs two at a time, the steps disappearing behind him, finally reaching the upper floor where his room was located.

A passenger pigeon was waiting for him at the window,

cooing and pecking at the glass. "Palmer," said Correk, opening the window, still able to find everything without having to make it visible. Still, he wanted to see his world. He bent his fingers and waved at the room, watching the familiar symbols appear on his outstretched arm. The room became visible again and Palmer stepped through the window, dropping the mail on his desk.

"I never know how the gargoyles can tell when someone is back." Correk picked up the note. It had the royal seal of the Light Elves on it.

See me first. It was signed by the king.

"Thank you, Palmer." Correk held out the card to the bird. The words started to wiggle, transforming into worms. Palmer gobbled them up and fluttered his wings in thanks, launching out the window again, back to the post office.

Correk went in search of the king, using a simple spell to locate him in the library. The gnomes looked up from their work and grunted, tipping their hats at Correk. A familiar greeting after someone was away. Most of the flowers on their hats did their usual raspberry. Only one or two snarled, instead.

The king was standing by the window and when he turned Correk could see that his crown was starting to bloom. For him, at least, the grief was passing. It would be time, soon, to return to the more familiar crown of silver vines.

"Correk," the king sang. "You've returned! The gargoyles said your arrival was imminent!" The king beamed with pleasure.

"My king," said Correk, bowing slightly. "You asked to see me."

"Yes. I know you're only here to gather magic before you go back. The prophets will insist you return to Earth. They're determined to ensure that these years before the gates open are not wasted. How long are you staying?"

"Just the day, with Your Grace."

"Of course, of course. But there is something you need to know. There are rumors everywhere about a dark force growing in our midst. I have sources who frequent the dark bazaar and someone is stirring trouble."

"I've already heard the same rumor."

"That is worrisome. You've only been back a moment and it's already reached your ears. No one will give details about who it might be or if it's a group. Did you hear more?"

Correk gave a firm shake of his head.

"Whoever it is," said the king, "they have managed to buy loyalty with fear or money, or both." The king moved his fingers in a pattern that Correk knew was to protect the room from eavesdroppers like a stray Willen looking for something to bargain with later. "The queen does not know, and I'd like to keep it that way for as long as possible. My source tells me the necklace is back on Oriceran. This dark force, whoever they are, they must have plans for us all."

Correk thought about telling him about the Willen's cryptic message, but without proof it could turn out to be a dangerous distraction. There was always the chance Correk was putting the pieces together wrong. It would have to wait until he knew more.

"What can I do to be of service?"

"At the moment, there is nothing any of us can do but stay vigilant. I'm glad you'll be on Earth. You will be my eyes and ears there. That gives me comfort, my old friend. The gates will be opening sooner rather than later, and we cannot risk starting off with dark forces threatening."

CHAPTER EIGHTEEN

The general was always being underestimated because of his small stature. He heard all the jokes about Napoleon or dynamite in a small package. He decided a long time ago to use all of it to his advantage. Too often, people underestimated his resolve and tried to test him. They never saw him coming.

He got great pleasure out of clearing up their misconceptions. Today was going to be no exception. He sat across the desk from the director of the psychiatric hospital and waited patiently. The director was leaning on the desk, his ID badge dangling over the particleboard disguised to look like oak. There was a smarmy smile plastered on his face. The fluorescent light overhead glared off his bald head where the comb over didn't cover.

On the desk between them were the discharge papers for Eireka Berens and a report that repudiated her mental illness. That was the part that was sticking in the director's craw. He was willing to release the patient but with conditions.

"We have integrity here, you understand. This woman has issues. She's clearly got schizophrenic tendencies, talking about elves and fairies and *entirely* other worlds. We can't just say that never happened, now can we? We have to consider the public's safety."

Still, the general waited. He knew when someone was making a case to get what they wanted. The director didn't give a shit about the public's well-being or Eireka Berens sanity. He wanted something. Something big.

The director swiveled in his chair, pulling blueprints off the credenza behind him, rolling the rubber band off and opening them, laying them over the general's papers.

"Now, if Ms. Berens had an adequate place to check in and still receive care on an outpatient basis, let us know that she's still responding to all our care, we would feel better. I'm sure my fellow lodge brother, the mayor, would agree with me." He tapped the drawings and smiled, the gap in his front teeth visible.

The general raised his hand, his eyes still on the director. An aide placed a folded piece of paper in it. No one in his entourage looked very happy.

The general carefully opened the paper and put it on top of the blueprints and pointedly slid it forward.

"I don't know if you realize, but my time is valuable, and you are wasting it. As you can see from the paper in front of you, you are a government employee at a government-sponsored institution. And somewhere in the chain of command, way above your head, there is me. That means that you have been wasting my time for quite some time."

The smile slipped off the director's face. The general tapped the paper again.

"Read the last line," he said in a low and menacing tone. "As of this moment, consider your ass fired. You are no longer employed by this institution." The general's anger was kept in check only by his satisfaction at firing the director and watching the realization sink in.

The director sank back in his chair, his ego deflating.

"But...but...but..." he sputtered, spit flying onto the front of his crisp white lab coat.

"What's that?" The general was starting to enjoy his day. There was a cockroach under his shoe, and he was having the pleasure of hearing the crunch.

"I need this job!" whined the director, slapping his hands on the top of his cheap desk.

"Now you want your job back?"

The general stood up and brushed his arm across the top of the desk, pushing the blueprints onto the floor. His face was hard, the pleasant mask he entered with, gone. He carefully placed a pen down on the form.

"The next time someone from my office comes in and asks you to sign anything," he said, in a slow, even, menacing tone, leaning over the desk, "you sign the fucking document."

The director took the pen with a shaking hand.

The aide came around and pointed at signature lines as the director nervously signed his name, droplets of sweat smearing the ink.

"Good!" The general clapped his hands, smiling. "Always a good day when everyone works together." He dropped the smile, sailing out the door without another word. Enough of his day had been wasted already. He hummed a song he heard on the radio as he headed down the hall. Leira Berens was one step closer to working for their side.

Leira read the paper again, trying to take it in. Her mother was declared sane and the government offered its sincere apologies for the error. A check was enclosed for $1,000,000 as restitution. The general was careful to point out that wasn't her salary or even a signing bonus. It was to be Eireka Berens' money. After all, it actually was a mistake to have ever locked her up. All over the country, others were being freed as well. All the government asked was that the whole matter be kept secret. That was exactly what Leira wanted, too.

She had dreamed of a moment like this a thousand different ways when she was younger. As she got older she stopped letting herself think about it at all. It always seemed like magical thinking.

She smiled at the thought, blinking back the tears welling in her eyes.

"Well, now," said the general in a fatherly tone, patting her shoulder. "Big moment." He cleared his throat and smiled at Leira.

If I could find my grandmother this day would be perfect.

She put the thought out of her mind. One victory at a time. The rock was rolling in the right direction.

"How soon?"

"Tomorrow. I know I told you by today but erasing her history is taking a little doing. It turns out there were a few agencies watching your mother. Apparently, they knew more than we realized, which puts them on our radar. Nonetheless, by the morning any trace of her will be gone from their system and if they try to look her up again, we'll be notified. You not only have my word, which I assure you is inviolate, you have my gratitude for what you are about to embark on for us. Your country, in fact *your* world, Earth, will always be grateful, even if most inhabitants will never know anything about it."

"Exactly the way I want it."

"Always a good feeling when a plan comes together and everyone feels like they won." He smiled. "Now, we have all of your paperwork to sign so we can make it official and get your clearance. There are benefits as well. Medical, dental, and a decent 401k. My aide will show you where to sign. Enjoy your evening Leira Berens, special attaché to the United States government. You've earned it.

Leira made one other condition before she signed. It was written in the agreement that she could tell several specific people about her new job. She agreed to leave out Oriceran, her complicated DNA, and her own magic in general. But she wanted to be able to tell them something close to the truth. After all, they were family.

She stood in her small living room surrounded by all the things that were so familiar, thinking about how things were about to change. *My entire life, everything is changing.* She twisted the sapphire ring on her finger. *Will I even be able to live here anymore? There's no room for my mother, much less a troll, Correk and my mother. Let it go, Berens. You're getting more than you ever imagined possible. The rest will sort itself out.*

"This is going to be one of the weirder conversations I've ever had to start with anyone." She looked at the troll sitting on the edge of the couch. He kept cocking his head from one side and then to the other as if he understood, cooing and trilling. "Hello everyone, I've quit my job with the police department to become a ghost hunter. No? How about witch doctor. Or vampire slayer. No one's mentioned any beings like that, yet."

She shook it off and watched the troll give a shake as well. He grinned, showing even rows of sharp, pointy teeth.

"Okay, now or never." The troll slid off the couch and came over to stand next to her. "Oh no, you're not coming. You're not part of the bargain I made. Your whereabouts will have to remain hidden. Come on little fella." She leaned down and held out her hand, waiting till he crawled onboard. She placed him in the center of the couch and whispered, "Nesturnium." He settled in, sighing as he sat back against a pillow. Leira looked at him and wondered if he was bored, despite the spell. She grabbed the remote and turned on Netflix, starting the movie Gremlins. "You'll like this one. I have a feeling these are cousins of yours."

She twisted the ring one more time and reminded herself,

everything changes tomorrow, before opening her front door and heading out to the patio. She weaved her way through the mostly empty tables over to where the regulars could always be found.

"Leira!" The familiar chorus went up from the people huddled around one end of the bar, laughing and telling stories. Estelle was at her usual post, standing on her stool, already handing someone what they wanted to drink before they had a chance to order. Smoke swirled around her bouffant.

Leira hesitated, surprising herself. She never ran from a fight. *Maybe that's the problem. This is all good news. Who knew it would be harder to face good news than it was to deal with the bad.*

"You okay?" Margaret shushed the others, batting at them, sloshing the martini in her other hand. Craig stopped mid-sentence and turned around to look at Leira, along with Mike and Scott.

Mitzi picked up Lemon and smiled at her. "What is it, sugar?

Leira felt her throat tighten and fought the tears welling up in her eyes.

Mike got off his stool, shaking out a pant leg as Scott stepped over to Leira. No one dared to touch her. They had never seen her so vulnerable.

"What is it? Are you sick? Did someone die?"

"Drink this, it'll help," said Estelle who had migrated over to them with a shot of bourbon.

"It's my mother. She's coming home."

Not the words she had expected to start with but there it was. She wanted to tell someone that it was real. It was official. And she couldn't think of anyone else, besides Correk. He was due back any moment. *My cousin.* I want all of my family to know.

"My mother is coming home. Tomorrow."

"Well, I'll be damned."

"Fucking amazing!"

"That's the best news I've heard in a month of Sundays."

"Beer's on me!" Estelle was loading up the bar with a beer for each of the regulars.

"Damn, this is a big occasion. Estelle is buying!" Mike started grabbing bottles and passing them around before Estelle could change her mind.

"And I quit my job." *Damn, that was not the way I wanted to say any of this.* She smiled as a tear rolled down her face. "Oh fuck, I'm not good at happy."

"Okay, so, you're happy you quit. I'm not sure I get that."

"I got offered another job. With the Feds. I'm a new agent in paranormal." She wiped her face on the edge of her shirt. "I start Monday." Everyone started talking at her at once.

"That makes all the difference, honey. You should have started with that."

"Holy crap, you're joining the X Files!"

"Does that make you Fox or Scully?"

"Scully, smart guy. The woman."

"The feds really do believe something's out there. Wow!"

"Here, take your beer!"

"Is it a party?" Correk strolled up next to her as if he was always on this side of the veil, his feet on Earth. He looked well rested and calm.

"Her mother's coming home!"

"Tomorrow!"

"And aliens really do exist!"

"And Leira Berens is going to track them down."

"Here, take a beer! They're on Estelle."

"Just the first round!"

"That is a lot of news to take in." Correk smiled and held up his bottle. "To Leira Berens. May she always know friends, family and all good things!"

"Hear, hear!"

She curled her toes, determined not to do the ugly cry.

Fucking feelings. She smiled as she took a nice large swig of her beer. *To all good things.*

"Correk if you ever think about joining a bowling team, you have to go with the Pin Pushers." Estelle cackled, looking up at the scoreboard. "Damn, boy, you are bowling a near perfect game."

Leira got up to take her turn, a lopsided grin still plastered on her face. Everything seemed a little easier. She stepped up to the line and rolled the ball, feeling a whizz of energy course through her as the ball sailed down the alley, curving just so, taking out all the pins. She smiled with satisfaction and went back to sit down.

"You might want to try and get a couple of spares," Correk whispered. "Now that you know what you can do, you have to show discretion."

"I'm just so damned happy."

"That's a combination of magic, beer and a little good news for a change. You're high as a kite." He looked at her sitting there, sipping her beer, smiling and waving at people. "Never mind. Enjoy your night. Life will intrude again, soon enough. Everyone deserves a night like this, and you have earned it, and then some."

"Feelings are not all bad," Leira snickered.

Correk leaned in to tell her, "Like I said, you're high on magic. Enjoy it. The hangover is a bitch. But I have to say, it's generally worth it. Just don't go making strikes from here without getting up. No, Berens, that wasn't a suggestion."

CHAPTER NINETEEN

Leira stood in her mother's room shaking with rage. Her mother stood quietly next to her, holding her hand as she looked around the room. An old wooden dresser painted white and a single bed with a metal frame. Not much more than a cot with a thin mattress. It didn't help that she was fighting a magic hangover and was seeing the world through a fog. It felt like she was moving through mud.

Correk paced around the room, grunting and swearing under his breath as he stopped at various points in the small room. He touched the windowsill, rubbing off grime with his finger, shaking his head.

He was doing his best not to unleash a fireball and send a horde of nits down the pants of everyone who worked there. Leira considered it but in the end vetoed the idea. Still, she was saving the idea for later, in case she changed her mind.

Eireka Berens was determined to be very still until she was safely on the other side of the many locked doors. There was nothing worth saying that she couldn't rant about later. Right now, she just wanted out.

Still, standing there feeling the warmth of her daughter's hand in hers was something to savor. Fifteen years. She had held her hand many times in the years since she was first locked up. But never with the knowledge of freedom just on the other side. She smiled at her daughter, channeling small bits of magic to soothe and calm her. To mother her.

"Alright, well, your paperwork is certainly in order." The floor nurse, a large woman with a short bob wore a tight, pinched smile. Her lips were a garish red. She blocked their exit for a moment but Correk stepped forward, willing to lift the woman over his head and throw her like a javelin, if that's what it took to leave the place.

She took one look at him and quickly shuffled out of the way, holding the papers to her chest. "Haba, haba, haba," she mumbled, opening and shutting her mouth like a fish.

Leira squeezed her mother's hand and led her out of the room, feeling the pulses passing from her mother and into her palm, and up her arm into her chest.

"It's going to be okay, Mom. That bitch will not stop us. Not today. No one will."

Eireka smiled at her daughter. At the word Mom. It was worth the wait. It was worth every fucking year. "I knew you'd figure it out. I knew."

"Go on out to the car. I want to find the doctor in charge. The man who kept her in here all these years." Correk was so angry his eyes were flashing light out of the corners.

"Not a good idea. You'll turn him into a donkey."

"Old wives tale, but if I could... Go on, I just want a word. We're leaving, but all these other people are not. Go. I'll only be a minute."

"I'm coming in, fireballs blazing if you get yourself stuck in there."

"These motherfuckers cannot hold a fully charged adult male Light Elf," he snarled.

"Nice time to finally pull out all the big words. I like it."

"I met your father," said Eireka, smiling at Correk.

He stopped mid-swear and looked at her, searching her face like he couldn't have heard her right.

"It's true. I recognized you the minute I saw you. You look just like him."

Leira saw the pain on Correk's face. "We can all talk about this later. We need to get out of here. I don't like being here one minute longer than we have to. Go say your piece. Don't injure anyone and get the fuck out of there as soon as possible."

Leira didn't wait for an answer. The reprieve felt fragile standing so close to the door. She put her arm around her mother and gently pushed her forward and out, into the air.

They made their way quickly to the green Mustang but as Leira held open the passenger side door, Eireka hesitated. She threw her head back, closing her eyes and breathing in deeply. "Fifteen years," she said, softly, barely above a whisper. "The air really does smell sweeter out here."

Correk watched them walk down the stairs, stunned at what Eireka had said. "How is that possible?" he muttered. "No one gets out of Trevilsom Prison."

"Can I help you?"

An orderly eyed him up and down as if he was trying to decide if he was looking at a visitor or a new patient. Correk tapped the visitor's badge clipped to his jacket.

"I want to see whoever's in charge."

"Do you have an appointment? If you don't have an appointment, that won't be possible. I suggest calling on the phone first and then come back."

Correk let the magic rise up in him, his eyes starting to glow and the fiery symbols scrolling across his skin.

The orderly stumbled back, reaching for the wall behind him.

"Never was, never will be." Correk spun a fireball over the man, leaving just a few nits in his pants. "A compromise."

He spun another fireball and whispered into it, following it as it rocketed down the hallway and up a flight of stairs before stopping in front of a door. He called it back to him, letting it dissolve in his hand and went up, and opened the door.

"What the hell?" The director stood up, splashing his coffee. "Dammit!" He mopped at it, pulling a wad of Kleenex from the box on his desk.

Correk quietly closed and locked the door behind him. Without saying a word, he spun a fiery red ball of light in his hands, his eyes aglow, the symbols returning. He stepped forward and whispered into the ball, sending it spinning around the director.

"You will work tirelessly for the rest of your life to improve the quality of care for everyone who comes through these doors or I will return." The fireball spun faster, finally slamming into the man's chest and seeping into his shirt, and under his skin. "Think of it as a GPS that will not only tell me where you are, but what you're doing. I will always know. Veer from your mission and I will get angry. You don't want to see me angry. Tell anyone, and prepare to join the people you have treated so miserably and become one of their own. This I swear."

Correk let the magic subside within him and opened the door, striding out and down the hallway. The director collapsed into his chair, throwing up his breakfast into his metal wastebasket.

Correk kept going till he got to the parking lot. Once he was there he turned around so that Leira couldn't see him and sent one more fireball back toward the building full of a thousand tiny insects. "One outbreak of nits among the staff is not even a start at being enough."

Mara Berens was getting better at navigating through the ether, pushing her will in front of her and letting her body follow. The poltergeist kept his word and showed her how to talk to the living still in the world. She kept hers and agreed to hide him long enough for him to visit his family. It turned out he was too afraid to get near them and reveal their whereabouts to the darker forces caroming through the world in between.

If you want it to work, I have to go with you. It was true, but she also wanted to be sure he wasn't going to try and drag someone into the world in between with them. That was more than she could bear.

Suit yourself. They moved through the world in between, pushing aside wormholes that led to different places until they got to one he recognized and went through. She could feel how eager he was to get to where they were going.

On the other side was a bedroom with faded wallpaper and a matching set of oak furniture.

That's my wife. We would have been married fifty-two years this year.

He found his wife folding clothes and putting them away in their old bedroom, whistling a song from a commercial playing on the TV in the background. *Can't startle her. I need to start slow.*

What are you going to do? Mara still wasn't sure this was going to end well.

Watch and learn. He focused his attention and let go of his will, sending it out ahead of himself to the wilted cut flowers in a blue ceramic vase on top of the dresser. They sprang back to life, lifting their heads, the leaves turning green again.

His wife turned and stared at the flowers, clutching a pile of underwear.

He turned his attention to the towels still jumbled in a pile on the bed and let his will fold one into a perfect square.

That should impress her. Couldn't get me to do laundry when I was alive. I wasn't the best around the house.

The woman sat down on the edge of the bed and slowly reached toward the towel, gently touching the edges.

See? Now she's ready. He pushed his will out again, his expression softening as he touched her hand. She shivered at the sudden cold blast of air in the room.

"Edward? Is that you?"

He smiled, pushing further and a small drawer at the top of the dresser opened. The contents flew into the air, tumbling in a sudden wind until a card separated itself out, falling gently into his wife's lap. Inside it read, Happy 40th Anniversary! To the most beautiful woman I will ever meet. Thank you for loving me. With all my heart. Edward. xoxo.

He put his chin down to his chest, smiling, sending out his love to surround his wife.

"I never... where did this... why Edward," she said pressing the card to her chest, looking up at the ceiling.

They always think you have to be up there. Isn't she beautiful?

"Drew! Elizabeth! Look what I found!"

A man and a woman came rushing into the room, followed by small children who climbed on the bed.

Grandkids.

Mara looked at him and realized all he had lost. *I'm sorry.*

My fault. I stepped off a curb too quick. Didn't look. Thanks for this. Now I can go.

Mara turned to go but as she did a bright light opened up a tear in the world in between, bathing Edward in it. His head was round again and his teeth were no longer broken.

Don't come too close. It's not your time yet. Find whoever it is you have to, but be careful. There are always darker things in here looking for ways to amuse themselves.

He let himself fall into the light and was sucked out of the world in between as if he was drawn into vacuum. Mara was all alone. *There's a way out.* The loneliness was overtaking her. Alone.

Except for the people in the room. They were hugging and holding hands and admiring the card.

Leira. Mara focused her will and felt herself get pulled back through the wormhole. She moved steadily through the gelatinous ether, searching through different wormholes, feeling for something familiar until finally she found it. She had no idea how much time it had taken or where she would come out.

But she knew. Leira was near. The energy was strong.

She peered through the ether and saw the green Mustang in the parking lot of the hospital. Leira was sitting behind the wheel.

Focus.

She sent her will out ahead of her, through the windows of the car, moving around Leira and the other occupants.

There's something else here that's familiar. The memories flooded back into her. She pulled herself closer until she could see who else was in the car.

Eireka! She tried to focus and send her will around her family but it was gone. The wormhole pulled her in, spinning her around and dumping her in an old train station somewhere in New Jersey.

In the Mustang, Eireka felt the swirl of cold energy move around her and looked up, recognizing the traces of magic it left behind. "Mama." She reached out, putting her hand on the window but it was too late. The feeling was gone.

CHAPTER TWENTY

"I get it. It's okay. You didn't have to buy me breakfast tacos." Hagan and Leira were sitting at one of the picnic tables set up around the food trucks in the lot on Rainey Street.

"Think of it as more of a celebration breakfast than anything else. I didn't get to buy you that drink last night.

"Date night with Rose, you know," said Hagan.

Leira gave a crooked smile. "Thanks for meeting me here. I don't want to get too far away from my mother for a few days. She may have magical abilities but she was still confined for fifteen years."

"I get it, kid. You know, it takes time. The worry. It'll take a while before you stop tensing every time you don't find her right away or she doesn't answer the phone. Phones! Have you shown her your iPhone yet? For that matter did you show the big guy one of those? Blow their minds!" Hagan took a hearty bite of his taco. "Still, I get it. It was a nice change of pace clearing those cases like we did."

"Chew a little more, would you?"

"Sorry. So used to getting five bites and then having to dump the whole thing and run somewhere."

"I've never seen you dump food the whole time I've worked with you."

Hagan laughed, taking another bite. "Sounded good, though, didn't it?"

"You know it's not about the government job."

"I hear those jobs pay well. Better than here. It's okay."

"It's not the job. It's the magic. Eventually, I was going to get found out. I couldn't use magic on the force, and I was finding it impossible to not help someone by pulling out a little something. This way I can use the magic and do some good without getting into some kind of bad situation."

Hagan stopped eating and licked his lips. "You got them to let your mother out, didn't you? That was what you wanted." He nodded his head. "Well done, kid. I like a partner who sticks up for their family first. I would have done the same." He took another bite, pulling Leira's tray toward him. "You still made them pay you some real cha-ching though, right? Good job!"

"No, go ahead. I can get more." Leira watched him take one of her tacos. "Surely, Rose lets you eat."

"I was in a hurry this morning. The captain said I had to find you before I could come in. I didn't know if it was good or bad news. Found it hard to eat."

Leira raised an eyebrow. "That *is* news."

"You gonna stay in touch? Send me a picture from the steps of the Lincoln Memorial."

"I'm not going to D.C. Another condition of mine. I'm staying right here. You and I can still catch a beer once in a while."

"And if I ever need some help?"

"If you or Rose ever need help, I'm your first phone call. Don't insult me. If you mean, with a case. I'm sure there will be times we need to work together again."

"Then we're all good. Hey, do you have to leave the car? Don't tell me. Another condition. I taught you right, kid. You went for the gold." He licked each of his fingers, smacking his lips. "I only have two problems left. Whatever mook they stick me with next that I have to break in and well," he looked down at his lap before looking up at Leira, "I might have run over a section of Rose's flowerbed. She is not happy with me. Mostly because I tried to replace them with some flowers I got at Lowe's. Apparently, there was more of a system to the whole thing than I realized. She said I messed up her placement. Anyway, I'm in the doghouse for now." He rolled his eyes and shrugged. "What are you gonna do? She's stuck with me."

"There's something I can do. Just this once!" Leira held up her finger. "A gift for teaching me everything I ever needed to know."

"Well, at least everything I know. Be still my heart. Are you gonna?" He fluttered his fingers.

"Not the magic hands again. Promise me you'll retire those."

"Berens, you put Rose's flowerbeds back to what they used to be, and I will never wave my hands around again!"

Leira closed her eyes, focusing on the energy.

Hagan watched but he didn't see anything happening.

Leira concentrated on his backyard, letting the magic lead her, choosing what to do next as she followed behind it. Green shoots erupted, growing into flowers in full bloom, arranging themselves in a pattern of purple, yellow and pink. Leira smiled at the image in her mind, letting the magic drain back into the Earth. She opened her eyes.

"Go home. Yes, you can take my tacos with you. Then get to work. You're going to be late."

"You are the best, kid, I'll see you soon!"

Hagan pulled into his driveway and was met by Rose on the front steps. She grabbed him around the waist and kissed him hard. Hagan started but caught on and kissed her back.

"You wonderful man! How did you do it?" She pulled Hagan

by the hand through the house and out the back door to admire the garden. "I never would have believed you could do it! I didn't even know you were paying any attention to my garden, but you must have been! You remembered every detail!"

Hagan stepped around her, down the few cement steps that led to the yard and stepped over the dog.

"It's even in full bloom! The old flowers were starting to go into hibernation, but you brought them all back. It's like we get a second spring before it's even spring!"

"It's beautiful," he whispered. The garden was in full bloom from one end to the other. Not just in the swath that Hagan had mowed down. Everything had come back to life, stretching upwards to meet the warm Austin winter sunlight. If he didn't know better, Hagan would have even sworn there was a kind of glitter.

"Nah, must be the light," he said, scratching his head. Rose came down the steps and wrapped an arm around his waist, admiring the garden with him. "You wonderful man! I love you."

"I love you too, Rose. I love you too."

Correk made his way across the patio, ignoring the shouts from the few regulars who were already gathering around the bar. Estelle blew out just enough smoke to create a haze around them, staring them down till they went back to their beers.

He went inside the small house without knocking. Eireka was pacing back and forth in the small living room, her fingers pressed to her forehead. "Are you alright?"

"What?" Eireka looked up, distracted. "Leira's not here. She's still at the station."

"I know. I came looking for you."

She stopped long enough to take a good look at Correk. "Thank you... for everything."

Correk opened his mouth to say something but Eireka beat him too it, blurting out, "This is going to sound crazy, but I think I know where my mother is being held." She held her hand out in front of her, shaking them. "I didn't know Leira was alone all this time. And my mother…"

Correk took her hands in his, holding them tight. "Leira was never alone. She found family, even if she didn't quite see it that way."

"She wasn't always like that, you know. You should have seen her when she was little. A regular chatterbox."

"That's a little hard to picture."

"Still swore like a sailor."

"Okay, now it's getting easier."

"She got that from her grandmother… my mother." Eireka's voice caught and she blinked back tears, wiping her eyes. "Sorry." She swallowed hard and looked away for a moment. "Leira was such a curious child. Always wanted to know how everything was made, where it came from. She took apart the microwave and I would have been mad, but she put it back together and it worked even better." Eireka gave Correk an uneasy smile.

"Sounds like the Elven side of her was already showing through."

"Maybe… probably. But all that ended when I was taken away." Eireka waved her hands. "Enough. It's in the past and you two have pulled off a miracle. Not just for me, but so many others." Eireka's brow furrowed. "Didn't you say you were looking for me? What did you need?"

The smile faded from Correk's face and he cleared his throat. "You said you knew my father."

Eireka's eyes widened. "Oh, of course. Harkin, yes. We were friends at one time, a long time ago. It's a wonder you and I never met. I heard stories about you, but by then you were already serving the king.

Correk looked pained, hesitating but Eireka took his hand

and squeezed it. "Harkin was a complicated man. He was a genius and magical and..."

"And liked a lot of women." Correk suddenly was embarrassed and started to apologize.

Eireka laughed and let go of his hand. "It's true, he did like a lot of women. I was not one of them. We were just friends. He was always a good friend to me, too. He could tell a story better than anyone I've ever met. Most of them probably weren't even true but I didn't care. However, he wasn't always the best judge of character and that got him into a lot of tight corners. That last one, I don't know."

"The one that got him sent to prison."

"Yeah, I think his intentions were good. He was trying to save Raphael, but something went wrong. He always claimed someone tampered with the machine, but no one really believed him."

"He made his own super villain."

"And paid for it. Not just with prison, but with the loss of his best friend. I lost touch with him once he was sent away. Trevilsom doesn't even allow messages to be sent. What did become of your father?"

Correk's hands were balled into tight fists. "I don't know. I always assumed he died in prison. There's no sighting of him since he was sent away, no word from anyone."

"I'm sorry, Correk. That has to be so hard not to know. No wonder Leira feels a bond with you."

"What?"

Eireka gave a small smile at the corners of her mouth. "You two are a lot alike, you know. You're so good at spotting an injustice but miss the good stuff right under your nose."

"I don't know what you mean."

Eireka laughed. "Yeah, I know. All in good time."

The Gardener of the Dark Forest held on tight to the mane of the lion, his legs pressing against the great beast's sides as they ran quietly through the deeper parts of the uncharted woods. Trees bent out of his way and animals scurried to the sides as he rode even further into the depths where no magicals dared to venture.

"Whoa," the Gardener whispered, the lion coming to a stop outside a thatched roofed building well hidden by a stand of trees growing up around the outside of it. The lion rubbed an antler against a nearby tree, waiting patiently for the Gardener to alight on the ground. Bees circled his head, buzzing at the blooming vines crawling through his hair.

He trudged into the building, making his way into the back where it opened into a pristine laboratory and a lone figure standing over the plans for a design. The Gardener cleared his throat and waited for the Light Elf to turn and notice him.

"Harkin, there's word your son has gone to the other world to help Eireka Berens' daughter. Don't you think it's time you let him know what really happened?"

"No, I've made my peace with it all. He's better off without me. I need to focus on fixing my mistake." He tapped the blueprints for a new CAT scan machine. "I almost have all the parts I need from the Dark Market. Soon, I'll be able to start rebuilding. Then, maybe..." He rubbed his weary face. "I can rescue Raphael and figure out what went wrong."

"You mean, who betrayed you."

"Maybe I do. But first things first."

"You were stubborn then, you're stubborn now."

"Look who's talking. I'm so close. I have to try."

"But your son... He thinks you're dead."

A pained expression passed across Harkin's face. "Then he has already grieved for me. Let it stay there. Let me stay in his past where I belong. Besides, I promised the king that I would let him go."

"If Correk ever finds out about the deal you made."

"He'll feel betrayed all over again but this time by the king and he'll be robbed of one more person." He shook his head. "No, don't tell anyone about me. This is easier for everyone."

"Not for you, old friend."

"I told you. I made my peace."

The Gardener hesitated but said nothing else and made his way back out to the lion. He gently petted the large head, listening to the great cat purr. "Someday, the truth will need to be set free. Then things will be set right, for everyone."

Leira and Eireka sat outside on the patio in the late morning, enjoying the sounds of the birds. Estelle told everyone the patio was closed to give them some time to be alone. Eireka sat with her chin tilted up toward the warm sunlight, smiling.

Her daughter's hand rested in hers. Leira kept watching her mother, trying to believe in her good fortune and let go of the small feeling deep inside that wondered what trial was coming next.

Things could just be good for a while.

The air stirred, blowing the hair off Eireka's face. It was turning colder in Austin and there was the possibility of frost. Leira knew Rose's flowers would survive. Let her wonder why they did so well this winter.

Another current of air blew across them as the temperature dropped. "Should we go inside? Strange weather." Leira pulled out her phone to check the weather report.

Eireka's eyes popped open and she looked around, side to side.

"Mom, what is it? What's wrong?" Leira's stomach clenched and she looked back at the guesthouse where Correk was still sleeping, the troll in a small box on the floor next to him.

Maybe he'll hear me in his head. She wrinkled her forehead, but nothing happened.

"Mama." Eireka stood up, holding out her arms.

"What are you doing?" Leira stood up with her, trying to see what was out of order.

"Not with your eyes," said Eireka. "Feel it in here." She tapped her chest.

The votive candle holders on the nearby tables rattled and the wind blew Eireka's long hair into her face. Leira felt a growing sense of panic but forced herself to focus, center herself.

Eireka grabbed her hand, flowing energy into her, connecting them. Leira closed her eyes and felt a new energy flowing through her.

A connection reaching out to generations of women in her line that had come before her and to those yet to come. She was connected to *all* of them.

A peace came over her and she smelled the scent of lilacs. It had been years, over four years to be exact, since she had smelled them last. She snapped her head to the left, her eyes still shut, to the line of women who had come before her and in her mind she saw an image that was more real than imagined. More present than past.

Her eyes widened. "Nana," she whispered. "You're alive."

Her mother inhaled suddenly, eyes open in surprise. "She's trapped. In the world in between."

"But she's alive," Leira's eyebrows narrowed in concentration. "I can *work* with that."

She felt the magic go out ahead of her, reaching out toward her grandmother, getting closer. A sense of relief came over her.

Suddenly, a look of surprise came over Mara's face as she was abruptly sucked backward into the void of the world in between. Leira jerked forward, hoping to feel her grandmother's energy but she was gone.

The last thing Leira saw was her grandmother reaching out toward her, her hand outstretched.

Sorrow seeped into the space instead and Leira yanked back her energy, recoiling from the sensation. The face of a young woman appeared in the dense mist, her energy grasping at Leira.

Leira knew that feeling all too well from her time as a homicide detective. Someone desperate for her help. Only this time it wasn't the murder victim's family, it was the dead woman reaching out for answers. Now they're sending me cases from beyond the grave. Fuck, I miss Hagan.

"No, family first, for once. I find my grandmother." She felt her mother squeeze her hand.

"We do this together," said Eireka.

"Together," said Leira.

The story is far from over. Leira's adventure continues in
PROTECTION OF MAGIC.

Get sneak peeks, exclusive giveaways, behind the scenes content, and more. PLUS you'll be notified of special **one day only fan pricing** on new releases.

Sign up today to get free stories.

These were some of my favorite author notes. Mostly because Michael kept telling me I author blocked him. "Who's gonna read my notes after they get through with yours?" he asked. Compliment accepted.

But he's also been my biggest cheerleader these past three years and has taken some pleasure in pointing out that for 30 years the traditional land of publishing didn't know what to do with me and then... voila!

And along the way I've had the best time creating stories of adventure that have great friends traveling all over the globe (and often returning to Austin, Texas), fighting side by side and always believing in a solution. That's kind of how I do life in general with a sense of wonder and optimism about what's around the next corner.

By the way, Michael's also fond of saying I based the troll on myself. Not entirely wrong on that point either. More adventures to follow.

Original Notes August 12, 2017: I was watching America's Got Talent last week. I'm a sucker for any reality show that helps someone get closer to their dreams. This season there are two acts that have made it to the live shows – a singing group and a lone singer – who are older. Great singers, beautiful harmonies, great stage presence. Just never made it.

Yet.

The singing group had been trying since the 1960's and gotten close... so close... but missed the mark. Now, they are on TV in front of millions and being recognized as great artists – no matter *what* happens next.

I was moved to tears and thought, good for you! But a half a beat later, it really struck me.

Hey, that's you and *you've finally made it.*

It's still coming over me like a wave that there are a lot of readers, FANS! who are loving the Leira Chronicles and asking...

Where's the next one?

Back when I first started writing seriously, almost thirty years ago, I was a newly divorced single mother with that baby boy, Louie. My entire family said, this is stupid. Go sell real estate. It became an echo inside of my brain. Your dream is stupid. I was already dealing with the destruction of the rest of my life plans. What now?

Just when I needed it, an older cousin of mine, Virginius Dabney, a Pulitzer prize-winning cousin, stepped in and did this amazing thing. He quietly took down a book of his and wrote something in the cover, and without saying anything else besides, "Great idea!" he handed it over.

I looked inside and it read, "To my cousin, Martha Carr, a great writer. Virginius Dabney."

I hadn't written a word yet. But I knew the magic and the power of what he had just done. It was my golden ticket. Everyone in my family sat back, stunned – even calling each other on the phone.

And they all *shut the hell up.*

He bought me a chance at my dreams. The road was still long

– I mean, it's 30 years later – but every step was worth it. Every adventure. Better to struggle on the road to my dreams. And right next to me for all of that trip has been the offspring, Louie – watching me.

Never…give…up. *Never*.

Then, in 2010 I was diagnosed with terminal cancer. Totally unexpected. I didn't see it coming or I wouldn't have let Louie sit next to me in the surgeon's office when he casually spit out the news. "You have less than a one percent chance of living longer than a year."

The doctor flipped through a notebook with picture of what the next year would look like. I purposely looked away. No need to know what horrors awaited me. My entire body did a low-level shake. It was all I could do to maneuver my way out of the tiny room.

I was doing my best to pull it together for Louie when he looked at me and said, "Weren't you listening? He said there was hope!" That kid, who was only 21 at the time and his entire family pretty much consisted of me, heard *hope*.

I still remember looking at him thinking, he'll be okay. It's alright.

I calmed down and started putting one foot in front of the other. Long story short – surgery, appointments, learning to walk again – and a very strange phone call in the middle of an ordinary day.

The nurse called and said, "Are you sitting down?" I thought the cancer had spread and braced myself. "We can't find it anywhere. We can't explain it. You're in remission." Later, they even studied my case at Northwestern and would shake their heads at appointments. "We can't explain why you're here."

I asked them to stop saying that one.

These days, Louie refers to me as a one-percenter…. Offspring is very good with the humor. There's a little more to this story. The same kind of cancer – new diagnoses – keeps coming up. Last surgery - #6 - was last October. I know it worries Louie – he's asked me to do videos for all the big moments in his life that have yet to happen... just in case. It's on my to-do list.

But writing - took a week off, got right back to it. There was a thriller series to finish. Of course I was going to get up and write.

It's that dream that just lives inside of me and has since I first discovered books.

I have something to say, to hopefully inspire or make someone laugh, or the best – feel better about their day. I hope I'm living up to my cousin, Virginius's gift – that golden ticket.

My cousin only lasted another year or two after that and never got to see that I finally made it – because of all of you. It's only a couple of weeks old (can you believe it!) but it's here. At last... it's *here*.

BIG THANK YOU for all the wonderful reviews – I read all of them and do my best to acknowledge each and every one of you (even the UK and Canada!) on my Facebook Author page. Lots of you can even attest – you write me – I write you back. It's like hearing from a friend who I've just been waiting for all this time. Thank you so much for all of it!

Worth the wait – *definitely* worth the wait!

I have to admit that the reason I believe the Troll is I.M. (Inner Martha) has to do with the unabashed humor she has for life in general, and YumFuck's love for all things D.C. Comics.

(I'm a Marvel type guy, Martha is a D.C. Girl. Except for Wonder Woman, I'm fond of that character and not too fond of the Fantastic Four on Marvel's side. I would suggest a trade between the companies.)

Based on the timeline of the original author notes, Martha goes on to Author Note Block Me a few more times. However, a couple of times for heart wrenching reasons and frankly I'm only sad those events happened.

However, spoiler alert, she makes it through!

You have many awesome stories with these characters ahead of you, so kick back, get your favorite beverage and enjoy yourself!

Original Notes August 13, 2017

First, THANK YOU for not only reading this book, but ALSO reading these author notes at the end!

Seriously, I JUST got through talking about Author Note

blocking in the back of Rogue Mage w/ Brandon Barr and his cancer story. Only to get ANOTHER cancer story with Martha and I told her, *how the hell am I supposed to even come close to the awesome story she has?*

She just laughed.

Not so much *at* me, as I think she is humored that I was complaining and between you and me, *that was my plan.*

I've done over fifty of these author notes in the last two years. I've audio transcribed nine of them for Audible releases and have about twenty-five on my task list.

I never thought when I wrote that first Author Note, that doing them would become something a little iconic. I am well aware that other authors have done them in the past as well, but for some reason, it feels like the byplay and fun we have here in the Kurtherian and Oriceran Universes have been amped up to a new level.

Now, I get called Yoda by all of those who read Ell Leigh Clarke's Author Notes from The Ascension Myth. I have fan's poking fun at me on the Oriceran Facebook page about the wall-paper and I can look in the mirror with a scowl on my face and tell that guy...

Mike, you only have yourself to blame.

And, I'm good with that.

It means the fans have gotten involved and they hopefully realize we are all in this together. We feed on YOUR interaction, and I can honestly admit that without the fans supporting me, asking when the next book is coming out, Bethany Anne WOULD NOT be as far along as she is today.

We (myself, my little publishing group) have grown because the fans had helped push us emotionally, supported us by reading the books, reviewing the books on Amazon and of course buying and just been a kick-ass group of people to be around.

In 2018, I'd like to figure out a way to do something special, meetups, whatever. I'm going to be in Frankfurt Germany this

October, so if you are in Europe, and care to meet during the Frankfurt Book Fair, let's get something going, ok?

It's time for Publishing 2.0 to explode, and I know *JUST* the people to make it happen.

And it's going to be *you*.

In the next 60 days, we will be releasing four new series in the Oriceran (Or-eh-sair-ehn) Universe and we are *SO* excited you are reading and enjoying as we work hard...

To Bring You The Truth...

Thank you, again, for making our lives possible.

Michael Anderle

For Hire: Teachers for special school in Virginia countryside.

Must be able to handle teenagers with special abilities.

Cannot be afraid to discipline werewolves, wizards, elves and other assorted hormonal teens.

Apply at the School of Necessary Magic.

<u>**AVAILABLE ON AMAZON RETAILERS**</u>

If smart phones and GPS rule the world - why am I hunting a magic compass to save the planet?

Austin Detective Maggie Parker has seen some weird things in her day, but finding a surly gnome rooting through her garage beats all.

Her world is about to be turned upside down in a frantic search for 4 Elementals.

Each one has an artifact that can keep the Earth humming along, but they need her to unite them first.

Unless the forces against her get there first.

AVAILABLE ON AMAZON AND IN KINDLE UNLIMITED!

CONNECT WITH THE AUTHORS

Martha Carr Social

Website:
http://www.marthacarr.com

Facebook:
https://www.facebook.com/groups/MarthaCarrFans/
Michael Anderle Social

Website:
http://www.lmbpn.com

Email List:
http://lmbpn.com/email/

Facebook
https://www.facebook.com/LMBPNPublishing

Made in the USA
Coppell, TX
07 August 2020

32618463R00152